Blood

Marked

Pages

Iain Cameron

DEDICATION

To all the health and care workers of every nation who worked tirelessly throughout the Covid-19 crisis, despite the obvious risk to their own health - this book is dedicated to you.

ONE

The train pulled into Brighton station, engine wheezing and brakes squealing. Stuart Livermore had been asleep since East Croydon, booze and tiredness leaving him exhausted. He wasn't aware they had arrived until the woman beside him banged into him with her bag as she rose from her seat.

'Oh, sorry about that,' she said. 'I can be so clumsy at times.'

He looked at her through half-opened eyes, a ghostly apparition. 'It's all right,' he managed to blurt out, 'I've got another arm.'

'Ha, ha. Very funny. Be seeing you then,' she said, giving him a regal wave.

Not before I see you first, he thought but didn't say.

It was evening, on a Sunday, he thought. The first part he could tell by the darkness outside the station, the other a rough guess. Where had he been? His brain slipped into gear with all the speed and agility of an old grandfather clock. He'd been a guest speaker at a literary event in Norwich, the Noirwich Crime Writing Festival. Today had been the final day, so yes, it *was* Sunday.

Afterwards, he and a couple of other authors had gone out for a few drinks before he had to catch his train. It was unfortunate, but he didn't possess the control that normal people possessed - a stop button. It didn't matter if this was in connection with biscuits, puddings or alcoholic beverages. When someone asked if he wanted another, his mouth answered instead of his brain.

He collected his bag and stepped off the train. He liked Brighton station - its high vaulted glass and steel roof and long platforms, making locals and tourists alike feel as if they were coming into an important place. The variety and quantity of theatres, cinemas, hotels, and all the rest which the city had to offer existed, not only to feed and amuse the local populace, but the numerous visitors as well.

If he'd arrived in daylight, he would have walked home; his house in Queen's Park wasn't far from the train station. Instead, he headed towards a bus stop and, a few minutes later, boarded the number seven bus. It was a short journey, but the vibration from the engine and the occasional puff of diesel fumes was making him feel queasy. He was glad when it reached Eastern Road, and he could get off.

He walked up Park Street, through the stone gates marking the entrance to Queen's Park, then along South Avenue to East Drive. He loved living here. It gave him the sensation of city life with the fine pubs and restaurants of Kemptown on his doorstep, and the impression of country living. This, courtesy of the trees, grass, and flowers of the park which could be seen from his front window.

He turned up the garden path and glanced towards the house of his next door neighbours, hoping to see

Steph. More often than not it was her partner, Mark, at the window. Tonight, there was no one; the house was in darkness. The houses in this part of the road were large and semi-detached. Livermore could choose the colour scheme for each room in the house, and what to plant in the borders around the back garden. Unfortunately, he had no say in the people who lived on the other side of the dividing wall.

Stuart Livermore and Mark Wallace did not see eye to eye. Mark's wife, Steph, on the other hand, was thirty-one, a decade younger than Livermore, with a pretty face and a stunning gym-honed physique. He liked her; she was sparky, a keen observer of the quirky, and possessed what his father would call, a docker's sense of humour. She was not averse to making fun of her own, or her husband's bodily functions, or giving Livermore the cut and thrust of what went on in the bedroom. Mark, however, was a big guy, who liked a drink and had a large jealous streak. If Livermore was as smart as he purported to be, he should only talk to Steph when Mark wasn't around.

He turned the key and stepped inside. He bent down and picked up the mail from the mat. Flicking through the small pile, he noted that his girlfriend, Hannah Robbins, hadn't visited the house while he had been away, despite his suggestion that she might. There had been several burglaries in the area, and he didn't want to return to a house cleaned out of all its valuables, or finding two hundred people gathered inside, drinking and smoking themselves into a stupor.

He placed the bag containing his weekend clothes, information picked up at the festival, and his laptop in the hall and walked into the kitchen. He put the mail on a worktop, a job that could wait until tomorrow, and took a bottle of beer from the fridge. Opening a cupboard, he pulled out a packet of Jaffa Cakes.

He knew what he needed to do was open the packet, remove a couple, then return the rest to the cupboard. If he took the packet into the lounge, as a normal person might do, it would be empty by the time he went to bed, with the inevitable negative effect on his waistline. The booze had made him reckless, though, it always did. He picked up his beer and, tucking the packet of Jaffa Cakes under his arm, headed to the lounge.

The lounge door was shut, making him pause for no more than a second to wonder why. He never closed the door except when sitting in there. Perhaps Hannah had come over and done her good deed after all. He turned the handle and walked inside.

'Well, if it isn't that famous scribe, Stuart Livermore. Come in, park your arse over there.'

Livermore shuddered in surprise at hearing the disembodied voice in the darkness, spilling beer over his hand. Had he imagined it? Or was there someone outside? Perhaps it was his neighbour, Mark Wallace, hiding below the window, trying to play a trick on him. He was about to write it off as that, or the holler of a drunk in the park, when the lamp in the corner of the room burst into life.

Livermore screwed his eyes up at the sudden glare, but when he finally focused, he recognised the ugly and evil individual sitting there at once. 'You!' he cried. 'How did you get into my house? What are you doing here?'

'Shut the fuck up, you stupid fuckwit and stop asking me all those bloody questions. Park your arse over there in that chair like I told you,' he said pointing. 'First, you're gonna listen to what I've got to say.'

TWO

The noise of the ringing phone invaded Detective Inspector Angus Henderson's dream. It was so vivid, he thought the sound had to be part of it. It took him a couple of seconds to realise it wasn't his mind playing tricks. He moved an arm out of the duvet and pulled it straight back as the bedroom was freezing cold. He tried again and retrieved the still-trilling lump of annoying electronic components.

'Yes?' he said.

He listened while the controller at Lewes relayed the information. 'Right.' He tried to sit up, no easy task with slippery pillows, and pins and needles running up his left arm.

'Where?'

He jotted down the details on a pad that he kept close to the phone, also noting the time: 01:40 in the morning.

'Who else has been alerted?'

After hearing the response, he said, 'Okay. I'm on my way.'

He ended the call, left the phone on the bed and headed into the bathroom. God, it was cold. He walked into the shower and switched it on. He didn't need the revival qualities of a cold shower to wash away a hangover, he didn't have one, but he did need the effects of a warm one to wake him up. It had been a late night, as he'd been in the company of a few colleagues playing poker.

He made it to the car in less than half an hour after receiving the call, and ten minutes later he was pulling up outside a house bordering Queens Park in Brighton. It was a quiet road with most of the houses in darkness, but one was lit up like a Christmas tree with numerous parked vehicles, giving the semblance of a used car dealership.

Climbing out of the car, he spotted Detective Sergeant Carol Walters walking towards him.

'Evening gov,' she said, 'or should I say good morning, as it's...' she looked at her watch, 'two-twenty. The time when most good people should be in bed and fast asleep.'

'This has got to be the easiest commute you'll ever have. What is it, three streets away?'

'Close enough for me to leave my car behind for once.'

'What do we know? Lewes Control said it's a male with multiple stab wounds.'

She pulled out her notebook and flicked to the appropriate page. 'The victim's name is Stuart Livermore. He's an author.'

'Who found him?'

'Hannah Robbins, Livermore's girlfriend. She'd rung him several times during the evening without success. He'd been away for a few days at some literary event and was due home about eight-thirty. She got fed up waiting for him to call her back, so she made her way here from Hove and opened the door with her spare key.'

'Where had Mr Livermore been?'

'To a literary festival in Norwich.'

'I'd like to speak to his girlfriend after I take a look at the crime scene.'

She shook her head. 'No can do, I'm afraid, gov. She didn't take the sight of her dead boyfriend well. The doc sent her home in a patrol car with a couple of sedatives.'

He sighed. It wasn't a good start. 'In that case, let's take a look at the body.'

They crossed the road to the house. Henderson knew not to look for the Austin Healey car belonging to their regular pathologist, Grafton Rawlings. He wouldn't be here today. He had another death to attend, one much closer to home; that of his mother.

The road seemed quiet and well-maintained. Even though the house was semi-detached, it looked substantial in size, and with such fine views of the park, Henderson imagined it wouldn't come cheap. Clearly, Stuart Livermore had been successful at the work he did. At the door, Henderson and Walters donned oversuits, boots, and gloves before stepping into the hallway.

The bulk of the activity seemed to be coming from the door to his right. He walked inside and found himself in the lounge, in the company of enough people to start a party: scene of crime officers - SOCOs, a police photographer, the Crime Scene Manager, the pathologist and, under his expert gaze, the inert figure of the victim.

Henderson headed over to the pathologist who, on hearing his approach, looked up.

'Morning, I'm Detective Inspector Angus Henderson, Senior Investigating Officer,' Henderson said, offering his hand.

'Howard Emerson.'

They shook hands.

'Another Scot. I can't seem to escape from you lot.'

Henderson bristled at the 'you lot' reference. 'What do you mean?'

'My wife's from Edinburgh, you see, and we've got a load of her family staying with us at the moment. Wall-to-wall teuchters and enough empty whisky and beer bottles to start my own glass recycling service.'

Henderson bent down to examine the victim. His face had been bashed up, as if he'd gone a couple of rounds with a heavyweight boxer. A large patch of blood had bloomed on his chest. There was blood on his jeans, not the bleeding of a single wound, but multiple blobs of dark staining, as if made by a leaking fountain pen.

'What do you think happened?' he asked the pathologist.

'He has a broken nose, compression of the right cheekbone, and bad bruising to his face. It suggests to me a concerted beating.'

'Before or after death?'

'Most definitely before, perhaps to subdue him. He was stabbed in a succession of thrusts to the arm, the leg, and the chest. I don't know the exact order of the wounds, but one thing I am certain about, even after a cursory examination, is that the chest thrust is the one that killed him. The position of the wound suggests the knife went straight through his heart.'

'So, these wounds to the arm and leg could have been what? Signs of a struggle?'

'I don't know and it's for you, Inspector, to try and find out.'

The pathologist's on-site examination complete, stretcher bearers were called to move the body to the mortuary for the post-mortem. Henderson stepped aside to let them in. When the body was stretchered out, and with the room now less crowded, he started to look around.

THREE

Stuart Livermore's house was a traditional red-brick, semi-detached with bay windows top and bottom, not much of a garden out front, but modern inside. The floor was of grey wood, the television stand, coffee table, and lamp all chrome, and the sofa and chair light brown and contemporary in style.

'He's a crime author,' Walters said from behind Henderson.

'How do you know?'

She pointed to a row of books on the bookshelf, built into a recess at the side of the chimney breast. 'These are all his.'

Henderson could tell that the bookshelves, with two cupboards at the bottom, had not been a DIY job. The shelves fitted flush with the space available, and the wood and fittings used were of such quality, he imagined they would still be standing in twenty- or thirty-years' time.

Henderson removed a book and, without opening it, reckoned he knew what it was about. The cover was dark, bearing the image of a dead body, and the strap line, 'You Can Run, But You Can't Hide', a giveaway to the contents inside.

'Is he popular?'

'I looked him up on my phone. One of his books has been made into an eight-part drama for television.'

'I would certainly call that popular. What was it called?'

'*Black Night.*'

'That's a song by Deep Purple.'

'Who?'

'It doesn't matter. I think I watched it, or at least some of it.'

Henderson remembered the programme. He'd watched one episode and soon got bored with the intricate story line: a serial killer preying on children. Serial killers were rare in the UK, although he could excuse their inclusion in a television drama, but what he couldn't abide was the perpetrator leaving clues; in this case, pages ripped from a scrapbook.

In his entire police career, he had never heard of any criminal deliberately leaving clues that could be used to catch them. In fact, some criminals knew more about forensics than many police officers and were meticulous in avoiding leaving anything behind. Either way, every criminal he had ever come across would do anything to make sure they weren't implicated, even blaming their best mate or a family member.

'This room looks a bit of a mess,' Henderson said. 'Do you think the victim was the untidy sort, or is this the work of the killer looking for something?'

Many items from the bookshelves to the right of the chimney were strewn across the floor, as were the contents of the two cupboards at the base. A standard lamp was also on its side, and framed pictures had been taken from the walls and smashed. By way of contrast, the matching bookshelves and cupboards on the other side of the chimney looked untouched.

'Might have been a burglary, and the victim came back while it was still in progress. Could be they were looking for money or valuables.'

'It's not a bad assumption, given he's had a book serialised on television and, looking around this place, he doesn't look to be short of a bob or two.'

A few minutes later, the detectives moved into the hall. There were no signs of confrontation here, only a bag containing Livermore's clothes from his stay in Norwich, and his laptop. Later, SOCOs would remove the bag and send the laptop, and the phone which had been found in the lounge, to the high-tech unit in Haywards Heath for analysis. The only other item of interest they could see was in the kitchen where a fingerprint officer was dabbing the broken window on the back door with his brush. Henderson walked towards him.

'Morning, Eddy. Is this how they came in?'

'Morning, gov. Yeah, simple as. The intruder sticks a bit of tape on the glass to stop the fragments falling and to dampen the noise. After a quick whack with the side of a fist, he peels off the broken glass to reveal a decent-sized hole. He then sticks his hand inside and turns the key sitting in the lock. Couldn't be easier.'

'Any dabs?'

'A few, but if the guy used a glove to smash the glass, and I don't think anyone would be stupid enough to use their bare hand, I don't think they'll be his.'

'Cheers Eddy.'

Henderson turned to Walters. 'Let's take a look upstairs.' They climbed the stairs, feeling as if they were moving away from the core activity. From the upstairs landing, they could see the doors of each room had been pushed open, presumably by the SOCO team, although none of them were up here.

Henderson soon found out why. It was a four-bedroom place, but three bedrooms looked unused. They were fully-furnished with beds and wardrobes, but no clothes were hanging inside any of the wardrobes and no books or spectacles were lying on bedside tables.

The exception was the largest room at one end of the house. This was clearly Stuart Livermore's bedroom and it didn't take long for the DI to confirm that Livermore lived alone. There were only his clothes in the wardrobe and scattered around the room, and it was his shaving kit and toiletries sitting on the shelves in the en-suite bathroom.

He also noticed a comprehensively-stocked medicine cabinet. Not so much in the way of lotions and ointments for scrapes and burns to be found in most people's bathrooms, but plenty prescription meds for anxiety and depression. This he deduced from looking at the one or two brand names he recognised, but there were plenty more he didn't.

'His bedroom's a damn sight tidier than mine,' Henderson said.

'And mine, but I've got the excuse, I'm a woman.'

'Why is that an excuse?'

'We women have way more stuff than any man: moisturisers, face masks, hair colour, special shampoo, you name it.'

'Point made. So, what have we got? The killer comes in through the back door, turns over one of the bookcases and, in the course of his search, Livermore returns home. They fight and Livermore is stabbed to death.'

'That's about the sum of it.'

'It doesn't look as if the burglar came up here. I wonder why not?'

Walters walked to one of the beside cabinets and rifled through its contents. 'If someone broke in with the intention of stealing valuables, they've left behind Livermore's passport and a couple of decent watches.'

'What does that tell us?'

'Maybe the sudden appearance of Livermore spooked the killer and, after stabbing him, bolted before he could broaden the search.'

'It's possible, or...?'

'His rummage of the bookcase downstairs was successful. He found what he was looking for.'

'Until the evidence indicates otherwise, I favour the latter. There are two identical bookcases down there, each with books, DVDs, CDs, and various bits of paperwork. Our killer not only ignored the upstairs rooms, but he targeted only one of the bookcases. This suggests to me he knew exactly what he was looking for.'

'I agree.'

'I noticed when I arrived that next door's light was on.'

'Yeah, I sent an officer in there a while back to take a statement.'

'Good. Let's go over there and hear what they've got to say.'

FOUR

The cup of coffee handed to Henderson by Stuart
Livermore's nearest neighbour, Steph Wallace, was
most welcome. He'd given up on the idea of returning
to bed when they had finished here at Queen's Park.
With the time creeping inexorably towards four, there
seemed little point. He wouldn't fall asleep right away,
and he would feel even worse when he woke up a
couple of hours later. The extra caffeine might help
him to see the morning sunrise without flagging too
much.

Henderson had presumed that the cop who had
taken Steph and her husband's statements earlier had
explained the reason for the police presence at the
house next door. With all the lights in the Livermore
house ablaze, the coming and going of numerous
vehicles, the traipsing in and out of various SOCO
staff, and the movement of the ambulance crew, even
the heaviest of sleepers would now be aware of what
was going on.

'Mr Livermore was an author, we understand,' he
said as an opener to both of them. It was a safe
assumption that whoever answered first would be the
person most friendly with their neighbour.

'Yes,' Steph replied in a shaky voice, 'and a bloody
good one at that. I've read all his books, including his

early Science Fiction ones. Now I'll never know if Josh Needham gets hitched to Betsy, or stays with that swine, Edward.' She covered her face with her hands while she sobbed.

Henderson looked at Walters beside him, a questioning look on his face.

'I imagine Steph is referring to the characters from one of the victim's books, sir.'

'Bloody right I am,' Steph said, her face streaked in tears and lips trembling. 'Stuart didn't just write crime, you know, he wrote rom-coms as well. Dedicated the first one to me, so he did. He also promised to include me as a character in the new one.'

Steph was aged around early thirties with blonde hair, suntanned - not uncommon around Brighton in late summer - and pretty, although her face displayed several lines as if she frowned a lot. She had a terrific figure, slim and shapely, suggesting a gym or exercise compulsion.

Her display of overwrought emotions was common in the neighbours of murder victims. Until the police found out who committed the crime and why, it was natural for those closest to the victim, either in relationship or proximity, to feel alarmed. They would feel, but for a twist of fate, it could have been them, or their turn might be next. Of course, Steph's tears may also have been a sign of the affection she felt for Stuart Livermore, but he parked that thought for later.

Throughout the early exchanges, Steph's husband, Mark, sat impassive and brooding in a seat to one side of the cold fireplace. Either he was dog-tired at being roused at this ungodly hour, or he didn't like to hear his wife talking so affectionately about the man next door.

'What woke you?' Henderson asked Mark, not only to hear his answer, but to try and involve him in the discussion.

'What? How do you mean?'

'Did the arrival of the police vans wake you or was it something else?'

'I never heard anything until one of your lot started banging on the front door,' Mark replied.

'You didn't hear anything before?'

Receiving no response, Henderson looked at Steph. 'What about you, madam?'

'Like what?' she asked.

Henderson was getting tired of this. It was akin to spoon-feeding a toddler. He didn't want to put words in their mouths, but he needed to do something to ignite this discussion. Neither of them seemed quick on the uptake.

'Mrs Wallace, a man was killed next door,' he said slowly. 'The killer entered the house by smashing the window on the back door. Did you hear the sound of glass breaking?'

'No.'

'We think there might have been a struggle. There could have been some shouting or screaming. A few things are smashed in the lounge such as picture frames, so there might have been some noise. Can you see what I'm getting at here?'

'I do, but I didn't hear a bloody thing. We're in the bedroom at the back of the house. This place is double-glazed with a high-quality glass, thanks to a mate of Mark's in the building trade, so we don't hear much of what goes on outside. I'm a personal trainer, see, and I work out every day of the week. If you've got a fitness tracker, you'll know what I mean when I say I do between twenty and thirty thousand steps a day. When I fall asleep, I'm dead to the world.'

Henderson had bought a fitness tracker a few years back to monitor his running performance. He wore it every day, even at times when he wasn't running. With all the walking he did around Malling House: upstairs to see the boss, over the road to the staff restaurant, across the car park to his car, it bleeped most days to inform him he'd completed ten thousand steps. Now and again, when out on an operation, he would reach twenty thousand, but never thirty.

'What about you, sir?' Henderson asked the still brooding Mark.

'I'm a self-employed builder and when I finished work, I came back here. With her being out, I can't cook, so I went out to the pub for my dinner and had a few pints. When I came home, I downed a few cans while watching telly. I don't sleep well until I've got a couple of pints in my belly, so by about eleven, I was comatose, same as her.'

'What about earlier, Mrs Wallace? Tell me your movements from say, seven onwards.'

In common with many pathologists, Howard Emerson was reluctant to commit to a precise time of death. Not only was he examining the victim at the crime scene, and not in his well-equipped mortuary, but the science didn't allow him to be as accurate as they were on television crime dramas. In the real world, detectives often had to work with a wide time window. When Emerson finally got around to it, it was unlikely he would be able to narrow the interval down much between the time Livermore was expected to arrive home, around eight-thirty, and when his body was discovered, after midnight.

'I was working,' Steph said, 'and got back home about ten.'

'Where do you work?'

'At Virgin Active in Falmer.'

'Did you notice if the lights were on in Mr Livermore's house?'

'They weren't.'

'You sound sure.'

'I usually look over at his house on the way into mine as a matter of habit,' she said. 'He,' indicating Mark with her thumb, 'calls me a nosy bugger, but I think of myself as a responsible citizen.'

'And you, sir, you said you were at the pub?'

'Yeah, that's right.'

'Which one?'

'The Charles Napier, just along the road.'

'What time did you go out?'

'Why? Am I a suspect?'

Henderson shook his head. 'Nobody's a suspect. These are purely routine enquiries, sir. Information gathering, if you will. It's nothing for you to worry about.'

'I left the house around seven-thirty and came home around half an hour after her.'

'You're right, I think you didn't get in until around half-ten,' Steph said to Mark. 'I remember looking at the clock thinking it was time for bed, I was so knackered.'

Now, what made Steph jump to her husband's defence so quickly? Was it to reinforce his alibi, or was Henderson reading too much into the exchange? A husband-wife alibi was the most common a detective would come across in the course of investigating a case, and one of the hardest to break down.

'How did you get on with Mr Livermore?' the DI asked, looking again at Mark.

The question seemed to throw him; perhaps his mind was still on the pub, and for a moment he looked startled. 'He was all right, I suppose. He didn't make a lot of noise, didn't hold rowdy parties or anything, kept his garden tidy—'

'You bloody liar!' Steph exploded. 'That wasn't what you called him a few days back when you saw him out in the back garden. You called him a fucking twat!'

Mark sat up in the chair, looking animated for the first time. 'So, what if I did? He was a fucking twat! He looked down on us as if we weren't on the same intellectual level as him, and as for those stupid hats he wore when he was out in the garden. Thought he was bloody Alan Titchmarsh or something. But hey, that's between me and you, girl. It's not for their ears. Do you want to land me in fucking jail?'

'Do I get the impression you and Mr Livermore didn't get on?' Henderson asked.

'No, we bloody didn't,' Mark spat. 'I couldn't stand the sight of the man. I'd cross the street if I ever saw him coming towards me.'

'Did something specific trigger your aversion, or was it a build-up of a succession of small issues?'

'It was her doing!' he said jabbing a finger at his wife. 'She had the bloody hots for him, so she did. The two of them would be sniffing around one another like a couple of dogs in heat every time they talked over the garden fence. 'Ooh yes, I will Stuart, ooh you are so funny, Stuart," Mark said in a falsetto voice. 'They thought I didn't notice, but I did.'

'Don't be daft. I just liked the man, nothing more. You've got a bloody big jealous streak, that's your problem.'

'Yeah, but it's not my problem any more, is it? Boy wonder is away, and he ain't coming back. Somebody's just gone and done me a bloody big favour.'

FIVE

Henderson picked up a hot cup of coffee, his third or fourth of the morning, he wasn't sure. He tentatively took a sip. After visiting the murder scene at Queen's Park, he had returned home to shave and eat breakfast. It had been tempting to lie down on the bed or the couch for a spell, but he'd resisted. It would have confused the hell out of him when he woke. A short time later, he'd headed into the office.

He'd utilised the time between then and now to set up the necessary elements of a major murder investigation: open a murder book; decide who he would assign to maintain the Home Office Large Major Enquiry System, HOLMES2; appoint indexers; select the detectives he wanted on the murder team, and determine what help he needed from the uniform boys.

The first three items on the list were concerned with how data would be collected and collated, as well as making sure all procedures were being followed. This was so a defence barrister couldn't later have evidence thrown out of court due to a lack of proper housekeeping. The last two items were concerned with how the murder investigation team should be staffed, which would determine how the investigation was run and how effective it would be.

An hour later, Henderson walked into the Detectives' Room on the second floor of a building in the complex known as Malling House, the headquarters of Sussex Police in Lewes. The room could be subdivided to allow a major investigation team some privacy, and for this one, his Admin Assistant had corralled the strays into a space in the corner.

Before speaking, Henderson took a good look around at all the faces. 'I know it's been a hard few days, particularly for those of you working on the Patcham murder, but it should be myself and DS Walters who are looking washed-out, not you guys.'

'Some of us have a better excuse,' DS Vicky Neal said. 'We were at Terry Haldane's leaving do last night.'

'Ah yes, I'd forgotten all about that. Did you have a good night?'

'I think so, up to around ten. My memory after that gets a bit dim.'

'That's when they started the karaoke,' DC Phil Bentley said. 'I have to say, with a touch of modesty, my rendition of 'Old Town Road' went down a storm.'

'I hope nobody was filming that bit of the evening,' a horrified-looking Neal said. 'I seem to recall somebody coaxing me up on stage, or was this part of the bad dream I had last night?'

'It was no dream, Vicky, Rob Davis filmed everything. Your impression of Bette Midler was something else and if you really want to see the video for yourself, I believe he's already uploaded it to YouTube.'

'It sounds like one of those sorts of nights; I'm glad I had somewhere else to go.' Henderson had been invited, but he suspected they were just trying to be polite. The presence of a DI among the throng of sergeants, constables, and civilian staff would have taken the edge off the evening. It wouldn't have been much fun for him either, with the lot of them getting pissed as newts and him being on-call and having to stick to alcohol-free beer.

'Okay,' Henderson said, 'let's focus on this murder.' He turned and tapped the whiteboard behind him. There, he had posted several photographs taken at the murder scene, added a few comments, and joined any connections that were evident at this time with straight lines.

'The victim's name is Stuart Livermore,' Henderson said. 'He's the author of several crime novels, rom-coms and science fiction novels and lived alone in a semi-detached house in East Drive, Queen's Park. He died from multiple stab wounds, about eight or ten to his legs and arms before death, and a deep, fatal wound to the chest.'

'I get the stab wound to the chest, but what are all the other injuries about?' Vicky Neal asked. 'Does it suggest he put up a fight?'

'They don't look like defence wounds to me,' DS Harry Wallop said. 'It looks sort of vindictive.'

'Maybe what you're trying to say, Harry,' DC Phil Bentley said, 'is it looks like some form of torture. The killer asks him a question and when he gives the wrong answer, he stabs him in the leg or arm.'

'It's all speculation at this point,' Henderson said. 'Maybe the P-M will give us a better idea.'

'I've read a couple of Stuart Livermore's books,' DC Sally Graham said.

'Have you, Sally? Good. Can you give us a flavour of what they're about? It might save me some reading later on.'

'He's best known as a crime author, although around a year ago, he branched into rom-com. His books are a bit different from the other detective books I've read. I would say he's pretty accurate in the way he portrays the work we do. You know, the procedures we follow at crime scenes, the use of forensics, PACE, you name it.'

'It sounds like he was getting some help.'

'Yes, it's in the acknowledgement page at the back of his books. He worked with a retired Superintendent from Kent.'

'Was he successful as an author? The size of the house and the quality of the furnishings suggests that he was.'

'I did a bit of checking before I came into the meeting. He'd been sort of bubbling under the top twenty for a few years until his fifth book, *Black Night*, won the Crime Writers Association crime novel of the year.'

'This is the one serialised on the BBC?'

'Yes, as a result of the CWA award, an independent television company picked the book up and turned it into an eight-part television series, shown on the prime nine o'clock slot. Since then, his books have always made it into the top ten.'

'This may sound a bit left field, Sally, but was anyone in his books stabbed in the same way as our victim with multiple wounds?'

'I've only read two, but in the fourth book in the 'Black' series, *Black Poison,* one of the characters is stabbed three or four times in the street, revenge for stealing the killer's wife. It doesn't sound like the same manner as our victim, but like I say, I haven't read them all.'

'Thanks, Sally.' If Henderson decided to read one of his books, it would be this one.

'Now, judging from the mess left outside the bookcase and cupboards in the lounge, which you can see in this photograph,' he said pointing at the board behind him, 'it looks as though the killer was looking for something.'

'It's got to be money or valuables,' DS Harry Wallop said.

'It's a logical conclusion to draw, Harry, given the mess, and the same one DS Walters and myself came to when first viewing the scene. However, there are a couple of inconsistencies with that scenario which makes me think the killer might have been a bit more systematic in his or her approach.'

He turned and tapped the photograph of Stuart Livermore's lounge. 'This is the only room in the house that looks rifled. If this is a burglary, they would have pulled apart other areas like the medicine cabinet. It contained a range of sedatives, sleeping pills and tranquillisers–'

'Why so much?'

'I don't know; perhaps he was a depressive, or suffered from anxiety. It's one of the points I've noted down on your summary sheets that needs to be followed up. If it was a burglary, without doubt the killer would have searched the victim's bedroom. There, in the bedside unit, and without too much trouble, DS Walters found several watches and his passport.'

'Is there anybody who can give us an idea what might be missing from the house?' Neal asked.

'I think Livermore's girlfriend, Hannah Robbins, would be our best bet, but at the moment she's under sedation. The death of Livermore seems to have hit her hard.'

'Poor girl.'

'Now, if you see here,' he said pointing again at the board, 'so far we've identified a small list of people close to our victim. We have his girlfriend, Hannah Robbins, who's already been mentioned. There's an ex-wife that his neighbour told us about, Ellen Jacobs. There are still some question marks relating to the people who I expect will know him from a work perspective. Here, I'm thinking about publishers and television producers. Does anybody know if authors, like actors, have agents?'

'I think they do,' Sally Graham said.

'Right, so we need to add in agents. As an initial sweep, Carol, you and I will interview Hannah Robbins; Vicky, you and Sally will talk to Ellen Jacobs; Harry, I want you to coordinate the door-to-door interviews around Queens Park.'

'Righto,' Wallop said.

'By talking to Robbins and Jacobs,' Henderson said, 'we should get a handle on who else we need to speak to with regard to his writing career.'

'Who's this Mark Wallace character you've underlined?' Neal asked.

'I was coming to him. Steph and Mark Wallace are Livermore's next-door neighbours; they live on the other side of the semi-detached wall. When Carol and I spoke to Mark early this morning, his hostility for the dead man was evident, he doesn't try to hide it. It seems to be rooted in jealousy. He's convinced Livermore and his wife were more than just friends, and she gives the impression her mourning is for more than her favourite neighbour. I'm not suggesting they were involved in an affair, but it's something I want you, Harry, to explore when you interview her. Do it once the door-to-door is underway.'

'Will do,' Wallop said, looking pleased not to be left out.

'She's a fitness instructor at Virgin Active in Falmer, and I think Mark's a builder. Find out where he works. I think it would be better for you to see Steph at the gym, without her partner present. If the questions get too near the knuckle, he might be tempted to give you a thump.'

'Understood.'

'Now, this is as far as Carol and I've got. If you can think of any other avenues we haven't covered at this stage, let's hear it.'

He looked around the room, but seeing no takers, he gathered his papers. 'See you all at six-thirty.'

SIX

Henderson returned to his office following the initial murder team briefing. In quiet moments he was monitoring his tiredness levels and, so far, he didn't seem to be flagging. A combination of strong coffee and the adrenaline rush brought on by a new murder investigation was doing a good job of keeping him alert.

He sat down at his desk and picked up the phone. Sergeant Bob Davis at John Street police station answered on the second ring.

'Hi Bob, it's Angus.'

'Oh shit, I wasn't expecting to hear from you today, Angus. I told you last night, mate, I don't have the money.'

'What the hell are you doing playing poker with money you don't have?'

'I know, I know, but I just sort of got carried away with the game.'

'If it was just me, I'd let it go until pay day, but you've got to consider what the other guys will think if word gets out. Your name will be mud and you'll never be invited to another session.'

'Yeah, I get it.'

'I can lie and tell them everything's cool, but if it happens again, it will be my reputation on the line as well as yours.'

'You're right, I know I messed up.' He sighed. 'I'm sorry, Angus, I really am.'

'Okay.'

'I think there's a place where I can get it.'

'Not a payday lender, I hope?'

'Nah, I wouldn't be so daft. My girlfriend. I don't usually involve her too much with my finances, you know how it is, but it looks like now I've got no choice. It will cost me more than money to pay her back, but who said penance was easy?'

'Good man. So, when are we talking about?'

'Well, it's Monday today, so if we say... by Friday?'

'Sounds good. Talk to you then, Bob.'

'Cheers, mate and thanks.'

Henderson put the phone down feeling cross at being forced to make the call, the first of its kind since joining the poker school over four years before. It was reckless for anyone to enter any gambling arena with money they didn't have. If people like Davis weren't careful, poker was the sort of game that could sweep you along in the thrill of the moment and empty more than your pockets. People had been known to throw in expensive watches, bracelets, phones, and even the keys to their beloved car, forcing them to hike home. He had never reached that stage, but if he did, he hoped he would recognise the signals in time and walk away.

'Morning, Angus.'

Henderson looked up. Detective Chief Inspector Sean Houghton walked into his office.

'Morning Sean, how are you?'

'I'm feeling a lot better than you, I imagine.'

DCI Sean Houghton was the replacement for Lisa Edwards following her move to the Met's Anti-Terrorist Unit in London. Houghton didn't just walk into a room, he seemed to stride everywhere with a sense of purpose. Perhaps he would settle down once he'd spent a few months in the job.

'The murder over at Queen's Park. How does it look?' Houghton sat down in the chair on the other side of Henderson's desk.

'The victim, we now know was a successful crime author by the name of Stuart Livermore.'

'Livermore? I read a lot of novels including crime. I think I've heard of him. Didn't he write the 'Black' series featuring DCI Ed Yates?'

'You know more than I do, but I think you're right. All the evidence points to him being killed by an intruder who wanted something that Livermore had. The victim had various knife wounds on his legs and arms indicating what, we don't know. Perhaps it was in an effort to subdue him, to make him give up some piece of information or a sadistic bastard's way of prolonging his inevitable death.'

'The latter I would think. When you say, Angus, 'a successful author', are we talking here about a celebrity? I had to deal with a pop star's death in my last job and I can tell you, the pressure from all sides will keep you awake, not just for one night, but for every night of the investigation.'

'I don't think even top authors can be considered celebrities.'

'Why not?'

'It could have something to do with their readers being more mature than the people who follow pop or movie stars. Plus, books aren't an immediate adrenalin rush like a good pop record or in the way a blockbuster movie can be.'

'Even with that caveat, it sounds to me like, given the vagaries of journalists and the pressure to sell more newspapers, the press will be taking a greater interest in this one.'

'You could be right. They tend to latch on to anyone with at least a half-interesting background, so I guess even a dead author fits the bill.'

'That's all I need for my first big case. Let's hear the rest of your summary.'

'There's not much more to tell. Livermore was finally killed by a deep wound to the chest. The killer then ransacked the cupboards, but only in the lounge.'

'Only in one room? That's odd. What does it lead you to conclude?'

'Either he had been scared off before he finished searching, although there's nothing to indicate this happened, or he had found what he came for. If he hadn't and wasn't disturbed, I'm sure he would have turned the rest of the house over.'

'I agree.'

'The question is, what was he looking for? As yet, we don't know the answer to that one. Once we've questioned the people closest to him, we should have a better idea.'

'When is this taking place?'

'The team are heading out now.'

'You've got them organised quicker than I expected. Didn't you go back to bed once you'd finished at the crime scene?'

Henderson shook his head. 'No point.'

'In that case, I'm glad I caught you now. I don't think I'd get much sense out of you any time after lunch. Strong coffee can only take you so far.'

'There is another scenario I think we need to consider.'

'What's that?'

'The killer went there with the sole purpose of killing Livermore, and only pulled the cupboards apart to try and put us off.'

'If that were true, he would have made a better fist of creating a ransacked house, don't you think? He would also have spilled the contents of a few kitchen cupboards, and tipped his underwear drawer all over the floor. To me, it looks like the scenario you mentioned at the start. Livermore told the killer where to find the item he wanted, but he still stabbed him, either to silence him, or because he wanted him dead for other reasons. Listen, Angus, I'm not by nature a desk jockey, I want to be out investigating cases. This one sounds as good to me as any. What do you think?'

'Is it your intention only to take part in important interviews and house raids, or do you want to be more involved overall?'

Houghton was fast-track, a bright guy with a couple of degrees to his name. He'd worked on a number of high-profile cases: a large drug bust involving the import of new cars, and the capture of a notorious jewellery heist gang. He was forty-three, a few years younger than Henderson, with short hair and a chiselled face. He looked fit as if he went out running or attended a gym regularly. Henderson liked to run, and completed a 5k several times a week, but this guy looked as if such a distance would act only as a warm-up.

'The first one. I don't think the pressures of the job will allow enough time for the second. Are you meeting any witnesses today?'

'Tomorrow, I'm going to talk to the victim's girlfriend, Hannah Robbins.'

'Right,' he said, giving both his knees a resounding slap. 'It sounds important enough. We'll team up for it.'

'I don't recommend you coming on this one, Sean. She's in a fragile state. She was given tranquillisers by the doctor after discovering the body. If two male detectives turn up on her doorstep, so soon after finding her boyfriend dead, I think it might be too much for her.'

He considered this for a moment 'I think you're right. How about we do this? Oh, hang on.' He pulled the ringing phone out of his pocket.

'Morning, sir. Yes, I do have it.' Houghton stood and walked slowly to the door. 'It should be on your desk by the end of the day.' He mouthed to Henderson, 'See you later', before disappearing out the door and down the corridor.

Saved by a ringing phone, it had been a lucky escape. A new DCI keen for a quick result was one rod he would have to bear; he didn't need another, his boss sitting beside him in an interview room, or in the living room of a witness.

Henderson hoped the administrative demands of Houghton's job, not to mention the legendary high standards set by *his* boss, the Assistant Chief Constable, would keep him at Malling House a lot more than he expected.

SEVEN

It was a cold day outside. According to weather reports this was due, in the main, to winds emanating from Siberia. Still, the heating in Hannah Robbins' flat was beyond what was required to keep the September chill from the door.

Henderson, Walters, and Robbins were seated in the lounge of an apartment in a modern block at the bottom of Second Avenue in Hove. It was a stone's throw from the seafront, but it was clear Ms Robbins' budget didn't stretch to a sea view. However, if Henderson leaned out of one of the windows, he might catch a fleeting glimpse.

Hannah Robbins was slight in build, with shoulder-length brown hair and a youthful, elfin face. Knowing she was the girlfriend of Stuart Livermore, a man of forty-three, he would imagine she was of a similar age, but she could be anything between twenty-five and forty-five. The giveaway, perhaps, was the cardigan, long skirt and fluffy slippers.

'I'm sorry for the intrusion at what I know must be a difficult time, Ms Robbins,' Henderson said. 'The sooner we find out more about Stuart, the quicker we can catch whoever killed him.'

'I understand. I'll tell you what I can.'

'Thank you.'

'Stuart and I had been going out for nine months. Before this happened, we were planning our future together.'

'He's divorced, I've been told.'

'Yes, he divorced Ellen Jacobs about four years ago.'

'How did the two of you meet?'

'I used to be his editor.'

'How do you mean, used to be? Because he's...?'

'No, no. I'm talking years back. When Stuart started out as an author, he was science fiction writer. He came to us at Thor Books as we specialise in the genre. The books sold well for a time, but Stuart said what he really wanted to do was write a crime series, something we couldn't help him with. His agent, Lindsay Taggart, secured him a deal with Constellation, the big crime publishers. The rest, as they say, is history.'

'His career took off?'

'Oh yes, big time. Not at the start, it rarely does, but by his fifth book–'

'*Black Night.*'

'You've heard of it? Good. At the time, a friend of mine said he was looking for material for a television project. I recommended Stuart's book.'

'I thought it was because he had won some award?'

'The CWA Dagger?'

'Yes, that sounds like it.'

'It certainly lifted his profile, but sometimes these things need a push before anything will happen.'

'I see. Did the series make him rich?'

'Don't sound so sceptical, Inspector. Not every author is sitting in a draughty garret hammering away on a skip-rescued typewriter. Yes, it made him rich, his subsequent books even more so. You see, with film and to a lesser extent television, the bulk of the money received by an author doesn't usually come from the film or television programme.'

'No?'

'No, it's from the spike they receive in book sales. People will be attracted to the book after they see advertising for the film, or indeed, once they've seen the film itself. For Stuart, this increase in sales continued long after *Black Night* was no longer shown on BBC iPlayer and Netflix.'

'I see.'

Robbins appeared calm. This didn't mean she had come to terms with her boyfriend's death, but she had obviously slipped into a more familiar business mode while talking about Livermore's career.

Henderson had been convinced that Livermore was well-off, although perhaps not to the extent suggested by his girlfriend. It might provide a motive for his murder, but as yet, he couldn't see how.

'You mentioned Stuart's literary agent, Lindsay Taggart. Who else did Stuart deal with from a professional perspective?'

She paused for a moment. 'There are, I think, three main people. There's his editor at Constellation Books, Maisie Carruthers. His publicist at King Media, Jane Stevenson. Finally, the police consultant who reviews technical aspects of his books, retired Superintendent Craig Johnson.'

'I'd like to take them one a time. Could you tell me a little more about each of them?'

'I'll do my best.'

'Maisie Carruthers. What does she do?'

'If I can speak ill of the dead for a moment,' she said, stopping to wipe her nose with a tissue, 'Stuart was a good writer, but a messy sod. Not in everyday life you understand, he always dressed well and kept his house tidy, but in his head. His manuscripts were full of inconsistencies, grammatical errors, typos, you name it. Maisie's job was to knock it into some sort of shape, which she did brilliantly.'

'Did she and Stuart get on well together?'

'Maisie can be a dragon when she wants to be, I guess all editors can be at times, but I believe in everything she did, she had Stuart's interests firmly at heart. Of course, there were major disagreements. Nobody who has slaved over a manuscript for months and months would be pleased to have it torn to shreds, and Stuart wasn't the type to take criticism quietly. Away from the office, they were friends. They often had lunch together; she would appear at events where Stuart was speaking. He, in turn, would support her when she needed something, like a review for a new book she was championing.'

'Okay. How about Jane Stevenson? What's her role?'

'When his publishers are about to release a new book, Stuart would engage Jane to start a publicity campaign. She's very good and gets him invited on to radio programmes, literary events, and featured in weekend magazines. You know the sort of thing, where there's a picture of the author in their study, and they talk about the things that are dear to them.'

'Why does he use his own publicist? I would have thought a publisher would do that.'

'Let's just say that some publishers are better at it than others. If there was a chart, Constellation would come near the bottom. Stuart said it was to supplement his publisher's efforts, not to supplant them.'

'Very diplomatic. What's she like?'

'Jane? She's feisty and assertive. She can be rude at times, in terms of business dealings, and with people who don't do what she asks. Outside of work, she can be a bit of a cold fish. Stuart didn't socialise with her.'

'The last name on your list, Stuart's police consultant, retired Superintendent Craig Johnson. What's he like?'

'Do you know him?'

Henderson and Walters shook their heads.

'Well, let me tell you, he's an odious character. At times, I think he has more in common with the criminals he once pursued than any policeman I've ever come across.'

'That bad?'

'Yes. Our paths have crossed on several occasions. Every time, I come away feeling like I need to take a shower. He exudes bad vibes from the way he talks about previous cases he's worked on, how he treated criminals he used to deal with, and even the sloppy way he dresses.'

'I appreciate you telling us this Hannah,' Henderson said, 'the information you've provided will help enormously. Now, I need to know if anything is missing from Stuart's house.'

'Okay.'

'I imagine you're the best person to do it. Am I right?'

'None of his family, his son or daughter visit him regularly enough to know what's there. His closest friend, Ryan Allison, another author, used to go around there quite a lot. He's a man and, no disrespect intended Inspector, but most men don't see much beyond the beer glass they are holding in their hand. So, yes you are right, I'm the best person.'

'I think the best way to approach this is for me to meet you at the house, then we can go over it room by room.'

She seemed to shrink back into her chair. 'I'm...I'm not sure I'm ready to go back into Stuart's house just yet.'

'I understand your reluctance, but I wouldn't be asking you if I didn't believe this was important. We think the person who killed Stuart was looking for something. If we can discover what that was, assuming it's been taken away, we should have a better idea of who we are looking for.'

'I understand, but ...'

'When I say room by room, I'm making it sound like a lot of work, when in reality, it isn't. What I mean is I'd like you to take a detailed look at the lounge and a cursory look everywhere else. The other rooms look untouched, and if something is missing, I think it will be obvious.'

She took a deep breath which seemed to fortify her. 'When you put it like that, it doesn't sound too difficult. I suppose I could give it a go.'

'I don't think you'll find it too bad, but we need to do it soon.'

She looked into the distance, perhaps thinking of better times. 'Okay, yes, I'll do it.'

'Good. When do think you could manage it? The sooner the better.'

'Tomorrow afternoon? I'm back at work on Thursday, so I think to try and arrange it after that will be more difficult.'

'Thank you. Now, I know this question will not be an easy one for you to answer, but I have to ask. Do you have any idea who killed Stuart?'

'I have no idea, Inspector, that's the God-honest truth. I've asked myself the same question many times.' She paused, fiddling with her hair, before pulling it back behind her ears. 'If you'd asked me who within Stuart's large circle of friends and associates is *capable* of killing someone, I would say Craig Johnson. That said, for the life of me I can't think of any reason why he would. Johnson was well paid and Stuart often wheeled him out at literary events. In a way, the man was a star, and Stuart was responsible, in a good way, for hastening his early retirement. If anyone out there is more devastated by Stuart's death than me, it would be him.'

EIGHT

Steve Mitchell started the engine and drove, the remains of a Gregg's sausage roll still sticking out of his mouth. Not the vegan option for him, this one was packed with meat. He liked eating in the car, doing two things at once always gave him a measure of satisfaction.

The downside of his car snacking was all the discarded crisp packets, chocolate bars, and paper bags from the said bakery that littered the floor and filled the side pockets. The mess was easy for him to ignore, but he couldn't say the same for his girlfriend, Ellie. On several occasions, she had refused to travel in the car until he'd cleaned it up.

He joined the A57, heading south-west towards the Yorkshire Dales. In his latest thriller, the seventh book in the *Cobra Squad* series, as yet untitled, he had written a scene where a clandestine helicopter drops stolen, classified documents somewhere in the Dales. The drop site had to be close to water for the purposes of the plot, and he believed he had found the perfect place using Google Maps. Now, he wanted to see for himself.

It was for the same reason he had spent the weekend in the south of England, not an easy undertaking with bad weather around Nottingham causing serious tailbacks. Further south, the ring road around Birmingham was littered with a succession of small accidents, and he was held up for over an hour on the M25 for reasons he couldn't fathom.

The start of the Dales, at least from his side of Sheffield, was the village of Ringinglow. Passing through, he tried to keep to the 30mph speed limit, a tricky undertaking in a three-litre V6 Porsche Cayenne, never happier than when cruising in the outside lane of a motorway at ninety.

When driving in towns and villages, he tried to keep to the speed limit. This wasn't because he was a model citizen, or loathe to break the law, which he regarded as a set of loose guidelines and not rules. No, he'd been caught by a camera in this village before and, with nine points already in the bag, another speeding bust would mean he would be banned from driving for at least a year.

He passed the Norfolk Arms Hotel, bringing back happy memories of a hearty lunch and a few beers following yet another sortie into the Dales to take pictures and make notes. All his books were set in and around Yorkshire, two in the Dales itself.

His phone rang.

He was about to answer when he spotted the front bumper of a police patrol car jutting out of a side-road some distance ahead. With a muttered 'Fuck', he lifted his foot off the accelerator, allowing the car's speed to creep back from thirty-five to under thirty. He pressed the call 'accept' control on the car's steering wheel.

'How's Yorkshire's answer to Lee Child?'

'Sam don't be a fuckwit all your life. I was born in Waltham Forest, as you well know. When was East London even close to fucking Yorkshire?'

'Not in football terms at any rate. Sheffield Wednesday are in the top six and the Hammers and your beloved Orient are down there in the relegation zone.'

'You know better than to get me started on football.'

'I'm just messing with you, mate. How are you getting on with the new one? I wanna know what mess you've got the Cobra Squad into this time, and if you've done what I asked you and bumped off that annoying bastard, Commander Dave Mathews.'

'This sounds like your subtle way of asking, but no, I don't have a title for the bloody thing yet. Like rhubarb in the equally famous Yorkshire Triangle, it'll appear when it's ready.'

'Lighten up, mate, I didn't call just to bend your ear about the new book. It so happens I called to tell you some breaking news.'

Sam Ogden was Steve Mitchell's literary agent and, if he was being honest, one of his best buddies. He'd got him out of jail when Mitchell had decked a guy for touching up his then girlfriend. In addition, on more occasions than he could remember, Sam had guided him back to his hotel or Sam's apartment in Battersea when he'd drunk too much to see straight.

'Don't tell me you've passed your IQ? No, I lie. It's your driving test. How a man can call himself a man without a driving license to his name, I'll never know.'

'Steve, I need you to be serious for a minute.'

'I am being serious. Driving is a serious business, and owning a car like this one is as important to me as Ellie, maybe even more.'

'Don't let her hear you say that. Are you in the car at the moment?'

'As I live and breathe.'

'Pull over into a lay-by mate, this might come as a bit of a shock.'

'I'm a big boy, I can handle it.'

'Suit yourself, but slow down at least. Stuart Livermore is dead. He was found murdered on Sunday night.'

'Whoa! Oh, fucking hell.'

'What's wrong? I didn't think you two were so close, or is there something you're not telling me since your last spat with him?'

'Don't be wet, we could never be close. I just about ran into a car on the other side of the road, seconds after I passed a fucking parked cop car.'

'I told you Steve, you need to pull over to the side.'

'I will, I will.'

In the rear-view mirror he watched the patrol car for any movement. To his dismay, it slid forward. The car emerged from the side street and turned his way. Shit! Up ahead at the edge of the village, Mitchell spotted a row of terraced houses. He turned into the lay-by in front of them. A few moments later, the patrol car pulled up behind him.

'If I get booked for this, I'm sending you the fine. Call you later, Sam.'

'I'll be on the lookout for your arrest on the news feeds. Then, I'll put out a press release: 'Steve

Mitchell, Yorkshire's answer to Lee Child sent to a high-security jail."

'Fuck off you idiot.'

Mitchell reached into his pocket, pulled out his wallet and fished out his driving license. When one of the police officers approached, he lowered the window and held it out.

The cop took the proffered item and placed it on the clipboard he was carrying.

'Your driving was a bit erratic back there, Mr...' he looked down at the clipboard, 'Mitchell. Have you been drinking, sir?'

'No way. Too early, even for me.'

'Using a mobile phone then?'

'Yeah, I was on the phone, but I was using it hands-free through the car's speakers.'

'Was it your partner or mother giving you a hard time?'

'No, it was my literary agent. I'm an author, you see. He'd just told me one of my... another author, has just been killed. Murdered.'

'Who would that be, sir?'

'Stuart Livermore.'

'I don't know the name, and don't recall hearing anything about the case back at the station.'

'It happened on Sunday night. He lived in Sussex, if it's any help.'

'You two were close?'

'I wouldn't say close. I've bumped into him at various literary events over the years, and we'd chat, but I was still shocked to hear about his death.'

Mitchell wondered where this conversation was heading; he couldn't complain. All the time they were discussing Livermore, the cop wasn't thinking about issuing him with a ticket. Maybe he'd forget.

The cop said nothing for a minute or two while he tapped out something on a device Mitchell couldn't see.

'My first reaction on seeing your misdemeanour back there,' the cop said, 'was to issue you with a ticket for careless driving. On listening to your story and checking its validity, in this instance, I'm instead inclined to let it go.'

Mitchell's annoyance at being stopped, and the cop's intrusive questioning about a man he didn't like, seemed to evaporate on hearing the words 'let it go'. A charge, then a conviction, would put points on his driving licence. Ergo, he would no longer be able to drive his beloved Porsche Cayenne, reducing his pride and joy to a plaything for the spiders in the garage for a large proportion of the following year. Hooray for common sense.

He listened as he was given a lecture. First regarding the use of a mobile phone in the car, and then about paying more attention while travelling through villages where elderly residents and small children could wander unexpectedly onto the road. Sermon over, he handed the licence back. Mitchell was so relieved, he could have kissed it; the license, not the hand of the cop.

He bade a grateful farewell to the patrol officer, and instead of carrying on into the Dales to conduct his research, Mitchell decided to call it a day. His new book could wait. He executed a tame U-turn and headed back the way he had come. There, he would dump the car at home, head down to his local, and celebrate today's good fortune with a few jars of Yorkshire's finest.

NINE

DS Vicky Neal was driving on automatic despite sitting behind the wheel of a car fitted with a manual gearbox. She was in the final stages of buying an apartment in Brighton. Only this morning, she received a letter from her solicitor, that not only ruined her breakfast, but would do the same to the rest of her day.

The apartment she was trying to buy was on the first floor of a beautiful, white, Georgian-style building in Portland Place, close to Brighton seafront. It was modern inside with a newly-fitted kitchen, fully-tiled bathroom, and wooden flooring throughout. Problem was, the lease she had been due to sign in a week or so, prohibited the use of wooden flooring on any apartment above the ground floor, due to noise.

'You okay, gov?' DC Sally Graham asked from the passenger seat. 'You're not often this quiet.'

'Sorry, Sally, I'm miles away. It's this flat-buying process. It's getting me down.'

'I know what you mean. These old buildings with complicated leases can tie lawyers up for months.'

'Just when I appear to be close to completion, something else jumps up to put a spanner in the works.'

'The thing never to forget is the seller, estate agent, and lawyer all want it to happen, just as much as you do. If it doesn't, they don't get paid. All the same, you need to be on their case or other priorities will get in the way.'

'Good advice,' Neal said. She paused, turning the car around a corner. 'I seem to say this wherever I go, but I've never been to Lindfield before.'

'A former boyfriend used to live here, so I've been here a few times. To me, it started out as a separate village, but now it's sort of been absorbed into Haywards Heath.'

'There's some pretty large houses around here.'

'I know, and there's a duck pond, cricket club, and a couple of decent pubs. It's what estate agents would call a picturesque village.'

A few minutes later they turned into Noah's Ark Lane. The houses here looked smaller and newer. They stopped outside a short row of terraced houses.

'The Jacobs' house is the one on the end,' Graham said. 'They can pretend they live in a semi.'

'Still, it's not a patch on the big place her ex owns.'

'Or, used to own,' Graham corrected.

'Quite.' She sighed. 'Okay, let's go and hear what she's got to say for herself.'

The former wife of Stuart Livermore, Ellen Jacobs, was on the phone when she opened the door to the two detectives. She ushered them inside after giving their warrant cards a cursory glance. Neal would never be so casual if two strangers arrived at her door. It wasn't as if they were wearing uniforms to corroborate their story, although she knew some con artists used appropriate clothing to disguise their true intentions.

The officers let themselves into the lounge, while Jacobs dallied in the hall, phone glued to her ear. This gave Neal a chance for a nose around. A quick poke among the items in a bookcase, and a glance at the garden through the rear patio windows, could often tell most detectives a lot about a person.

First impressions weren't promising. The books in the bookcase, some by her former husband, were messy, dusty, and looked as though they hadn't been taken out for years. Clothes were scattered around the room, not as a result of Jacobs being caught mid-ironing when the phone rang, instead it looked like a couple of teenagers lived here. This was confirmed upon Neal's examination of several framed photographs which featured a boy and girl aged around fifteen or sixteen.

A few minutes later, Ellen Jacobs entered the room. She had straggly brown hair, a pretty face, and was wearing jogging pants and a sweatshirt, suggesting she was about to embark on an exercise session, or had already done so. The podgy frame, pasty complexion, and the empty cup and plate with the biscuit crumbs lying on the coffee table, suggested otherwise.

'Sorry about that,' she said. 'Everything about my friend Sarah's life is a crisis, but it fair keeps me grounded. First off, can I get you anything, tea or coffee? Please say yes, because I'm desperate for another.'

'The death of her ex doesn't seem to be bothering her as much as it did Hannah Robbins,' Neal said in hushed tones when Jacobs had disappeared into the kitchen.

'I was thinking the same thing. Maybe they've been apart a long time.'

'Could be.'

The source of the biscuit crumbs was revealed when a half-finished packet of McVitie's Chocolate Digestives was placed in front of the officers, alongside two coffee mugs.

'As I said on the phone, Ms Jacobs–'

'It's Ellen. Nobody calls me Ms Jacobs except the man from the council.'

'Ellen it is. Can I assume you've heard about the death of your former husband?'

'Yeah, I did. A journalist told me.'

'Oh.'

'Yeah, a woman called and asked if I had any recent pictures of Stuart and to give her some background.'

'I see. Please accept our condolences for your loss.'

'Thank you.'

'We are part of the team investigating his murder. We're talking to everyone who knew him, trying to build up a picture of what he was like. Does that sound okay?'

'Yeah, no problem.'

'If I can make a start. How long were you and Stuart together?'

'We were married fifteen years. We've been divorced for four.'

'Did you have any children together?'

'Yeah,' she said nodding at the pictures Neal had been examining earlier. 'Daniel's fourteen, but big for his age, and Jodie, who's just turned sixteen. They're typical teenagers. He's worried about the spots on his face, and she has tantrums saying no boy will fancy her because she's so ugly.'

'I was looking at her picture a few minutes back, and I thought then what a pretty girl she was. She isn't the least bit ugly.'

'I'll tell her you said that. It might stop her getting so upset about it.'

'What do you do, Ellen, or what did you used to do before you had children?'

'Before I met Stuart, I was marketing executive with a couple of large companies, the likes of Disney and John Lewis. Like so many other stupid women at the time, I gave it all up to stay at home and look after the children.'

'Why do think it was stupid?' Graham asked. 'Do you regret having them?'

'No, no, that's not what I mean. What I resented was giving up a good career. I did it on the understanding that Stuart would look after me when the children were grown up and off our hands. It wasn't written in stone or anything like that, but who can abandon a good career in business and then go back twenty years later and pick up where they left off? Nobody, that's who. I don't have a clue about the technology they use, and even the language people speak nowadays is different to what I'm used to.'

'What happened between you and Stuart?'

'As soon as he got his first whiff of success, he fu...buggered off quicker than a dog out of the traps at Hove Greyhound Stadium.'

'Why, what happened?'

'Oh, it's the same old story. In fact, it could have been a plot from one of the stupid rom-com books he was starting to write. Books which I counselled him against writing, by the way. He left me for another woman; traded me in for a younger model. She wasn't just younger than me, she was ten years younger than him, and much more successful. Another bloody author, would you believe?'

'What was her name?'

'I can't remember, but she didn't last long, I do remember that. He dumped her after a couple of months, but the damage was done. No way would I have him back, even if he got on his knees and begged me. A month after, I filed for divorce. No sooner was the ink dry on the papers, when the bas...when Stuart signed a deal with a television company for them to make a series for the BBC of *Black Night*.'

'Did this annoy you?' Graham asked.

'Annoy me? I was bloody livid!' she exploded. 'It still bothers me. While he was struggling to make it as an author, we were living on the money I'd saved from the time when I'd been working, and from the sale of a house belonging to my parents. He was earning next to nothing from his books. You see, when you're not successful, publishers don't want to know and pay you peanuts. When a book takes off, like *Black Night* did after the programme aired, they throw everything at it. Stuart not only received money from the television company, his publishers were giving him big advances to write more books.'

'Did you feel like you'd missed out?'

'Of course, I bloody did! Do you think I like living in this box with that crappy car outside? I funded Stuart through all the lean times, the least I could expect is he would pay me back. Did he? Did he hell. I never saw a bean.'

'Have you gone back to work?'

'I needed to,' she sighed. 'No way could I clothe and feed two teenagers with the money I have in the bank. I manage a Customer Service Team at EDF Energy in Hove. It's not the level of work I'm used to, not by a long stretch, but it pays the bills.'

'Did Stuart make maintenance payments?'

'Yeah, it's the one good thing I can say about him. They're paid on time every month.'

TEN

Henderson picked Hannah Robbins up from her flat in Hove and drove her to Stuart Livermore's house in Queen's Park. She said little on the journey, the two days since the discovery of Livermore's body having done little to soften the pain. However, she did look less frail and vulnerable than previously, so with luck they might get through this without incident.

Scene of Crime officers were still working and would continue to occupy the house for the rest of the week. They hadn't as yet uncovered any clue as to the identity of the perpetrator, save for an unmatched footprint in the soil outside the back door. If he or she had been wearing gloves when they smashed the back door window, and again when they stabbed Livermore, Henderson's best hope would lie in a stray hair, or something else dropped by the killer.

They made their way past the bags and cases of equipment left by the SOCO team in the hall and walked into the lounge. The room was quiet and devoid of activity, the SOCOs work in this part of the house now complete. He could hear them moving upstairs.

'We should start in here.'

'Why, because Stuart was killed in here?'

'No, because the forensic team are finished with the lounge and the kitchen. We won't be in their way.'

'Oh, I see.'

'What I'd like you to do is take a look around this room. Try to picture all the items and equipment which were situated there the last time you visited. Then, I'd like you to tell me is if there's anything missing.'

'Okay, I'll do my best.'

She stood at the door and scanned the room for several seconds. 'On Sunday night when I came in here, there was a pile of papers scattered around the base of the bookshelves. They're not there now.'

'Don't worry about that. It's all been removed by my officers. We'll return everything in due course.'

'Why have you taken them?'

'For the same reason you're here, to see if anything's missing. If the paperwork is, as we suspect, typical for a single, divorced man, it should contain tax records, bank statements, investment details, publishing contracts and so on. If something has obviously been removed, we should spot it. Likewise, if something is there doesn't fit, it could be the item we think the killer was looking for but didn't find.'

'I see. So, do I ignore the bookshelves?'

'No, I'd like you to take a look at everything still in there. Try to visualise if anything's missing.'

To him, it sounded like he was repeating himself, like uttering a religious mantra to make him feel better, but it was no more complicated than that. The team were convinced the killer had taken something.

Identify it, and they were on the way to identifying them.

She walked slowly around the room, doing what Henderson asked.

'The television's still here, and the DVD player. Stuart watched a lot of DVDs, more than he did television programmes.'

'I do the same myself. I don't often find there's much on the box of interest.'

'His books are all there, so are his audiobooks and the translations done by foreign publishers. Why he kept them, God only knows. He didn't speak French, German or Italian.' She removed a book and began flicking through the pages. 'At least I've got something that very few other bereaved partners have. I can pick up one of those at any time and have Stuart talk to me as if he was in the room beside me.'

'Did he narrate his own audiobooks?'

'No, I'm afraid he didn't. If he did, I could listen to them now and hear his voice like he was still alive. They were narrated by an actor from *Game of Thrones*. If you've ever watched it, he was the beefy guy who wandered away from one of the big showpiece battles in series six. He was badly wounded with his face all bloody, and lay down for rest, only to be attacked and eaten by a pack of wolves waiting in the woods.'

'Grisly.'

'Yes, but his rich baritone was a perfect match for Stuart's writing which at times can be dark and brooding.'

She fingered her way through each of the DVDs and CDs. Reaching the end, she stopped and turned to face Henderson. 'Nothing's missing from this room that I can see.'

'Okay, let's move into the kitchen.'

The broken window in the back door was no longer visible, a sheet of hardboard tacked up, awaiting the arrival of a glazier.

'No, it all looks fine in here, but I don't suppose any burglar would be interested in taking his old coffee machine or kettle.'

'It would surprise you to hear the things that people will steal. Even builders have to lock up all their machinery on a site at night. Otherwise, they'd arrive next morning to find bulldozers and cement mixers missing.'

'Good Lord, I had no idea.'

They completed the review of the upstairs rooms in less than five minutes. The rooms looked as they did the last time Hannah had stayed there, the day before Livermore left for Norwich. With only a single man living in a four-bedroom house, all but the main bedroom lay unused and the other rooms contained only the minimum of furniture needed to accommodate any guests. This made it simple to see if anything had been disturbed.

'Thank you for taking the time to come here, Hannah,' Henderson said at the foot of the stairs. He reached over and eased open the front door. 'I know it can't have been easy for you.'

'Stuart's death was so violent, so grisly, it's affected me in ways I couldn't have imagined. I'll do anything I can to help you find his killer.'

'I'm pleased to hear you say it, but you've helped me enough today. C'mon, I'll give you a lift back to Hove.'

'No, that won't be necessary, Inspector. I'll walk, it will give me a chance to clear my head.'

'Are you sure? It's a fair distance.'

'I know, but I've done it plenty of times. I tend to walk everywhere as I don't own a car. Not that you can usually find a place to park around here, anyway. Goodbye, Inspector.'

Robbins turned and walked down the path.

'Goodbye, Hannah and thanks again,' Henderson said. He was on the point of closing the door when he heard Robbins say, 'Oh, Inspector Henderson. Can you hang on for a second?'

Henderson turned. 'Have you forgotten something?'

'No. I've been thinking about the question you asked me when you came to my flat. You said, could I think of anyone who might have killed Stuart?'

'I remember. Have you thought of someone?'

'When I was thumbing through Stuart's books earlier, there was something niggling away at the back of my mind. I've only just grasped it.'

'I'm glad you did. Who?'

'It's someone Stuart disliked, and that's saying something. He liked everyone. A few years back, Stuart accused a fellow author on Twitter, Steve

Mitchell, of 'sockpuppeting'. Do you know what that is?'

'No, never heard of it.'

'When we talk about it in terms of the book business, it's when someone uses a succession of aliases to write favourable reviews of their own books on sites like Amazon and Goodreads. They also create posts on a wide variety of book forums saying what a fine author they are.'

'Is this considered gaming the system, or simply cheating?'

'There's nothing illegal about it, I believe, but I think it's a heinous practice. It dupes the reading public into believing the perpetrator is a better author and more popular writer than they really are.'

'Stuart accused Steve Mitchell of doing this?'

'Yes. Mitchell's an author of a series of what I would describe as robust thriller books featuring a gang of odious characters called the Cobra Squad. They're big muscled hunks who drink, smoke, womanise, argue about who's got the most tattoos, and beat-up the bad guys in their spare time. You get the picture?'

'Yes.'

'Mitchell is an expert at sockpuppeting. He used over fifteen aliases, and on Twitter he bombarded users with recommendations for his books. On Goodreads and Amazon, he'd write dozens of five-star reviews for all his books. I could go on.'

'What went on between him and Stuart?'

'Stuart put a couple of posts up on Facebook and Twitter criticising what Mitchell was doing, suggesting readers should boycott his books in protest. Mitchell responded like a member of the Cobra Squad by turning both barrels on Stuart. Fake websites with reader testimonials panning Stuart's writing began to appear. Stuart received abusive Tweets and critical posts on Facebook. Only last week, a Tweet from an account which Stuart said he was sure came from Mitchell, advocated he should be cut into little pieces with a sharp knife.'

ELEVEN

A car containing DS Harry Wallop and DC Phil Bentley pulled into the car park at Virgin Active in Falmer, on the outskirts of Brighton. The weather had taken a turn for the worse, with driving rain and a blustery wind. Few words were exchanged as they made a dash for the entrance.

The gym was located close to the University of Sussex, Brighton and Hove Albion's football stadium, and situated in the grounds of the University of Brighton. Even without entering the gym, the areas they drove past: School of Health Sciences, sports fields, and the football stadium, spoke of youth, health, and nutrition. If Wallop, not the fittest of officers in the Serious Crime Team, was already feeling more energised, he wondered what effect it was having on his rugby-mad companion.

'This place is massive,' Bentley said, 'way bigger than the gym I use.'

'Every gym is bigger than the one I use,' Wallop said.

'Why?'

'I don't go to one'.

'Never?'

'Never joined one, never been to one even as a guest.'

'Maybe you should, Harry,' Bentley said, nodding at his sizeable gut. 'Christmas isn't so far away, you know.'

'Cheeky sod, but maybe you're right. Only last week a mate of mine dropped dead with a heart attack. He was four years younger than me.'

'Sorry to hear that, Harry. Were the two of you close?'

'Kind of lost touch with him over the years, to tell you the truth, but I still liked talking to him whenever we did manage to catch up.'

The trim-looking lass behind the reception desk at last finished her phone call. 'Can I interest you gentlemen in any of the offers we have available today?'

'No, we're not here to join the gym,' Wallop said. 'We're detectives from Sussex Police here to see one of your personal trainers, Steph Wallace. I believe she's expecting us.'

'Steph? Yes, she did mention it. Let me see if she's free.'

'This place looks bigger on the inside than it did outside,' Bentley said. 'Look at the number of rowing machines they've got; bloody amazing.'

He had to agree. It was a huge facility, some of which he could see with a view into the gym area and through windows out to tennis courts and pool. The direction board added a few more items to the list: spa, spin studio, and weights room.

The receptionist returned and, out from the shelter of the large desk, Wallop could see she had the figure of an underwear model.

'Steph will be here in a few minutes. What I'll do is take you to a room where you can have some peace. She'll join you there when she's finished.'

'Does Steph work long hours?' Wallop asked as they walked past a group of sweaty individuals pumping away on the rowing machines.

'She does, and a few of the other more experienced PTs do as well. They're self-employed you see, so the more they work, the more money they make. To tell you the truth, I'd be reluctant to go home if I had a partner like hers.' She opened the door to a small, glass-panelled room kitted out with a couple of chairs and a small table.

'Why do you say that?' Wallop asked. The officers walked inside.

'God, I don't want him arrested or anything.'

Wallop shook his head. 'That's not why we're here. We're just interested to hear more about Steph.'

'You sure?'

'You have my word.'

'Her partner's a brute, drinks too much and wants her to do what she's told.'

'Does he hit her?'

'I don't think so, but he's coercive, you know? He bullies her, not physical like, but more in her head, if you know what I mean? Oops, I'd better shut up, Steph's coming. Have a good meeting.'

Wallop and Bentley got up to shake Steph's hand when she entered the small room, and he hoped she didn't feel too intimidated. Wallop was of average height, but Phil Bentley was over six foot with the build of a solid rugby player. Their interview subject would be lucky to reach Bentley's shoulders.

'Did Sam offer you drinks?'

'She didn't, but nothing for me,' Wallop said.

'I'm okay as well,' Bentley said.

'Fair enough. As you can see, I don't go anywhere without my trusty companion,' she said, nodding at the pink bottle with white stars dotted all over, now sitting on the table. 'Got to keep hydrated.'

It was an effort for Wallop to look from Steph to the water bottle, as she was a stunning sight to behold. Blonde hair parted in the middle, not reaching her shoulders, a beautiful face, and a body that wouldn't look out of place as a museum sculpture.

'Mrs Wallace,' Wallop said, gathering up as much self-control as he could muster.

'Call me Steph. I hate Mrs Wallace.'

'Okay, Steph. We're following up the meeting you had with DI Henderson, late Sunday night, Monday morning.'

'I was pretty zonked at the time, I have to admit. I'd had a session here until about nine, so all I could do when I got home was grab something to eat and fall into bed.'

'How well did you know Mr Livermore?'

'He's been our neighbour since he moved there about four years back. Me and him sort of hit it off right away. You see, I'm quite sociable and so was Stuart. I can't say the same for Mark; he seemed to take an instant dislike. He's like the cantankerous old Labrador my mother used to have. If he didn't like the postman, that was it. We had chewed letters until they brought in somebody new.'

'What was it about Stuart that Mark didn't like?'

'He told your boss it was all because of me. Stuart fancied me, he said. Jealousy did the rest.'

'It sounds as though you don't agree.'

'It's part of it, but you see, Stuart was smart, well-read, educated. Mark just isn't. He's had a chip on his shoulder ever since I've known him. I used to think he took a dislike to politicians, newsreaders, actors, and people he knew, because of some fault they possessed. I only discovered later it was caused by something else.'

She stopped to take a drink from her water bottle.

'It was all because they'd spouted something he couldn't understand,' Steph continued, 'and there I could give you a long list of subjects: politics, economics, geography, history, women, to name a few. I mean, I don't think of myself as smart, but at least I've got a couple of A levels. Mark left school with four GCSEs and one of them was metalwork.'

'How did jealousy play a part?'

She puffed some air up towards her nose, ruffling her hair. 'He didn't like me talking to him.'

'How often did you see Stuart?'

'During the summer, I'd see him out in the garden a couple of nights a week, either sitting having a drink or doing some planting or weeding. I like gardening and, even if I say so myself, I've got the borders at the back looking nice. He would walk over and ask me about specific plants or how I managed to get the shrubs growing so tall and bushy, that sort of thing.'

'And at other times?'

'How do you mean?'

'Did you see him at other times, maybe in the street, in the local pub or out shopping?'

Her face reddened, making Wallop wonder why.

'I don't go into pubs much, in fact, I don't really drink.'

'What about cafés? Did you ever meet him for coffee?'

'I suppose I'd better tell you before someone like Sam at the desk blabs it out. At weekends, if I was working, he would sometimes come here to see me. He would treat me to coffee, or lunch in the café over there, or we would drive out to a country pub someplace.'

'Were you and Stuart having an affair?'

'What the hell has that got to do with anything?' Steph said, raising her voice for the first time. 'We're neighbours who like each other. Why does everything have to boil down to sex? Can't you lot think of any other subject to explore, or are you trying to get off on one?'

'Steph, please calm down. The reason we're asking is strong relationships between people, in particular when one of the parties is married to someone else, can cause tension. This can lead to conflict.'

'Yeah, but if I said me and Stuart were having an affair, you'd right away shine your bloody spotlight on Mark.'

'Not necessarily. The person we're looking for could be someone that Stuart knew, or perhaps a person working here who saw the two of you together and became jealous.'

Her face took on a pensive appearance followed by a resolved expression, as if someone in particular had come to mind. This wouldn't come as a shock. The instructors he had seen were in the main young, well-built, and took care of themselves. Some looked to be so full of their own self-importance they would try it on with every woman in the place.

'I see what you're getting at,' she said at last.

'Well, were you?'

'Was I what?'

'Steph, were you and your next-door neighbour having an affair?'

'I liked him a lot, you know? I looked forward to him coming here to pick me up, take me out, and afterwards, it made me feel good.'

'C'mon Steph.'

'Yeah, I admit it, we were having an affair. Happy now, are we?'

TWELVE

Henderson returned to his office after the six-thirty team update. He wasn't ready to go home just yet. In fact, he didn't have much to go home to. His relationship with Dr Claire Fox had come to an ignominious end when he and her daughter had become embroiled in a stand-up argument.

This time, her gripe had been about the police, a mixture of the Gestapo and SS rolled into one, according to Daisy. It was an extreme viewpoint, driven by left-leaning political opinions, not uncommon amongst young people in Brighton, plus a dose of teenage angst. He shouldn't have risen to the bait, but rise to it he did. In the end, neither he nor Claire could see an easy solution; walking away seemed the only option.

The team had now interviewed Livermore's girlfriend, Hannah Robbins, his ex-wife, Ellen Jacobs and his next door neighbours, Mark and Steph Wallace. In addition, the SOCO team had finished their examination of the crime scene. They'd done this in three days, a bit of a record. The job was made easier since all the action had taken place in the lounge, with a little in the kitchen, and because only one person lived in the house.

The information contained in the forensic report was so lacking in substance, it wouldn't make a bottom slot on page six of *The Argus*. No unknown fingerprints were discovered and no hair samples or other items had been dropped by the perpetrator. Henderson's only hope now was on the examination of the articles removed from the house, in particular Livermore's phone and laptop. However, he wasn't holding his breath. This was one they would have to do the hard way.

The interviews had thrown up an unhappy ex-wife and two 'persons of interest': Mark Wallace and Steve Mitchell. Ellen Jacobs lived in a small house in Lindfield, while her ex had a large four-bedroom house all to himself. They'd split up before Livermore had hit the big time, and this grated on Jacobs, who denounced the divorce settlement at the time as derisory.

She deserved more, she claimed, since it had been her earnings that had supported Livermore during the lean early years when his books weren't selling so well. All this rancour and angst raged on all the time Livermore was paying her full child maintenance every month; a situation many divorced women would happily settle for.

Despite this, he didn't consider Jacobs a suspect. Due to the laws of inheritance, she wouldn't benefit directly from her ex-husband's death, but he imagined child maintenance would cease. This, of course, was subject to the terms of his will, providing Livermore had written one. Not a forgone conclusion for a man of forty-three.

Where Jacobs could benefit was if the bulk of his estate, or a willed amount, had been left to his two children. This money could be used to pay for clothes, their first cars, and later, their first homes, obviating their mother in the long-term from funding this expense. All things considered, he couldn't see her in the frame, either for killing Stuart, or hiring someone to do the deed for her. According to DS Neal, despite Jacobs initiating the divorce, she'd let enough slip to leave Neal with the impression that Jacobs still loved him and would have taken him back if he had asked.

Mark Wallace, the next door neighbour of Livermore and husband of Steph, had made his dislike of the author clear. At first, Henderson believed it to be a simple case of jealousy, because his wife had found Livermore so fascinating. This was modified by Harry Wallop's interview of Steph at her gym, when she'd told him it was also Stuart's perceived intellectual superiority that had exacerbated Mark's inferiority complex.

The subsequent revelation about Steph's affair with Livermore had shone a different light on proceedings. Mark's suspected jealousy could have been dismissed as paranoia, the contortions of an over-active imagination, but what if his suspicions were based on fact? He didn't strike Henderson as the brightest, but over time he might have joined the dots: Steph arriving home late, smelling of after-shave, stubble scratches on her face, or being protective about her phone. What if he'd finally snapped?

In some respects, it could be regarded as a classic case and the reason given for a spike in the murder rate one New Year holiday while Henderson was a police constable working in Glasgow. Such was the widespread alarm, the police issued a statement explaining that the sharp rise in the murder rate was due to a series of unrelated domestic incidents, which presented no additional danger to the wider public. They went on to outline a typical scenario. The man next door is invited into his neighbour's house for a drink. They get drunk together and the man becomes interested in his neighbour's wife. She responds. The husband can only take so much before he explodes and a fracas develops. It could stop there, but if one of them reached for a heavy ornament or a kitchen knife, murder would often be the end result.

He was mindful of this issue when he'd asked Harry Wallop to interview Steph. If Mark had murdered Stuart Livermore, it was the easiest thing in the world for his wife to provide him with an alibi. He wasn't convinced this was the case here. Steph professed affection for Livermore, and their alibis: Mark's evening in the pub and Steph's late-night working with personal clients, had both checked out.

Mark would be interviewed again. With no witnesses, forensics, or confession to connect him with the violence against the author, Henderson suspected he would remain a 'person of interest' for the time being. However, if one fingerprint or hair follicle of Mark's was subsequently found on any item that had been removed from the house, Henderson would have him. This would be all it would take. No way would he, a man who professed such hatred for his neighbour, ever step into his house.

Livermore's dispute with Sheffield thriller author Steve Mitchell looked a bit more interesting, although for the most part, it had been played out on social media. The one exception was an incident at the Harrogate Crime Festival the previous July, the details contained in a crime report uncovered by Sally Graham. At this point, Livermore had only accused Mitchell of sockpuppeting; Mitchell hadn't yet set up the nefarious websites that he later used to launch vitriolic attacks on Livermore.

Livermore had been drinking with four other authors in the bar of the Swan Hotel in Harrogate, when Mitchell walked in. Someone in Livermore's party had said in a voice louder than was necessary, 'Is this the real Steve Mitchell, or one of his aliases?'

Mitchell, not one to back down, according to officers who had attended the scene, strode over and headed straight for Livermore. He'd protested his innocence, but an argument soon developed about Mitchell's behaviour in creating false reviews for his books. Pushing and shoving followed, before Mitchell grabbed Livermore by the lapels and punched him twice in the face, breaking his jaw and knocking out two teeth.

The police were called, Mitchell was arrested, charged with assault, and banged up in cells for the night. When the case came to court, the judge took into account Livermore's inebriated state and Mitchell's sobriety, having just arrived at the bar. He let the accused off with a caution and a fine.

When the pugilists had returned to their respective corners, Mitchell to Sheffield and Livermore to

Brighton, the battle continued, albeit only with laptops and across the ether of cyberspace. In an effort to try to call a halt, Livermore had contacted Mitchell's publisher and informed them about the assault, requesting they tear up his assailant's contract. They refused and, in retaliation, Mitchell set up several websites posing as disgruntled fans. He began populating them with bogus testimonials, claiming Livermore was a crap writer, a misogynist, a racist, and any other abusive term he could think of.

All this would have been fine, if a bit unpleasant, until Mitchell had changed the rules of the game by making a death threat against Livermore, as Hannah Robbins had mentioned. Mitchell had upped the ante, leaving Henderson no choice but to take it seriously.

He picked up the phone and asked the operator to put him through to South Yorkshire Police.

THIRTEEN

Henderson reversed into a tight parking space and walked towards Station Street in Lewes. It was late September, and already he could see evenings were becoming darker earlier with a new, chilled edge to the air.

On the south coast of England, it wasn't the cold weather that residents feared, but high winds. He would be the first to admit that Brighton motorists weren't the best at adapting to snowy conditions on the rare occasions it fell. However, the wind could blow so strongly that turning into a street leading to the seafront could take a person's breath away and, for the unprepared, knock them off their feet. It also had a habit of throwing tons of stones from the beach on to the esplanade some two metres above, giving council workers a tough clean-up job every spring.

The Royal Oak wasn't a pub Henderson had ever been inside. It was a large place with lots of beers on tap and plenty of tables, most of which were empty as it was still early evening. He spotted his companion at a corner table and, as promised, he had already bought a pint for Henderson, now sitting in front of him.

'Evening Sean,' he said as he approached and sat down. 'Thanks for the drink.'

'My pleasure, Angus. Cheers.'

Henderson picked up the glass and took a drink, savouring the flavour. Nothing could beat the first mouthful of a decent pint. There were some men he knew who couldn't wait to glug half of it down, enjoying the boozy feeling it gave them on the way to losing all their inhibitions. It could turn socially-inept introverts into loquacious chatterboxes, and exuberant extroverts into loudmouths or aggressive bar drunks, as every young copper could testify.

'I know it's early days yet,' Houghton said, 'but how are things progressing with the Livermore investigation?'

Henderson outlined the main people they'd interviewed from Stuart Livermore's life, and mentioned the two 'persons of interest', Mark Wallace and Steve Mitchell. Talking about them now, neither man, on paper at least in the case of Mitchell, fitted the image Henderson had of the cold-blooded killer who had murdered Stuart Livermore. Perhaps he would change his opinion when he finally had a chance to speak to Steve Mitchell.

'Mark Wallace looks a better bet to me,' Houghton said. 'He sounds the jealous type, and there's no one but his wife to corroborate his movements on the night in question. I mean, the barmaid at the pub said he had been drinking there, but who looks at the clock when a customer leaves?'

'His wife Steph is a personal trainer and often stays late working with clients. Her employers have verified she left the gym at nine-thirty, and she says she came back to the house on Sunday night about ten, which more or less checks out. By which time, judging by the window given to us by the pathologist, Livermore may already have been dead, but it's not conclusive.'

'Forensics didn't offer up anything?'

'Not a thing we could use. Nothing's ever that easy, is it?'

'All we need is something to put Wallace inside Livermore's house, and we've got him. Wallace has made his antagonism for his neighbour pretty clear, and even though he's a builder, no way would he have gone into Livermore's house to do any work.'

'I agree.'

'What about the other guy?' Houghton asked.

'Steve Mitchell's got form against our victim, but as you said before, jealousy is a stronger motivation for killing someone than selling a few more books.'

'Nevertheless, interview Mitchell. Pick any holes you can find in his alibi.'

'Aye, I will.'

'As I said to you before, I was hoping to get involved in this case, but there's a meeting with the Home Secretary in a month. The ACC wants me to give a presentation on how forces like ours are using new technology.'

'Like what?'

'Some of it we have already, the likes of ANPR, CCTV, body cameras, and face recognition software. The one area he's asked me to concentrate on is AI.'

'Artificial Intelligence?'

'Yep, how we can use systems like predictive algorithms to select a likely culprit from the characteristics of a number of suspects, or to analyse the mountain of data we collect on HOLMES for every big case. It could churn out statistically significant areas for investigation.'

'If it works, it could replace a copper's nose, or what we detectives call intuition.'

'I wouldn't go as far as to say that, but it could be used to take the guesswork out of large-scale investigations. We've got HOLMES collecting huge amounts of data for each investigation, but it takes you and people from your team to make sense out of it. AI could take over this role, hand you reasoned arguments for taking a specific path, or give you grounds for arresting a particular suspect. Just think how it could have shortened the investigations into the Yorkshire Ripper or the Soham murders.'

'I'm not against technology. Anything that allows us to increase the rate at which we apprehend serious criminals has got to be a good thing, but is AI capable of handling lies and misstatements of truth? My understanding of the strength of AI is its ability to process large amounts of facts and data and turn it into something usable. In our line of work, we often don't know if someone, or indeed anyone, is telling the truth. They've been saying about computers ever since they were invented, garbage in, equals garbage out. I think that adage is still appropriate.'

'It's a good point, Angus,' he said reaching for his notebook, 'and something I'll include in my presentation.'

'Another drink?' Henderson asked.

'No, no. Let me. I invited you here.' Houghton got up quickly. Henderson, not wanting to cause a fuss and draw attention to themselves, let him carry on.

'Here you go,' Houghton said a few minutes later. He deposited two pints on the table, 'and some crisps to soak up the beer.'

'Thanks.'

'One of the reasons I wanted to talk to you, Angus,' Houghton said after resuming his seat, 'was to clear the air over my appointment.'

'Clear the air? There's no residual resentment on my part, or have you heard any different?'

'Why the hell not? You're an experienced DI with an excellent clear-up record.'

'You said it yourself, you want to be involved in this case, but you can't because you need to prepare a presentation for the Home Secretary. I like being hands-on with cases, it's where I think I can make the greatest impact. If I was doing your job, no disrespect intended, I would be climbing the walls with all the admin and paperwork.'

Houghton laughed. 'Luckily, I don't mind the admin side. So, you didn't interview for the job and got turned down by the board?'

'Is that what people are saying?'

'It's what I, not unnaturally, assumed when I first arrived.'

'No, I didn't put myself up for it. I did have another opportunity for a promotion alongside your predecessor, Lisa Edwards.'

Houghton nodded.

'She moved to the Met's Anti-Terrorist Command and wanted me to go with her.'

'You didn't fancy it?'

'While the work they do is exciting when they're involved in a big operation, it takes a huge amount of desk-based research to get there.'

'I once considered it myself, but I agree, there's too much desk work, even for me.'

'I like the job I do now. I'm not ready to move on.'

'I suppose the best option, when the time comes to move from Sussex, is for you to transfer to a smaller force. One where the DCI is directly involved in all serious cases.'

'Aye, I was thinking the same, but not yet. There's still a lot of work to be done in Sussex before I decide to move on.'

FOURTEEN

He stood at the bar, waiting to be served. He hated queueing for anything: shops, bookies, pubs. If he was beginning to feel agitated, because the barman was taking too long to serve him, or the waiting crowd too large, his leg would start to bounce up and down in a nervous twitch. If the barman served someone who'd joined the throng after he had, anything could happen. He could start a fight with the latecomer, nut the barman when he finally came around to serve him, or throw the drink straight in his face and start throwing the empty glasses littering the bar at his head.

Tonight, he waited his turn. He was in a sports bar in Brighton town centre where they were showing Manchester United v Liverpool. There was a telly in the crappy house he rented in Hollingbury, but it didn't have Sky. If he wanted to find out how the match ended - the score was 1-1 at half-time - he needed to curb his temper a wee while longer.

The useless barman, a spotty oik with a 1930s haircut, straight out of *Peaky Blinders*, and arms replete with David Beckham tats, finally spotted him.

'What can I get you, pal?'

'Pint of heavy.'

'Pint of bitter, yeah?'

'That's what I said. Are you fucking deaf or what?'

'Keep your hair on,' the barman said. He reached for a glass before shoving it under the John Smith's tap.

He wanted to respond with a sharp wisecrack, but it was a tad difficult as his own straight and long hair was in a lower division from beerboy's. In addition, there was a big bastard manning the door and it wouldn't be sensible to talk himself into receiving a nose-cruncher from him for starting some aggro with the bar staff.

He took his beer, bitching to himself about the price, dearer than his old local in Edinburgh, and re-joined the crowd watching the match. It was still half-time. The talking heads of overpaid ex-footballers, now overpaid match analysts, co-commentators and summarisers, were discussing what a great goal Liverpool had scored and the dubious one scored by Man U.

He was from Edinburgh, but had fallen out of love with Scottish football because of its tribalism. Fans didn't care if their team won anything, as long as they defeated their rivals. It wasn't only Rangers and Celtic, but Hibs and Hearts, Dundee United and Dundee, St Mirren and Greenock Morton. He'd grown up in the Fergie era, when Man U were a team capable of beating anyone they came across. This was something he could relate to.

The match restarted. Ten minutes in and Man U scored, releasing an outpouring of joy from him and the majority of those around him, since Liverpool fans were in the minority. The game see-sawed for the next fifteen minutes, but despite the tension, the score stayed the same.

He felt a hand on his shoulder and turned. He was ready to knock the head off the bastard who had dared to impinge on his personal space and spoil his concentration on the feast of football in front of him. It was the ugly bugger who guarded the door. A big slab of a bloke, wearing a dark suit and with an earpiece in his ear, looking like an overweight agent who didn't make the grade at Quantico.

'Tone it down a bit, pal. You're winding up the Liverpool supporters,' he said nodding at a small knot of red-shirted Scousers, 'and you're annoying some of the neutrals. Okay?'

'Aye, right mate, I hear you.'

Slab-boy waddled back to his station while he turned back, a puzzled expression on his face. Why pick on him? He could see plenty of blokes getting animated and shouting at the screen. The Scousers didn't look the least bit bothered; perhaps they had lived too long in the south and no longer felt the pull of their roots. He returned to the action and did what he was told for a spell, but it was hard, as Man U were all over Liverpool for the final twenty minutes.

At the end of the match there was a loud cheer when the reds from Manchester walked away with the spoils. He joined in and didn't care if it upset anyone: a win was a win, sweeter still when it was against the reds from Merseyside. In any case, he didn't intend staying in this boozer once the match was over. He finished his pint, his fourth of the night which was a low count for him, and would join his mates who would still be in the Royal Oak in Hollingbury.

He walked outside, sauntering past slab-boy who gave him the evil eye, and made his way towards North Street, where he knew he could catch a bus home. While waiting, a group of three Liverpool fans who had been in the same pub as him, crossed over to his side of the road and looked over. He didn't fancy the odds, but he wouldn't run away. They might not be armed, but he was.

They carried on walking and were soon swallowed up by the crowds, heavy at this time of night with events finishing and people moving between clubs, pubs and restaurants. Minutes later, his bus arrived. He loved the way electronic boards on modern trains listed station names, and the way noticeboards in buses informed passengers about the forthcoming destination. He was an inquisitive traveller, always taking note of landmarks, woods, and open spaces, but Ditchling Road was a long thoroughfare with nothing much to catch his eye.

A few minutes later, the bus came to a halt. Several people alighted before him. In front of him was a young woman, fiddling with something in her handbag while walking slowly. In time, she had left a long gap between her and the other passengers. She was wearing a light jacket and a dark-coloured dress hiked up to reveal a nice pair of legs. Lovely. He hadn't made any plans to do anything tonight, but when an opportunity presented itself, who was he to say no?

He dallied, walking quietly to ensure she didn't realise there was someone behind her; a favourite ploy. Up ahead, the entrance to Hollingbury Bowling Club, closed at this time of the night. A few metres after, he knew there was a footpath leading into woods.

Picking the right moment when there were no cars or people about, he pulled gloves out of his pocket, put them on, and sped up. He approached the woman, his trainers masking the noise of his footsteps. He grabbed her and placed a gloved hand over her mouth before bundling her into the deserted entrance to the footpath. In a deft movement, he shuffled her behind the car barrier and into the darkness of the woods.

He dumped her on the grass and jumped on top of her. A gloved hand covered her mouth as a knife was passed in front of her face.

'Make a noise and you get this!' he hissed. 'Don't think I won't. It was used earlier in the week. Understand?'

She nodded, her eyes wide and pleading. Just the way he liked it.

He put the knife to one side and shoved his hand up her dress. She wasn't wearing stockings or tights, just skimpy, thin panties. He made to grab a handful of material and rip them off, when something cold hit him in the face. In an instant, it felt as though his skin had caught fire.

What the fuck! His eyes were stinging, his lips tingling, and there was a weird smell filling his nostrils. What the hell was happening? He leaned down, wiping his hand over the damp grass and rubbing moisture into his eyes. He did this ten or eleven times before his vision started to clear and the throbbing behind his eyes abated.

There was no group of riot police standing there with tear gas launchers in their hands, nor had a warplane dropped a magnesium flare. He couldn't feel blood or the pain of being hit by anything solid. What was obvious was that the girl had gone. There was only him, on his knees with tears streaming down his face. The knife lay to one side, as the lights of Ditchling Road twinkled indistinctly through the trees.

FIFTEEN

'DI Henderson, DS Walters? I'm Sergeant Nathan Yates. Welcome to Sheffield.'

They shook hands and started walking.

'It's a shame the weather didn't behave for your visit. It's hard enough trying to convince folks in the south that it's not always pissing down here in Yorkshire.'

'I'm from Fort William,' Henderson said, pushing through double doors, into the bowels of Carbrook House, South Yorkshire Police HQ. 'I doubt Yorkshire could match us for rain.'

Yates laughed, revealing white and perfectly aligned choppers. It was an age thing, Henderson felt. Anyone under forty had no excuse but to have perfect teeth. Dentistry had advanced markedly since he was a boy, when the main treatment on offer was drill, fill, or extract. Nowadays patients could have braces, whitening, implants, ceramics, and much improved filling materials. In addition, parents were now more aware of the dangers to their children's dental health from eating too much sugar.

Henderson and Walters were shown into an interview room, which looked more modern than anything at Malling House.

'Give that a whack,' Yates said, pointing at the red button on the wall, 'if you need any assistance. I know this is only a fact-finding meeting, but your man is a big lad and he has some form.'

'Point taken,' Henderson said, taking a seat on one side of the table. Walters sat down beside him.

'I'll be off and get him for you,' Yates said.

'Thanks for all your help, Nathan,' Henderson said.

'Any time,' he said as he walked away.

'I like this,' Henderson said, looking at the control panel in front of him. 'No creaky old recording equipment to deal with. A simple press of a button and all the gear lights up.'

'At least with the old kit we've got, you know when it's recording. You can see and hear it. In this set-up, it's not so obvious as the control is somewhere else.'

'That's progress, you have to embrace it.'

'What do you mean?'

'If you don't, you and the other luddites will get left behind.'

'Luddites? I'll have you know–'

'In here, sir,' they heard Yates say from the corridor.

Steve Mitchell walked in and, for a moment, Henderson was taken aback. His idea of an author was a slim guy of average height, bookish, a spectacle wearer with a pale complexion from staying indoors too much, a bit like Stuart Livermore. By way of contrast, Mitchell looked like an amateur boxer, or a rugby player. He was tall, broad-chested, and muscled. His hair was tightly cropped, and he sported a slightly skewed nose, once broken but seemingly not repaired properly.

They introduced themselves and sat down. Yates left, but said he would come down periodically to make sure everything was all right.

'Thank you for coming in to see us, Mr Mitchell.'

'No problem.'

'We're detectives investigating the murder of Stuart Livermore in Brighton last Sunday night.'

'Your colleague, Yates, told me.'

'Good. How did you become a writer, Mr Mitchell?'

Mitchell seemed momentarily thrown by the question, his mouth opening then closing as if he was about to say something but thought better of it. Perhaps he was expecting the DI to launch into an interrogation about his whereabouts the night Livermore was killed.

'I'd always wanted to be a professional footballer, and signed schoolboy forms with my home town club at the age of eight. By the time I was eighteen, nineteen, I was playing for a number of lower division clubs, the likes of Tranmere and Rochdale. By twenty-six, I was at Portsmouth and doing well, top scorer in the league, but then I ruptured knee ligaments.'

'How long did that put you out for?'

'It ended my career. The treatment for loads of football injuries like bone breaks, cartilage tears and ruptures has improved immeasurably over the years. Back then, the surgeon said he could patch me up, good enough to get me back in the first team, but I'd be left with a permanent limp when I'd finished playing. Alternatively, I could pack it in now and be able to walk like a normal person for the rest of my life. I took his advice and packed in playing, stopped doing the job I loved, the thing I'd been working towards since I was a kid. It's a helluva choice to give any sportsman, don't you think?'

'I agree.'

'Washed up at twenty-six, I attended sports college where I was awarded a degree in physiology and psychology. I used it to give me a start on a new career as a football coach. Highlight of that period was becoming coach at Leyton Orient.'

'You're from the area?'

'Yeah, it was my local club, the place where I'd been playing as a schoolboy, but they didn't offer me a professional contract. Armed with the degree, I worked there as the coach for the under-eighteens, before a promotion to the first team. It was probably the best years I've ever had in football. This lasted until a string of bad results, when the club decided to sack the manager I was working with, and brought in Gino Maldini, the Atalanta boss.'

'I've heard of him.'

'He, at the time, was one of those new analytical managers and surrounded himself with statisticians, doctors, physios, coaches, nutritionists, the whole shebang. Everybody does it now, but back then it was revolutionary. He brought with him all his own people from Italy, so me and everybody I worked beside got the heave-ho. It's the side of football they never discuss on Sky, or in the sports pages of newspapers. It happens every three or four years at some clubs, when the entire backroom staff are cleared out and all their graft is consigned to the dustbin. I've known people so traumatised by the experience, they never work in football again.'

'In your case, I imagine it was something of a blessing in disguise,' Henderson said. 'I would think you make more money from your books now than you ever did as a footballer.'

'You're right, I do, but it doesn't mean I don't miss it. I loved being outside in all weathers; the smell of freshly-cut grass; working with a large group of young lads, and the unbelievable feeling when everything comes together and you win an important game or a tournament. A big part of my life as an author is to sit on my arse behind a bloody computer screen for eight hours a day. To keep me sane, I use any excuse I can to get out of the house. It's the reason the books I write contain so much research.'

'I can imagine, but you've also used your football experience to good effect.'

'You're referring to the Ben Cohen series?'

'Yes.'

'I suppose it was some sort of catharsis, writing about a coach who solves crimes while working for an East London football club. If I can't be involved, I can always write about it. That's what my agent told me at the time, anyway. After publishing three books featuring Cohen, I seemed to have purged the football bug out of my system, so from that point of view, it was worth doing.'

'Talk to me about Stuart Livermore.'

'There's not much to say. It must be obvious, even to you, I didn't get on with the bloke. Livermore thought he could snitch on me because I was a working class guy, not a private school educated knob like him, and lived miles away in faraway Yorkshire.'

There it was again, Henderson noticed. Not only did Mark Wallace have a chip on his shoulder about Stuart Livermore's perceived social standing and intellect, here was Steve Mitchell thinking the same. Why did Livermore succeed in winding these two men up when Hannah Robbins said he was such a nice man and got on with everyone? It perhaps wasn't an important point, but he would talk to Walters about it later.

'Snitch on you for what, sockpuppeting?'

'I'm impressed.'

'Don't be. We do our research thoroughly as well.'

'Touché.'

'Did you do it?'

'Guilty as charged, but the last time I looked, it's nothing to excite you guys.'

'You're right, it's not a criminal offence, but I can see how it would give you an unfair advantage and annoy some people.'

'Unfair!' he exploded. 'Don't talk to me about fucking unfair! Bastards like Livermore are in a club with loads of other authors. You promote my book and I'll do the same for you. They do this on social media and at literary festivals. They'd say to readers, 'if you like my book, you should read Damien's.' That sort of shit. I didn't go to the same toffee-nosed school or university as they did, so I wasn't included.'

'Is this a formal organisation, this club?' Walters asked.

'I call it a club, but it's more like a cabal, a loose association of like-minded patronising pricks, if you want my definition.'

'So, sockpuppeting was your way of getting back at them?'

'Not so much a way of getting back, as a way of ploughing my own furrow. They had their way of obtaining a leg-up for their writing careers, I had mine.'

SIXTEEN

The intercom buzzed. Hannah Robbins put down the book she had been reading, this time for pleasure and not for work, and walked over to the door entry unit. Seeing the slim and genial features of Ryan Allison on the video screen, she buzzed him up.

A few minutes later she opened the front door and the tall, gangly frame of Stuart's best friend sauntered in.

'Oh, Hannah,' he said taking her in his arms and giving her a hug. Ryan was never one to step over the bounds of impropriety and somehow gave her a hug that felt like it was coming from a brother and not from a dear friend. It reminded her too much of hugs from her mother, when the word 'aloof' often popped into her head.

'I'm so sorry to hear about Stuart,' he said into her ear. 'I would have come earlier, but Holly's been off school with measles.'

'No worries there,' she said pulling away. 'I had them myself around the same age.'

'She wasn't feeling too bad, but you know what schools are like when someone arrives all covered in spots.'

'Yes, before you know it the World Health Organisation has declared a pandemic. Let's move into the lounge. Can I get you anything before I sit down?'

'Do you have any beer?'

'I'm sure I can rustle something up.'

'Good, I'll have a coffee then.'

She looked at him before bursting out laughing. 'You idiot.'

'Anything to try and cheer you up.'

'Well, you've succeeded. It's the first time I've laughed since Stuart died.'

'There you go then.'

Ryan wandered into the lounge, she into the kitchen. It was a modern apartment, completely refurbished before she moved in two years previously, with freshly painted walls and ceilings, new carpets, a swish door entry system and a slick kitchen filled with numerous labour-saving devices. It was an easy place to maintain and keep tidy, which was one of the reasons why she'd bought it; working in London, she didn't spend a lot of time there. This week she had, but she didn't have the energy to lift a finger to cook or clean.

She took a beer out of the fridge for Ryan and removed a bottle of Canadian Club from one of the lower cupboards. Before opening it, she glanced at the clock: 7:15 pm. It was force of habit. Her mother had a rule, passed on to her daughter, no alcoholic drinks before six. In the last few days, that rule had been broken several times.

She poured two fingers and topped it up with ginger ale. She was about to walk into the lounge with the beer bottle and whisky when she remembered

Ryan liked his beer in a glass. It was something she could never understand about men. Ryan, and many of her male friends and colleagues, would happily neck from a bottle in a pub, but at home they would throw their toys out of the pram if it wasn't served in a glass.

She walked into the lounge and placed the drinks on the coffee table. Ryan had taken a seat on the settee. He was being a gentleman by not occupying the chair she had previously been sitting on, even though she wasn't precious about it. It didn't stop him, however, from lifting the book she had been reading.

'I see you're reading Bill Bryson,' he said flicking through the pages. 'Makes a bit of a change from the pointy hats and pale faces of your usual fare.'

She retook her seat. 'Don't be so sniffy about science fiction and fantasy, or I'll be forced to give you a list of all the authors in those genres who sell a lot more books than you do.'

'Point taken. I do apologise. What's it like?'

'Have you read it?'

'No. You know me, I stick to crime and thrillers.'

'You should give it a go. Read too much of the same stuff that you write and you might find it creeping into your own work. Before you know it, you'll be accused of plagiarism.'

'That's what Lucinda says, but I don't believe everything she tells me.'

'Well, if you won't listen to me, you should listen to your editor. She knows best.'

Ryan tossed the book down on the settee, the subject closed. He was in many ways, an open book. Whenever he had something on his mind, he couldn't wait to reveal it.

'What's the latest on the police investigation?' he blurted out. 'A couple of detectives came to see me, but because I've been at home most of the time looking after Holly, I had nothing much to tell. Have you heard anything?'

'You know as much as I do. Just because Stuart and I were going out together, doesn't mean they share any breakthroughs or new developments with me. In fact, based on my scant knowledge of police procedure, the people left behind are often the last to know when anything happens. The only thing I do know is there doesn't seem to be anything missing from Stuart's house.' She went on to explain about her visit there with DI Henderson.

'Hannah, do you know if they've talked to the Yorkshire rat, Steve Mitchell?'

'Inspector Henderson said he would be doing so this week.'

'Good. I wouldn't put it past Mitchell. He's big, he's been in trouble with the law before, and he's got a vicious temper.'

'I don't think it sounds like him, do you? Breaking into Stuart's house and waiting for him to come home before attacking him? It all seems too subtle and premeditated for someone like Mitchell. He's a seat-of-the-pants sort of guy, and more likely to confront Stuart in the street to give him a punch or a kick than stab him with a knife.'

'He does seem to thrive on confrontation. I would even go so far as to say he seeks it. But you're right, sitting in Stuart's house waiting for him to return from Norwich requires a subtlety Mitchell doesn't possess. Well, if not him, who?'

'I've been giving it a lot of thought,' she said. 'It could be one of his readers, someone in receipt of one of Stuart's spiteful emails. You know how he could be, if someone insulted him, he would do the same right back.'

'He did, but it sounds a bit lame to me.'

'Could he have upset someone during the recording of the *Black Night* programme? When the wind machine broke and everyone was getting agitated, he was more annoyed than anyone else. He was calling people names and shouting at any poor sod who came near. It wasn't as if this was the only incident.'

He considered this for a moment. 'You're right. Stuart thought the television programme was his baby, even though the production company had bought the rights. At times, he accused them of deliberately trying to foul things up.'

'It could also have been a stalker from a literary festival. He told me before about this couple who appeared at every event he attended, but they never wanted a book signed or came up to him for a chat. Or it could be someone who identified with a character that Stuart killed off. He didn't think twice about killing off characters he didn't like or once they had served their purpose.'

'It's a long list,' he said, 'and only people from the literary side of his life. You don't think it could be someone from his personal life? Could it be a neighbour? I know he didn't get on with the guy next door, or maybe the boyfriend of his ex-wife?'

'Those are the places the police will look, and as they haven't uncovered anything–'

'That they've told us about.'

'Since they haven't found anything, we need to look further afield.'

'Won't the police be doing that when they've exhausted the obvious?'

'Perhaps they'll get around to it eventually, but will it be done before they cut the number of officers on the case and scale the whole investigation back?'

Ryan sat up, a startled look on his face. 'Is that a possibility?'

'I've read enough true crime and fictional crime books to believe it is.'

'What are you suggesting? We should try to cajole them into looking in the direction of someone from the *Black Night* production company, or a stalker from a literary festival?'

'Maybe, but if they're not interested, or won't commit the manpower, then I'll need to do it.'

He looked at her intently. 'You can't be serious? Hannah, you're not a detective. You haven't got any experience of police work.'

She sighed as if dealing with a slow child. 'Thank you, Ryan, for stating the blinding obvious. I have a better understanding of the world that Stuart inhabited than they do. It won't do any harm for me to do some digging.'

'I understand where you're coming from, and if you're determined to do this, and I can see by the look on your face you are, let me offer a word of advice. I hope, Hannah, you'll heed it. Whoever killed Stuart is still out there. They may take exception to someone else sticking their nose in. Have your phone with you at all times and carry something you can use in self-defence. I'm not suggesting you carry a weapon or anything, but even a noisy attack alarm is better than nothing.'

SEVENTEEN

'Kent looks a lot like Sussex except for those funny houses with the pointy tops,' DS Vicky Neal, driving the pool car, said to her companion, DC Sally Graham.

'They're called oast houses.'

'Why do they look so weird? It's like houses for wizards.'

'They were originally built to dry hops, you know, for beer making.'

'Now there's a subject I do know something about. I like a drop of beer now and again.'

'The pointed bit at the top is a chimney to let the smoke out.'

'They grow hops in Kent?'

'They did, and still do to some extent, but it's not as it used to be. Way back in the 1930s, Kent used to be covered in hop plants.'

'Really?'

'Yeah, so much so, they'd run trains to Kent from the East End of London, and farmers would use their trucks to ferry hundreds of families down to Kent to pick hops during the summer months.'

'I never realised. How do you know all this? You from the area?'

'No, I saw a documentary on BBC 4 about it.'

They were driving through the village of East Farleigh, but despite the assistance of the satnav, they still couldn't find the place they were looking for. This was either because the postcode was shared by a number of addresses, or the house didn't exist.

They approached an unmarked road leading off to the right, the only one they hadn't investigated.

'We might as well try this one, we've been down every other,' Neal said.

'Why not? Even though there isn't a sign to say if there's a house or farm up there. We've run out of options.'

Neal waited for a car to pass before making the turn. She almost wished she hadn't after the car whacked a deep pothole.

'Shit! I hope I haven't burst a tyre,' Neal said, her expression anxious. 'I'm not sure the AA man could find us out here.'

'There's nothing coming up on the car's information system to suggest any malfunction. Does the steering feel okay?'

'Just the same. It doesn't feel like it's pulling to one side.'

'You're probably all right. We'll check it when we stop.'

'God, if this is where Johnson lives?' Neal said, her teeth chattering together as if watching a scary horror movie. 'He needs to drive a monster SUV with huge tyres, or get the bloody road fixed. There are so many undulations and potholes, it feels like we're sailing a boat.'

'I know there's a history of coal mining in Kent, I wonder if they did much of it around here?'

'I've been to villages in Yorkshire, right in the middle of the coalfields, and it's more pronounced than this. There, they've got small rounded hills which are green and look like hills, but they're former slag heaps, made with the spoil from the mines. There's been so much underground work, the roads in the area have huge dips and rises caused by the land subsiding over time. If this didn't exactly fill my head with confidence, I positively freaked out when I saw warning signs about roads that could suddenly collapse.'

'It does sound scary. I hope it doesn't happen here.'

'I think we're more likely to be knocked unconscious than fall into a big hole.'

Away from the village, they were now surrounded by fields and the occasional copse. They hadn't travelled far off the main road, but it felt like they were in the depths of the countryside with no human or dwelling for miles around. This hadn't been Neal's experience of living in the south. A few miles outside Manchester, it was easy to feel alone and isolated, and if she became lost, she would die there. In the south, she had never been to a place where a house or hamlet had not been within walking distance.

Minutes later, the road started to widen, enough to allow two cars to pass if they were foolish enough to use this road, or had got lost which she felt they were. Above the tree line, she could now see several chimney tops.

'Hallelujah, we're not taking a short-cut to the Kent coast,' Graham said. 'There is a house up there after all.'

'Thank the Lord. I think I was getting white finger just trying to keep hold of the blooming steering wheel.'

The track became tarmac and the trees disappeared to reveal a large house surrounded by paved areas, with a loose stone section, big enough to park several cars. By way of contrast, the garden to one side resembled a ploughed field and, sitting in the middle, was an idle cement-mixer.

'The house looks new,' Neal said. She drove slowly towards it. 'The garden's a bit of a work in progress. There's no building company sign. I wonder if the owner built it himself.'

'It does look new. You can tell by the clean slates on the roof.'

Before they got out of the car, two dogs came bounding over, barking and slavering as if their lives depended on it.

The dogs were Doberman Pinschers. To Neal, the sort of dogs favoured by the heads of criminal gangs and drug dealers. They used them to protect what they had acquired from ill-gotten gains: be it a drug-filled warehouse, a laboratory manufacturing Spice, or a large house. The dogs could be trained to be obedient, but they never lost their aggressive instinct, and despite being a dog lover, she could never take to them.

'My God, look at them,' Graham said. 'I think they want to eat us for breakfast.'

'I think they've just finished breakfast and now they fancy a snack. I love dogs, but no way am I getting out of the car to talk to them.'

'What do we do?'

'I dunno, peep the horn until someone appears?'

Before Neal could do anything, a man appeared and called the animals to heel. Instantly the pointed ears fell back. The two Dobermans slinked back towards their master. When the dogs were lying docilely beside him, Neal opened the car door and got out.

'I hope you're not going to say they're a couple of softies and love children.'

'No chance, they're guard dogs, pure and simple. Tear your throat out if I wasn't around.'

'What a comforting thought. I'm Detective Sergeant Vicky Neal, and this is Detective Constable Sally Graham. We're from Sussex Police.'

'Craig Johnson,' he said extending his hand for both women to shake. 'I'm sorry, I forgot you two were coming, otherwise I would have locked them in their kennels.'

'No harm done.'

Retired Superintendent Craig Johnson spoke with a scouse accent, tinged with a hint of Kent, not surprising. He had spent most of his career in the south. His hair was swept back over his head, accentuating its retreat from his forehead, but it still retained much of its colour and looked natural, not out of a bottle. He was tanned and stocky, although the flabby face suggested a former boxer gone to seed.

'Let's go inside.'

They walked towards the front door. 'Did you build the house yourself?' Neal asked.

'No, not me personally, I got a local firm to do it. I'd owned the plot for years, which I bought from a farmer who was about to be made bankrupt. If you look over there,' he said, indicating a spot to the left of the house, 'you can see over to the North Downs and the skyscrapers of Canary Wharf.'

Neal walked over. Sure enough, the view was spectacular and expansive. The house was situated at the top of a small rise, a rare find in flat Kent. She could see for miles to the north, east, and west. No wonder he had built a house there. 'It's a great site.'

'I think so too. C'mon, let's move inside. I'm gagging for a cup of coffee.'

EIGHTEEN

DS Neal thought Retired Superintendent Craig Johnson looked scruffy, dressed in stained jeans and ill-fitting sweatshirt. The kitchen where he led her and DC Graham was the complete opposite. It was fitted with all modern appliances and she couldn't see a cup, crumb, or scrap of paper out of place. It felt a shame to sully it with their presence, but nevertheless, they entered and took seats around the kitchen table.

While Johnson organised some hot drinks, Neal looked out over the garden. At least, she assumed it to be a garden. She could see grass rolling out into the distance, but the area closest to the house, the place where she presumed a patio was due to be built, looked no better than a ploughed field.

'I can build fences and patios well enough,' Johnson said, echoing her thoughts as he placed coffee mugs on the table, 'no way could I build a house. I'd erect a wall before realising I should have put in water pipes or electrical wiring first.'

'I wouldn't know where to start. Mr Johnson—'

'Let's not stand on ceremony here, we're all colleagues. Call me Craig.' He took a seat.

'Okay. Craig it is. We're here today as part of the team investigating the murder of Stuart Livermore in

Brighton on 22nd September, approximately a week ago.'

'Christ, his death came as a shocker, I can tell you. He liked a drink did Stuart; we both did. I'd always imagined his early demise would be under the wheels of a car or a train while drunk, not stabbed to death by some fucking lowlife. Excuse my French.'

'How did the two of you meet?'

'Let me think, it was a long time back. Yes, he was witness to a stabbing in Canterbury town centre about ten years ago. I was the investigating sergeant. He'd been in the town lecturing at the university, his alma mater as he called it, on creative writing. We got talking. He said he was a writer, and asked if I would be interested in helping him. I thought, yeah, why not?'

He took a drink from his coffee mug. It didn't seem a gesture designed to buy him time to try and remember the next part of the story, more to savour the details of an oft-told tale.

'I imagined it would be a bit of beer money, you know, but it just got bigger and bigger. Eventually, he shoehorned me in as police advisor on the *Dark Night* television series. The money from the programme built most of this,' he said, pointing upwards with his thumb.

'Impressive. How did you get on with him?'

'Like a bloody house on fire.'

'Really?'

'It's surprising when you think about it, him being university-educated and so clever an' all, and me a hairy-arsed scouser from Toxteth. He is, he was, a funny guy, and generous to a fault. If ever I needed a sub until payday, or a lift anywhere, Stuart would be happy to oblige. I kept telling him he had to harden up. People will take advantage, I said, but you couldn't change him.'

A woman entered the kitchen and nodded in their direction. The term 'brassy blonde' was often used to describe a mobster's girlfriend in an East London gangster movie, and this lady looked straight out of central casting. In addition to the large and conspicuous barnet, she wore a tight pink dress that did everything to accentuate her big bum and pneumatic boobs.

'The missus,' Johnson said a touch unnecessarily. 'Angela.'

'I thought you were retired,' the new entrant said in a voice posher than her appearance suggested. She began making herself a cup of coffee.

'They're detectives from the team investigating Stuart's murder. I'm helping with enquiries.'

Angela stopped what she was doing and strode over. Neal noticed she was wearing killer stiletto heels; around the house, how decadent.

'What's happening with the case?' she asked in earnest. 'Do you have anyone in the frame for it yet?'

'She was fond of Stuart,' Johnson said by way of explanation. 'I used to think it was only about the money, but now I'm not sure.'

It was meant as a playful comment, but it still earned him a rebuke, a smack on the shoulder.

'There's no one yet,' Neal said. 'To be honest, and I'm only saying this because of your background,

Craig, Stuart sounds such a lovely man. It's hard to think of him having enemies. Not enough to kill him, at any rate.'

'He was a lovely man,' Angela agreed taking a seat at the table. The close-fitting dress gripped tight. All credit to the quality of dressmaking, the seams protested, but refused to budge. 'He would do anything for you, for us. He would drive over here from Sussex to make sure our builders were doing what they were supposed to, whenever we went to our villa in Portugal.'

Neal glanced at Craig and detected the slightest hint of annoyance. The newly-built house had been adequately explained away, but what had paid for the Portuguese villa?

Rich coppers were a source of continual speculation in the force. In particular, those involved in fields where large sums of money often changed hands, such as counterfeiting, fraud, and drug enforcement. It looked easy for those on the outside to imagine someone working there slipping a couple of thousand into their pockets from a cash stash, or a few bags of cocaine into the boot of their car at a drug bust.

Johnson had worked in those areas, coming into contact with many unsavoury characters. Money could also be made by passing information to criminal friends or by doing the opposite, making sure damaging material never saw the light of day.

'If he didn't have any enemies, and I don't think he did, why would someone kill him?' Angela asked.

'Could it have been a random act, or a case of mistaken identity?'

'It doesn't look random,' Neal replied, 'although we haven't discounted mistaken identity. However, there are some indications that lead us to believe this is not the case.'

'What indications?' Craig asked.

'I hope you understand, Craig, but I'm not at liberty to say. Some aspects of this case are not public knowledge.' The stab wounds to Livermore's arms and legs had not been widely reported as they could not be easily explained. Her view was he had been maliciously attacked or even tortured. If so, that didn't suggest mistaken identity or a random act.

'Yeah, I understand,' Craig said, 'but you can tell me—'

'Craig, what about some of your old buddies who come around here now and again?' Angela said. 'Did any of them have dealings with Stuart?'

'Don't be daft woman. They had nothing to do with him.'

'You say that, but I remember seeing Stuart in the garden during a day in summer, talking to Dean whatshisname.'

'Everybody was outside that day. It was a hot day.'

'Clarke. It was Dean Clarke.'

'Angela, I think you should leave now, allow us to get on with our meeting. You're distracting these officers from their enquiries.'

'But I really want to find out what happened to Stuart.'

'We all do, but you're not going to find it here, are you?'

'No, I suppose not, but I want to do whatever I can to help.'

'The best help you can give us at the moment is to leave us alone.'

She stared at her husband for a couple of seconds before she got up from her seat and walked out of the room.

'What was this meeting Angela was talking about?' Graham asked, getting in quick before Johnson could change the subject. 'The one in the summer with Dean Clarke and Stuart Livermore?'

'Stuart often came over here to talk about some procedural stuff he wanted to include in his new book. While he was here one day last August, a few of my buddies turned up for a social call. Stuart's a sociable guy and afterwards he said that talking to them gave him the inspiration for a couple of new characters he was thinking of putting in a future book.'

'Do you remember if there was a falling out with anyone here, or if Stuart became involved in an argument with someone?'

'Nothing like that went on. It was a relaxed afternoon and many beers were drunk. It happened only the once. I like to keep the various bits of my life separate.'

Jealously guarding the golden goose, more like, Neal thought.

'As a good friend of Stuart's, a former police officer, and someone who worked with him closely, what do you think happened to him?'

'I think I'm better qualified to answer that question than almost anybody. I've known him for over ten years, I've been in meetings with his publisher, I've met his agent, been present in television studios when they filmed his book. For the life of me I can't think of anyone who would do him any harm. He is, was, a super nice guy. He was an author, for Chrissakes, not a criminal, a soldier, or a detective. In some ways, he was the best friend I ever had. I will miss him terribly.'

NINETEEN

Henderson collected a pile of papers from his office and strode into the Detectives' Room for the 18:30 update. The team were already gathered. Without wasting time, he got down to business.

'It's Tuesday, just over a week since Stuart Livermore was found murdered. Tell me we're closer to finding his killer.'

He let the silence pervade for a few seconds before saying with a loud sigh: 'Phil, you make a start.'

'Right boss. Yesterday, Sally and me met with Lindsay Taggart, the victim's literary agent.'

'For the benefit of the rest of us, what is a literary agent?'

'This is the author's first point of contact if he or she has a problem, or they want to discuss a new book or contract. Generally, when an author's written a new book, he and the agent sit down and make changes to improve it. This is to ensure the publisher sees only the polished jewel, and not the rough diamond, as Lindsay described it.'

'Now we're clear on our definitions, what did she have to say?'

'She and Stuart had what she called a tempestuous relationship.'

'Did she indeed?'

'Yes, she said he was precious about the words he wrote and took exception when she or anyone else tried to alter them.'

'I would imagine it's the same for most other authors. If I'd slaved for five or six months over a manuscript, I'd be annoyed if someone took a red pen to it.'

'Let's just say that, according to her, some are better than others at accepting criticism.'

'What's Taggart like?'

'She's a big lady,' Bentley said. 'I don't mean in the, you know, chest department, but she's almost as tall as me, and big boned.'

'Intimidating?'

'I'll say. She speaks loudly and is hard to interrupt. She liked Stuart. He always delivered his manuscript on time. Despite him having problems with her making changes, when they were done, he was always quick to praise her, especially if he believed the alterations made the book better.'

'So far, so normal, I imagine,' Henderson said, sensing another dead-end. 'What about enemies?'

'She was aware of Livermore's spat with Steve Mitchell and dismissed it out of hand. She'd discussed the matter with Mitchell's agent, Sam Ogden. He was in agreement about Mitchell's dislike of Stuart, but he'd known Mitchell for almost ten years and doesn't believe him capable of murder.'

'Interesting. Anything else?'

'No, nothing else, boss.'

'Did Ms Taggart offer up the name of any other likely perpetrator?'

'No, but she did say she didn't believe the killer would come from the book side of Stuart's life.'

'No?'

'Nope, even though some authors climb on their high horse by refusing editing suggestions, and condemn what they see as blatant commercialism at literary events, she believes most agents and publishers have the author's interests at heart. If what they are proposing is aimed at selling more books and making more money for the publisher, it would do the same for the author. It's a win-win for all involved.'

'I'm coming to a similar conclusion,' Henderson said. 'Which means we're either missing something, or we need to dig deeper into his personal life. Let's move on. Thanks, Phil.' He caught Vicky Neal's eye. 'Vicky, how was the retired Super?'

'For those not aware, former Superintendent Craig Johnson was the police advisor on Stuart Livermore's books. He helped him to make sure police procedure and terminology was right. We had an interesting discussion. He was guarded at the start, but this was before his wife came into the room and upset the apple cart. As if to make amends, he became more open and admitted Stuart was one of his best friends.'

'Did he indeed?'

'I said his wife had upset the apple cart. Johnson was telling us about his and Stuart's business relationship, when she blurted out about owning a villa in Portugal, and that she saw Stuart talking to some of Johnson's criminal buddies in the summer. Johnson, it appears, still hangs out with some of the old informers and criminals he used to deal with on the job.'

'Does he? Who?'

'The one name his wife mentioned was Dean Clarke. I looked him up. He used to lead a criminal outfit in Forest Hill, South London, said to be engaged in importing drugs and offering protection to local businesses. He's retired now, it seems.'

Henderson's eyes opened wide in surprise. 'What's Livermore's connection to them?'

'Maybe none. He was seen one afternoon talking to Clarke is all we know. It could mean Livermore was there to discuss book issues with Johnson when Clarke and his buddies showed up. It's the way Johnson tells it, or it could have been a regular occurrence. Perhaps Livermore was thinking of including him as a character in one of his books, or considering writing a true-crime story based on his exploits.'

'What's your take?'

'From what we know of Livermore and Johnson, I think it probably happened more than once, but no more than a couple of times. Everyone we've met says Stuart was such a nice guy, they couldn't see him getting mixed up in any nefarious activity, or hanging out with hardened criminals. On the other hand, if Stuart was contemplating severing his relationship with Johnson, the former Super might have used someone like Clarke to persuade him otherwise, and maybe he went too far.'

'Was the association between Livermore and Johnson mutually beneficial?'

'You bet. It wasn't only books, but the television series on which Johnson was police advisor. He lives in a new, substantial, detached house in West Farleigh in Kent, in its own grounds and looking over a large slice of Southern England. He said the work he did for Stuart Livermore paid for it.'

'I didn't realise this sort of work was so lucrative. I think I need to find an author I can advise. Did you detect any rancour when he talked about Livermore?'

'Quite the opposite in fact. He became a bit emotional when talking about Stuart's death.'

'Yeah,' Carol Walters said, 'but don't forget, he's ex-job and a former uncover officer to boot. He's seen more liars than most of us can shake a stick at. I'm sure he could fake it if he wanted to.'

'I agree, Carol, but Livermore's connection with Johnson still needs to be fleshed out. Although, I don't believe we've got enough to put the former Super under surveillance. If we're not careful, we'd find him drinking with former criminals because he misses the buzz, or he's engaged in some scam which doesn't involve our victim.'

'Point taken.'

'I'll do some digging with a few contacts I've got in Kent and see what it throws up.'

'Okay.'

'Carol,' Henderson said, 'why don't you let the rest of the team hear your take on the meeting we had with Steve Mitchell in Sheffield, and tell them about your latest discovery.'

Walters filled in details about Mitchell's background, the former professional footballer turned thriller writer. Nothing provoked a reaction from the team until sockpuppeting was mentioned.

'What the hell's that?' Harry Wallop asked. 'Sounds like something you'd see in the Punch and Judy show on Brighton seafront.'

'According to Wikipedia,' Walters said, 'sockpuppeting is creating an online identity used for the purposes of deception. In the case of Steve Mitchell, he adopted a number of aliases to promote himself and his books on Twitter, Facebook, and Instagram. Posing as Joe Bloggs or whoever, he writes a Tweet or a Facebook post saying he'd just read one of Steve Mitchell's books and thought it was brilliant.'

'It's reprehensible,' Sally Graham said, 'as it misleads readers, but it's not illegal, is it?'

'No, it's not illegal, but I think if you'd bought something from Amazon or eBay based on the recommendation of a fake review, you'd be mightily pissed off when it didn't work.'

'For sure.'

'It's the same thing with books, and considered by many of those in the industry to be morally wrong. Stuart Livermore took this stance and outed Mitchell. To cut a long story short, there followed a war of words between Mitchell and Livermore before Mitchell punched our victim in the face at a literary festival. He subsequently threatened to kill him.'

'Sounds like handbags to me,' Wallop said. 'A storm in a teacup, as my mother used to say.'

'It looked that way until a few days ago, Harry,' Walters said, 'until I discovered Mitchell was in the south of England the weekend of Livermore's murder.'

'Was he?' Wallop said. 'How did you find this out?'

'I called his agent about something else, and he let it slip.'

'Do we know where he went or who he came to see?'

'After hearing he'd been down here, I got the researchers to do a bit of digging. We got the reg of his car from the South Yorkshire force and tracked it on ANPR. On the Saturday afternoon prior to Livermore's murder, the car was picked up by CCTV cameras in Brighton.'

TWENTY

Henderson headed back to his office after the evening team update. He was keen to follow up on the Craig Johnson and Steve Mitchell leads highlighted in the meeting. He sat at the desk, woke up his pc and loaded his contacts file. Running down the list of names he found the one he was looking for. He picked up the phone.

'Rudi Cavell,' a voice said when the phone was answered.

'Rudi, good evening. It's Angus Henderson in Sussex.'

'Angus, good to hear from you. What can I do for you?'

'I'm in the middle of an investigation into the murder of a man here in Brighton Our enquiries have uncovered the name of a former Superintendent from your neck of the woods.'

'Now you've got me interested. Who are we talking about?'

'Craig Johnson.'

'A murder enquiry and Craig Johnson? I might have guessed.'

'Why do you say that?'

'You know how it is. Some detectives behave as if they're undercover even when they're not, reluctant to tell you what they're doing, and turning their computer screens away if you come too close. They might not be looking at something dirty and dangerous, but then again, they just might. What's your interest?'

'The murdered man was the crime author, Stuart Livermore. Johnson was his police advisor.'

'Ah, I remember the story now. He used to brag about it around the office, all the money he was making. If the television programme he was consulting on, ach I've forgotten the title...'

'*Black Night*.'

'Ah, yeah. If *Black Night* ever made it to the BAFTAs, we were to look out for him. He'd be there in a new penguin suit and dickey bow, and in his top pocket would be his speech, ready to face the cameras if the production team were called up on stage.'

'What was he like as a cop?'

'Ask anyone. The first words coming into their heads would be 'old school'. He'd only just started to trust DNA testing by the time he left, but when it came to analysing social media, smartphones, and laptops, he didn't have a clue. He'd delegate the lot. 'Don't give me all that technical gobbledygook,' he used to say, 'just tell me what it means.''

'What sort of cases was he working on?'

'Mostly drug enforcement, cross-Channel stuff, part of it undercover. He got his promotion to Superintendent following his involvement in gathering intelligence about a forty-million-pound heroin haul aboard two lorries importing flowers from Holland.'

'It's difficult and dangerous work.'

'Yeah, you can say that again. It brings you face-to-face with hardened criminals. One word or gesture out of place and you're toast.'

'He was obviously good at it.'

'No, you can't fault him there. The best of those guys, and I would put Johnson in the same category, are so convincing there comes a point when you can't tell them apart from the criminals.'

'Rudi, how did he behave around the office?'

'When he returned here to HQ, there were rumours about him being on the take. He said the money he was chucking around came from his work as a police advisor, not from any of his criminal buddies he was often seen with. There was an internal investigation, but nothing came of it.'

'So, he retired with his reputation unblemished?'

'He did, all thirty years of it. Most guys, when they retire, take security jobs or work in the warehouse at Sainsbury's, trying to make ends meet. The pension they tell me, doesn't stretch to paying all the bills. Johnson said he was making so much from working with Stuart, and on the television series, plus his own books, he didn't need another job.'

'His own books?'

'Yeah, he not only assisted Livermore with the technical stuff, they started writing a thriller series together. It was based on the work he did while working undercover. It's Johnson's name on the cover, but as anyone will tell you, if they've ever read one of his reports, it had to be Livermore writing them. Johnson's grammar and spelling were beyond crap.'

'Is he successful?'

'Last I heard, he's now got three published, and they're all doing very well. I spoke to him about nine months back. He told me he was now making more money from writing than he ever did as a cop. Said he wished he'd retired ten years earlier.'

A few minutes later Henderson put the phone down. He woke up his pc. He loaded the Amazon website and keyed in Craig Johnson's name. The former Super now had four thrillers published, and a quick glance at the number of favourable reviews and the position of the books in the sales charts only confirmed what Rudi Cavell had told him.

Henderson sat back in his chair and sighed. He realised all the theories he'd harboured about a South London gang and a vengeful Craig Johnson had turned to dust. No way would the retired Super harm a hair on golden boy Stuart Livermore's head. In fact, he suspected the opposite was true: Johnson would do damage to anyone who threatened Livermore.

His own, growing literary career probably accounted for the villa in Portugal which Vicky Neal had mentioned. It wasn't pay-outs from low-life criminals at work here, but the hard graft of hours spent hammering away on a laptop keyboard. Mentally, Henderson ran a line through Johnson's name.

He left his office and walked towards the staff restaurant. He would buy a coffee now, and something for an evening meal. He couldn't think of going home any time soon. There was still a load of work he had to get through.

Twenty metres or so from the door leading into the restaurant, he could hear laughter and the hubbub of numerous conversations. It wasn't as raucous as could be heard around lunchtime. Then, the numbers inside were swollen by admin staff, but tonight there would be a sufficient number of late-shift patrol crews, IT staff, and telephone operators to fill many of the seats.

'Ah, it's you Henderson. I'd like a word.'

He turned to see Jim Hegarty striding towards him. Hegarty, a DI from John Street in Brighton, dealt with serious crimes in Sussex below the level of murder, those being the preserve of the Serious Crime Team in Malling House. Henderson didn't like him. He could be an officious prat and was known to bully junior officers.

Henderson stopped. Not because he wanted to speak to Hegarty, but as he appeared earnest, Henderson would prefer to have this conversation in the relative quiet of the corridor and not in front of everyone enjoying an early dinner.

'Where were you last Wednesday night?' Hegarty asked.

'Why should anything I do, be of interest to you? Are you checking up on me?'

'C'mon, Angus, it's a serious question.'

Henderson sighed and decided to humour him to get this stupid Q&A session over with. 'Let me think. Wednesday. I was in a pub in Lewes having a drink with my new chief inspector.'

'Who's that?'

'Sean Houghton.'

'Never heard of him, but I guess it counts you out.'

'Counts me out of what?'

'There's been a series of rapes in Brighton, and for the first time we think we've caught a breakthrough. The perp has said nothing to his victims before, but on Wednesday, things changed. It was fortunately only an attempted rape as the intended victim was armed with,' he coughed, 'an illegal pepper spray. Something she'd bought on eBay, apparently. She said her attacker spoke with a strong Scottish accent.'

'So, you thought of me?'

'Not just you, I'm asking everyone I know with a strong Scottish accent.'

'What if I couldn't have supplied such a cast-iron alibi as talking to a senior police officer? Would I be a suspect and taken in for questioning?'

'There's no need to get so annoyed, Angus. I was only joking.'

'Well, maybe I don't like your sense of humour,' Henderson said, walking away.

TWENTY-ONE

This wasn't the first day back in the office for Hannah Robbins. She had worked a couple of days the previous week, but she was still struggling to concentrate. She had a pile of manuscripts in front of her, some from literary agents she respected, others having been sent direct to her publisher on-spec by budding writers, this despite a website notice telling them not to. As punishment for this transgression, some editors would immediately bin the manuscripts. She, instead would look at them, but would give them short shrift.

Science Fiction and Fantasy, more than any other literary genre, attracted the young, whose obsessive interest could turn certain films, books, and TV series into a cult phenomenon. Often, she would pick up a manuscript and within minutes would know which programme or movie it was based upon, down to the main actors and a visual rendering of the setting.

Visions of Stuart began to flood through her head. Her concentration on the papers in front of her faded, like a movie switching between scenes. Hannah and Stuart had been going out together for nine months. It was a short time for her, as she was loyal and committed, but a long time for him. In the past, ever since his divorce from Ellen, he had been reckless, flitting from one relationship to another, like a bee in search of sweeter pollen.

Nine months was the longest he had ever gone out with anyone. He would often tell friends this was down to his and Hannah's shared love of books. This was part of the appeal, she couldn't deny it, but she would counter that he had gone out with several other authors and an editor in the past, and those relationships hadn't lasted.

For her, it was about so much more than books. Some nights they would switch off the television and just talk. They shared a love of walking on the South Downs, and both enjoyed candlelit meals at Beni's Bistro in Hove. Then, there was the banal: she had fond memories of travelling together in the train to London, she heading to work, he going to a meeting with his agent or editor to discuss a new book.

He'd asked her to move into his house in Queen's Park. It was a better prospect than her apartment in Hove, with more space and a decent-sized back garden, but she'd refused. It wasn't because she didn't love him, or didn't want to be with him, she did, but she wasn't ready. She needed to be sure he possessed the same level of commitment she did. Now she would never know.

She started sobbing, the tap-tap of tears falling on the weighty tomes of an alien invasion: a race of lizard creatures turning humans into zombies. She fished out a handkerchief and dabbed her eyes before wiping the tear-marked pages.

'Is this a bad time?'

She looked up, her teary eyes taking a second or two to focus.

'Oh, hello Celia. It's fine, do come in.'

Celia Cathcart, a freelance book designer and illustrator, walked in. She was in her late thirties, with shoulder-length brown hair, always neat and styled, and dressed in a flowing black skirt matched with a studded leather bomber jacket. Those who didn't know her, were often shocked by her drawn face and pipe-cleaner-thin arms and legs. She wasn't bulimic, or an avid dieter, but suffered from an overactive thyroid.

Celia stood in front of the desk hugging her artwork like a safety blanket.

'I heard what happened to Stuart, Hannah. I'm really sorry. He was such a decent human being and as you know, I've always loved his books.'

'Thank you, Celia. It's very kind of you to say so.'

'If you want to reschedule, I would totally understand.'

'There's no need, I'm fine, truly. Take a seat. No, tell you what. Let's go upstairs to the staff restroom. I fancy a change of scenery. I've been sitting in this office too long.'

'Sure.'

It was called the staff restroom, but this being Thor Books and not Google, whose offices she passed on the way to work in the morning, there were no beanbags, hammocks, smoothie makers or healthy food dispensers. Instead, it resembled a basic café in Stepney. To be fair, Thor wasn't a large company, only forty-seven employees all shoehorned into a tall, narrow building in a side-street off St Giles Street in London.

Moving upstairs was a welcome change from the confining four walls of her office. They found a clean table and Hannah left Celia to sort out her illustrations while she went to wrestle with the hot water urn.

The large silver cylinder delivered, almost at random, either piping hot water for a cup of decent coffee, or lukewarm stuff with no other use than to wash her hands. Standing there looking at the thing reminded her of her mother. Not the round shape of the vessel, her mother had never in her married life been larger than a size 8, but its temperamental nature.

When her mother had first heard of Stuart's murder, she was shocked. When this emotion receded, her true feelings swam to the surface like a stinging jellyfish. 'Well, I never thought he was good enough for you, dear. I've read some of his stuff, and I think he must have been a violent man under that veneer of civility to think up all that gore and violence.'

For the first time in living memory, Hannah had put the phone down on her, and didn't call back to apologise. She knew it would create an impasse, her mother never apologised for anything, no matter how long she waited.

If Hannah refused to pick up the phone, it would require her father to interrupt his deep perusal of *The Telegraph* crossword to intervene. He wouldn't think of picking up the phone himself to call. He would instead cajole his wife, like the haranguing shop steward at the place where he once worked, until she did.

'Is everything all right, Hannah?'

She turned to see Celia standing there. Hannah had spooned the coffee into mugs and added milk, but hadn't poured in the water. She had been staring at her distorted reflection in the urn's polished surface, wondering if this was how her mother viewed her: a mixed-up, mess of a girl who couldn't organise her life properly or choose the right man.

'Oh, I'm fine,' she blurted out. 'This can be a temperamental beast. You have to pick the right moment to pour.'

'I see,' she said in a reassuring voice, although her face still looked a little puzzled. 'Just shout if I can be of any help.'

'Will do.'

Hannah turned the tap and was pleased to see boiling water flowing. Sometimes, it would make her cross if it came out cold, but today she was in a 'bugger-it' mood. If it hadn't worked, they would have left the building and decamped to the nearest Starbucks.

She carried the mugs over to the table and placed them down with care. Celia had spread out her lusciously illustrated drawings, and no way did Hannah want to besmirch them with a rogue drip or spill. They were one-offs, unique and beautiful as a rock band's LP cover back in the days of vinyl, and couldn't be replaced. Celia was even-tempered to a fault, but Hannah would bet even she would blow her top if any of her pictures were damaged.

Hannah now found it easier to concentrate. The restroom was an airier and brighter place than her dull office, shadowed as it was by adjacent tall office blocks. For some reason, words on the page utilised neurons which could be easily interrupted by memories of Stuart. Pictures, it seemed, required the use of a different part of her brain, one into which disturbing thoughts could not easily intrude.

Celia's illustrations were colourful, lush, and strikingly beautiful: sleek spaceships sailing through an azure-coloured space filled with stars, comets and planets, the colours vivid and their edges seamlessly blended. In one book, the author's name and book title were etched in a font resembling liquid mercury, conjuring up images of Arnie's arch foe in *Terminator 2: Judgement Day*. Not a bad thing since the book was based on a similar story.

She spent the hours up to lunchtime immersing herself in time travel and interplanetary conflict, before marvelling at the sexuality imbued in a vampire figure without turning her into a porn character. Hannah suggested a few changes which Celia accepted with good grace. The illustrator walked away from the meeting happy to have matched her brief. Her hard work at the easel had been recognised, and she would soon be paid for all her hours of toil.

The effort of concentration for such a long period had exhausted Hannah, but she rallied when she left the staff restroom and returned to her office. Without sitting, she picked up her jacket and handbag, descended the stairs, and disappeared out of the front door.

TWENTY-TWO

The Oasis Brasserie was busy when Hannah entered. Not seeing her lunch companion in the thick throng, it took directions from a harassed and grumpy waiter to point out the correct place. She climbed the stairs to the mezzanine and wasn't surprised to find it just as busy as the downstairs area.

The restaurant was filled with businessmen in smart suits, trimmed hair, and eager-to-please expressions. Many were accompanied by over-made-up young women with slim bodies, clad in short, tight dresses, wearing impossible-to-walk-in shoes. All common in this part of London with so many publishers, legal chambers and accountancy practices in the area, as was the sound: everyone talking loudly as if to exaggerate their level of self-importance.

She found Lindsay Taggart at a table pressed against the wall, for once not holding court like a medieval monarch dispensing largesse. Instead, she was engrossed in reading something on her phone.

'Afternoon, Lindsay.'

Stuart Livermore's literary agent looked up, her deep blue eyes, coloured contacts some of her cattier colleagues suggested, focussing for a moment before her face broke into a broad smile. 'Hannah, darling, it's lovely to see you.' She rose from her seat and hugged her.

It wasn't a warm hug, a degree or two up the Celsius scale from Stuart's friend, Ryan Allison, but then warm was never a term to be included in the same sentence as Lindsay Taggart. Never married, but with a string of minor-celebrity lovers, she was a big lady; big in voice, big in her demands during contract negotiations and when raising her voice to remonstrate with someone who had disappointed her, often waiters in places like this.

'How have you been?' Lindsay enquired.

'Not too bad,' Hannah said. She squashed into the gap between their table and its neighbour. She took a seat with her back to the wall, now able to survey the room without turning around. She was surprised to find Lindsay had left this seat free, as she liked to notice, and be noticed. Hannah shrugged off her jacket.

'Busy in here,' Hannah said, and could have added how she hated the tables being so close together. She could not only see what the people in the next table had ordered, but she could watch them eating, and, if she was really bored with her companion, listen to what they were talking about.

'I probably eat lunch out more than you do, and I often find it's like this. Not always the same restaurant, mind you. The current flavour of the month changes like the wind.'

Hannah picked up the menu.

Lindsay's manicured fingers, replete with bright red nail varnish, eased the menu back on the table. 'I want to say how sorry I am to hear what happened to Stuart. I know what you must be thinking, what does she care? She's got another ninety-nine authors to worry about, she can replace Stuart easy as pie with some lucky sod from the slush pile. I want you to know, Hannah, I really liked Stuart.'

'I know you did, he told me.'

'We had our disagreements as happens in any business relationship, but twenty minutes later it would all be forgotten. You remember the time when he said he wanted to write a novel about a washed-up detective who has one last chance at redemption?'

'I do,' Hannah said, smiling at the memory.

'I told him it had been done a hundred times, but would he listen? The more adamant he became, the angrier I got. In the end we were both on our feet hollering at one another.'

'He could be as obstinate as a bull when he put his mind to it.'

'He could, but I had the last laugh. He told me he'd started writing it and, despite developing a detailed summary beforehand, he couldn't get past chapter four.'

'Have you decided, ladies?'

Hannah looked up. It wasn't the surly waiter from downstairs, but a girl with a pleasant, smiling face. Hannah appreciated the small gesture. Places like this were hectic from eleven-thirty in the morning to about three in the afternoon. She knew if she worked there, she would find it impossible to look happy.

'Mussels for me,' Lindsay said.

'Tagliatelle, with salad on the side,' Hannah said, despite not having looked too closely at the menu.

'And to drink?'

'A large glass of Chablis for me,' Lindsay said.

'I'll have a glass of sparkling water.'

'No, she won't,' Lindsay interjected. 'She'll have a large glass of Chablis too. She needs it. Don't worry,' she said to Hannah, 'I won't stand over you while you drink it if you don't want to.'

Hannah didn't complain. She didn't want to make a fuss and, as Lindsay had said, maybe she needed it. 'Okay, a large glass of Chablis for me,' Hannah said, 'but I'd still like a glass of sparkling water.'

'No problem. I'll bring your order over in a few minutes.'

They made small talk until the drinks arrived. Lindsay had been talking about a new author she had signed, and Hannah responded with the occasional supportive noise. When the waitress departed, Lindsay lifted her glass. 'A toast,' she said. 'To Stuart.'

Hannah picked up her glass and clinked it against Lindsay's. 'To Stuart,' she said.

Hannah spoke before Lindsay could regale her once again about her great 'new find'.

'Lindsay, you knew Stuart as well as anybody. What do you think happened to him?'

'The police asked me the same question.'

'They've been to see you?' she said, a tad surprised.

'Yes, they came to the office. A rather dishy young man with lots of upper arm muscles, and an attractive blonde sidekick. I know when they make cop dramas, including those written by some of my authors, they tend to make police officers gritty and unattractive. This is to make sure our attention isn't diverted from the plot, they tell us, but maybe they should use actors like those two. I know I responded better to his questions than I would have done if it was some ugly fat bloke with sweaty armpits and acne.'

'I imagine there's a large body of empirical research out there to back up your opinion. What did you say to them?'

'I told them about the internet spat Stuart had with Steve Mitchell over his sockpuppeting, but they said they knew all about it.'

'Yes, I mentioned it too.'

'Something else came to me while we were talking, an incident that happened a year or two back. During our discussion, it was at the back of my mind, and I couldn't quite grasp it. Since then, a few fragments have come back to me.'

'Which incident is this?'

'A tagliatelle, for you madam,' said the waiter, placing a plate of steaming pasta in front of Hannah, accompanied by a side salad. She was momentarily taken aback at the speedy service, making her suspicious that her meal had just come out of the microwave. No, she was being stupid, her pasta, and the meals on the table next to them, looked fresh. With such a large number of people in the restaurant, meals had to be made and delivered quickly, or some diners would be forced to wait hours.

Another waiter arrived holding a black pot. In a dramatic gesture, he whipped the top from the vessel and laid it upside down on the table, a depository for the empty shells. He then placed a basket containing a selection of breads, and beside it, a bowl of lemon-infused water.

'Can I get you anything else?' they were asked, but everything they had ordered was now sitting in front of them.

'No, thank you,' Lindsay said. Both waiters turned and walked off.

Lindsay set about attacking the mussels while Hannah sat there. She was waiting to hear a bit more than the teasing fragments she had been thrown, her stomach growling at the enticing smell, the first food of the day.

'Are you not eating, Hannah? C'mon, at least make a start.'

Hannah did as she was told, knowing her companion could not be rushed. Lindsay would tell her story in her own time.

A few minutes later, Lindsay put her fork down, giving the remaining molluscs in her pot a temporary reprieve. She took a large swig of wine and placed her glass back on the table, her fingers still toying with the stem. 'A few years back, two, maybe three, I should check in case the police ask me again, Stuart was signing books at a literary festival.'

Lindsay sat back in her chair, arms in her lap. 'It was Bloody Scotland in Stirling, I think. There are so many of those things nowadays I sometimes find it hard to keep up.'

'I know what you mean.'

'Stuart told me about it at the time, and later, I heard the same story from another author, so there's no doubting its authenticity. Stuart was sitting behind a desk signing books when a badly-dressed guy, who hadn't shaved for a couple of days, and perhaps a worker from a nearby building site, came up to him and started berating him.'

'What for?'

'The man accused Stuart of ruining his brother's life. He said it was Stuart's fault, and he was going to pay.'

'How awful. What was it all about? What did he want?'

'Stuart told me about it at the time, but for the life of me, I can't remember the details.'

Hannah's face took on an incredulous expression. 'Lindsay, I don't wish to sound rude, but you've got the memory of an elephant, everyone says so.'

'I know, I know, but I deal with over a hundred authors, and Stuart's not the first to be insulted at a literary event. I don't want to tell you something and give you false hope, when I might be confusing the detail of this incident with something else. It was several years ago, after all, and a lot has happened since then. What I do remember, and I'm certain about this. It had something to do with one of Stuart's television programmes.'

TWENTY-THREE

Stepping outside, the breeze felt cool, but Henderson's light jacket was adequate. The commemorative service he'd just attended in the Downs Crematorium was short, as only crematorium services could be. They'd started off with a bit of singing, a modern song, not a psalm, followed by three readings: Stuart Livermore's editor, Maisie Carruthers, spoke about his literary career; his best friend, Ryan Allison, about the happy times they'd spent together; and his tearful girlfriend Hannah Robbins of the love and affection she felt for him.

In the course of the investigation, the team had talked to Steph, Hannah Robbins and Ryan Allison, but not Carruthers. Henderson would try to rectify this shortfall now. Many of the mourners were standing outside admiring the flowers and the messages written by other visitors. Carruthers, he guessed, was in her late-forties, and at present talking to a woman about twenty years her junior. The two women were smoking, vaping rather than sucking on the real thing, billowing large clouds of vapour and everything else into the cool morning air.

'Maisie Carruthers?'

'Yes, I am. You must be from the police.'

'Is it so obvious?'

'No, I've been to several functions with Stuart over the years and met a number of his friends and relatives. I have a good memory for faces and I don't remember seeing you.'

'Guilty as charged. I'm Detective Inspector Angus Henderson, Sussex Police.' He held out his hand which she shook.

'A Scot. My father was from Scotland; Edinburgh. Although, I suspect you're from a place a lot further north.'

'Fort William.'

'Do you come to the commemorative services of all your murder victims? I thought that only happened in badly-made television dramas.'

Her friend laughed, choking a little on the e-cigarette smoke. 'Listen to you, giving this poor man a hard time. He's only doing his job. And in any case, what do you know about television dramas? You don't own a telly. Would you believe it, Inspector? I've been trying to persuade her to buy one ever since I moved in.'

'As always, Astrid, you are right. I stand corrected. I do prefer to read in the evenings.'

'It's just an excuse for you to continue working.' She turned to Henderson and held out her hand. 'I'm Astrid Hawkins, Maisie's guardian angel and partner.'

'Pleased to meet you,' Henderson said. 'In answer to your question, Ms Carruthers. I don't go to every funeral or commemorative service. I've come to this one as I'm still trying to get a better understanding of Stuart's life.'

His main reason for being there was to talk to Maisie. To do so at her office in London would take the entire morning or afternoon, a big chunk of time with no promise of a result. If, instead he managed to have a short discussion with her now, it would settle the matter one way or the other. If she did have something useful to offer, he could then arrange a more fruitful trip to London.

'How long have you known Stuart?' he asked Carruthers.

'Eight years, I worked it out while writing my eulogy for today. He used to write science fiction over at Thor books. Hannah Robbins was his editor at the time, but I suspect you know that already.'

He nodded. 'Do you know Hannah?'

'Oh yes. In this business everybody knows everyone else. The publishing industry is not as big as it looks, but punches way above its weight in marketing terms. I've met Hannah on and off at book fairs and conferences for about the last fifteen years. It was no surprise when she and Stuart started going out together.'

'What makes you say that?'

'I knew she liked Stuart while he was at Thor, but she wouldn't consider going out with him while they still worked together.'

'How did you get on with him?'

'Me? Like you, Inspector, I don't go to every funeral either. If you include all the authors I work with and all the people I know in the book business, I'd be doing this sort of thing every other week. You can therefore surmise from my presence here, that I really liked and respected Stuart. First and foremost, he was a bloody good writer.'

She stopped to have a puff of her e-cigarette. 'A lot of people, in the main those writing and publishing literary novels, are snooty about crime. They accuse the genre of formulaic plotting and predictable endings. Stuart's books were anything but. At times, his writing was as good as anything produced by a literary novelist, while his plots were always credible and well-thought researched.'

Carruthers was short and slim, hair barely down to her ears, with prominent cheekbones and a severe-looking resting face. She looked formidable and not the sort of woman many authors would get the better of.

'Second, he was such a nice person. He would do anything for anyone. Whenever we were about to publish one of his books, he would come into the office and thank everyone who had worked on it. At Christmas, he would send each and every one of them a gift. I could go on, but I'm sure you get the picture.'

'I do. Did he have any enemies?'

'In a word, no. The business we're in isn't like construction or demolition, where people affected by the route of a new road, or the destruction of a much-loved landmark can react with passion and violence in a bid to stop it. There are so many books out there, why would anyone care if Stuart's or someone else's novel wasn't published? It's not the kind of business where one garners enemies, Inspector, and before you say it, there is always an exception to the rule. In this case, the exception is Salman Rushdie, but he genuinely is a one-off.'

'What about Steve Mitchell?'

She shook her head, but her short hair didn't budge. 'It was a minor skirmish resulting in a brief bout of fisticuffs. Nothing more. Mitchell's a hot-tempered lout and Stuart picked the wrong guy to try and take a pop at. He accepted that and, as far as I'm aware, had moved on.'

The mourners were moving towards a bus parked outside the gates which was scheduled to take them to lunch at a local hotel. Maisie and Astrid were going, but Henderson would pass. The trio started walking in the direction of the bus.

'What about Stuart's police advisor, Craig Johnson? Have you met him? If you haven't,' he said, nodding towards the bus queue, 'I can see him up there.'

'Oh, I've met him all right. Stuart would bring him into town now and again, the country yokel having a look at the bright lights of the big city, he would say to me, but I suspect not to him. He came into the office a few times, and yes, he's a rough and ready character. More at home in dingy pubs in Kent than smart London eateries, I suspect, but he wouldn't lay a glove on Stuart, I'm quite sure. He knew which side his bread was being buttered. I told Stuart he was paying him too much for his services, but he wouldn't listen. He felt the man's advice was too valuable to risk losing it.'

'I understand Johnson still hangs around with some questionable characters, and Stuart met a few of them.'

They were now at the bus, behind a small, subdued queue waiting to climb aboard.

'I don't think you'll find the answer you're looking for there, Inspector. Yes, Johnson still likes to associate with a number of his former criminal associates, and invites them around to his house. The way Stuart told it, they're all as old as Johnson himself. Their best years are behind them and, in most cases, younger people have taken over their businesses.'

'That doesn't mean they couldn't still pose a danger.'

'No, it doesn't, but Stuart never felt there was any malice in those discussions. Quite the opposite, in fact. He liked talking to them and enjoyed his weekends over at Johnson's place. It gave him, he said, a greater insight into the criminal mind. I know of several plots that made it into his books which he gleaned from his time talking to those guys. Former criminals they might be, but I'm not convinced you'll find Stuart's killer there.'

The bus queue had disappeared, leaving only Maisie and Astrid. Carruthers turned to face the DI and stuck out her hand. Henderson shook it.

'Goodbye Inspector,' she said. 'I do hope you catch whoever did this. They, whoever they are, have killed a lovely human being.'

TWENTY-FOUR

After attending Stuart Livermore's commemorative service, Henderson returned to Malling House. When he reached his office, he stood at his desk munching a sandwich and drinking from a bottle of water. A few minutes later, Walters walked in carrying a folder.

'Ready?'

'I will be when I finish this. Any problems with our guest?'

'If you mean, did he deck the officers bringing him here? The answer is no, but he wasn't best pleased to be dragged all the way from Sheffield and the comforts of home.'

'Hardly dragged. He wouldn't be here at all if he hadn't been so economical with the truth.' He squashed up the sandwich wrapper and lobbed it into the bin before picking up the Stuart Livermore folder from the desk. The two detectives walked towards the stairs.

'How was the funeral? Did you see Maisie Caruthers?'

'Commemorative Service. It was at the crematorium and most unlike any other funeral service I've ever attended.'

'How so?'

'It was more modern than any I've been to. Livermore must have been an atheist. There wasn't one word from the gospels or a psalm uttered. We started off singing one of Stuart's favourite songs, a pop tune, and at the end, as we were walking out of the chapel, a Country and Western ballad was playing.'

'It does sound a bit different.'

'At least it was a happy service and not something maudlin, as a typical funeral can often be. We were celebrating a life well lived, not moping over the man's untimely death.'

'Hear, hear.'

'After the initial songs, there were tributes from Maisie Carruthers, Ryan Allison and Hannah Robbins.'

'Was Steph there?'

He nodded.

'How was she?'

'Tearful throughout.'

'Was her bullish partner, what's his name, Mark, with her?'

'No, otherwise I suspect there might have been a scene. The eulogies all focussed on Stuart's life and achievements. Nowhere did anyone mention how he'd died.'

'It sounds like the modern way to do it. What was Maisie Carruthers like, and what did she have to say for herself?'

They were out of the building now, walking towards the Custody Suite.

'We can count her out of any jealousy act. She lives with her female partner.'

'Maybe she's bi.'

'Don't complicate the issue when I think I've got my head around things. Suffice to say it's the only motive she could have had for killing Stuart. As she said, publishing is not about life or death, it's only books.'

'If his killer isn't involved in the book business, we're out in a boat without a paddle. Livermore didn't have a wide circle of friends outside of literary festivals and book signings. Most of his socialising and drinking took place there as well.'

'You're right.'

'Did she point the finger at anyone else?'

'I mentioned Johnson and Mitchell, but she dismissed them both. Johnson, because Stuart was providing his bread and butter, and Mitchell's harassment as a little skirmish that had since run out of steam.'

'Interesting,' Walters said. They walked through the security doors. 'Let's ask Mitchell and find out what he thinks.'

They pushed open the door of the interview room to be faced with the icy glare and folded arms of the former professional footballer. It was typical autumn weather outside, not too cold if you could avoid the wind. However, still a bit too chilly to be wearing a white t-shirt that looked a couple of sizes too small, stretched tight over substantial chest and arm muscles.

'Good afternoon, Mr Mitchell,' Henderson said as the officers walked in and took their seats. Walters began setting up the recording equipment.

'Is it?' Mitchell replied.

'Ready,' Walters said a few moments later.

'For the tape, this is Detective Inspector Angus Henderson...'

'Detective Sergeant Carol Walters.'

Henderson nodded at Mitchell. 'Steve Mitchell,' the man on the other side of the desk said.

'How was your trip from Sheffield?'

'The motorway around Sheffield was clogged after a bad accident, so for once I came down on the train. At least the buffet was operating.'

'Good to hear. Has anyone here offered you tea or coffee?'

'Yep, but I don't want anything. I had enough to eat and drink on the journey.'

'Okay, let's make a start. Mr Mitchell, I'm in charge of the team investigating the murder of Stuart Livermore in Brighton on 22nd September.'

'I know. You told me when I met you two in Sheffield.'

'The last time we spoke in Sheffield, you admitted the quarrel you had with the victim was about your use of aliases to promote your books.'

'Don't tell me you've brought me all the way to bloody Sussex to talk about that old chestnut. If you have, you can do the decent thing and give me an airline ticket so I can fly back.'

'This spat boiled over when you assaulted Stuart at a literary event in Harrogate.'

'This was all dealt with by the local plod.'

'Yes, and I'm willing to accept the judge's comments about Livermore and his party being the worse for wear and you sober, so there were mitigating circumstances.'

'That's very big of you.'

'You failed to mention when we talked to you, the death threat made in a Tweet about a week before Stuart died.'

'Is this all you've got?' he said in an angry voice. 'If it is, what the fuck am I doing here?'

'Your Tweet was in response to someone posting a picture of a shredded Motörhead jacket by a disgruntled fan. You suggested the same thing should be done to Livermore.'

'Yeah, yeah. What can I say? I was furious. I'd read a piece in *The Guardian* about unscrupulous authors gaming the system, and citing my name. What else was I going to think, but the article had been written by Livermore?'

'Fair enough,' Henderson said, sitting back and folding his arms. 'Is that it? Is there anything else that happened between you and the victim which you should be telling us about?'

'How do you mean?'

'Have you otherwise attacked, threatened, or cajoled Stuart Livermore in addition to the times mentioned earlier?'

'No.'

'You're sure?'

'Course I'm bloody sure. He was a royal pain in the arse, I'm sure you know this by now, but I didn't have it in for him physically. I'm not that kind of guy.'

Henderson snorted. 'The previous convictions for affray and assault were, what? The other guy's fault? The aberration of a misspent youth?'

'Yeah, okay, I admit it. I'm hot-tempered, I can't help it. When something riles me a lot, I explode, but it's not always at someone else. There's a punchbag in my garage when I feel things are coming to a head.'

'Fair enough, but can you explain why your car was spotted in the Queens Park area of Brighton on the 22nd September, the day Stuart Livermore was killed?'

'I'm laying out CCTV pictures for Mr Mitchell to see,' Walters said.

'This is you in your Porsche Cayenne, is it not?' Henderson said.

'Yeah, but—'

'What were you doing near Queen's Park in Brighton, Steve, close to the house where Stuart Livermore lived?'

'I don't know...I can't explain.'

'C'mon, Steve. Were you lost, casing the place, looking for an address, what?'

He shook his head. 'No comment.'

They gave him a few minutes, but no satisfactory explanation came forth.

'I need a lawyer,' he eventually said.

'I think you do too,' Henderson said. 'Steve Mitchell, I'm arresting you for the murder of Stuart Livermore. You do not have to say anything. But, it may harm your defence if you do not mention when questioned something which you later rely on in court. Anything you do say may be given in evidence. Do you understand?'

TWENTY-FIVE

Henderson and Walters walked towards the Detectives' Room for the evening briefing. When he pushed open the door, they were met by loud clapping and cheering from those present. He wasn't expecting this from hard-nosed, stoic detectives, so it was a moment to savour. He nodded in acknowledgement and headed over to the corner where the Stuart Livermore murder team were assembled.

'Evening everyone.'

'Well done boss,' Harry Wallop called, 'you nailed him.'

'Correction Harry, everyone involved in this enquiry can take credit for nailing him. This, and every murder investigation before it, and those coming after it, will always be a team effort. You all deserve the congratulations.'

This led to another bout of cheering and handshakes. Henderson let it run its course.

'Booze-up tonight, in case you haven't heard,' Phil Bentley said. 'Nag's Head from seven.'

'See me later Phil and I'll stick some money in the kitty.'

'Sure thing.'

'Now, getting back to the here and now, there's still some work that needs doing. As well as making sure files, interview notes, and HOLMES2 are up to date, we need a bit more on Steve Mitchell to make sure a conviction sticks.'

'Haven't we got enough already?' Harry Wallop asked.

'On a good day, Harry, and with a fair wind, the CPS believe they could get a conviction. They've been given his on-line spat against Livermore, the pub assault, the threat to kill him, and now CCTV of him casing the victim's house on the day of the murder. He hasn't given us a satisfactory explanation his presence there, and I can't think of one. My worry is his lawyer might come up with something to sow some doubt in a jury's collective mind.'

'Fair point.'

'As a first step, SOCO's are examining Mitchell's house at Watson Road in Sheffield. They will send down any laptops or phones they find. The HTCU will analyse them and the phone Mitchell had in his possession.'

'The laptop should tell us loads,' Sally Graham said. 'We only have Mitchell's word for it about the extent of his sockpuppeting and the furore it caused.'

'I hope so,' Henderson said. 'The results we got from the analysis of Livermore's phone and laptop were such a disappointment. It was almost as if Livermore had deleted all references to Mitchell.'

'Maybe as Maisie Carruthers said to you,' Wallop said, 'Livermore had moved on following his spat with Mitchell. Perhaps this was what she was referring to.'

'Might be,' Henderson said. He looked over at his Admin Assistant. 'Mel, any gear received from

Sheffield, get it off to the High Tech Unit as soon as it arrives.'

'Will do.'

'Right,' Henderson said, 'what else do we have scheduled?'

He listened while each of his sergeants itemised the meetings planned over the next few days, mainly with members of Livermore's immediate family: his brother, children, and father, who had been in hospital at the time of his son's death.

'As I said before,' Henderson said, 'with regard to obtaining more evidence against Mitchell, continue digging in these interviews. Don't let up just because we've got this man in custody.'

'When's his court hearing?'

'Next Monday. It gives us less than a week to find something conclusive to nail him with. Is there anything else?'

Henderson fielded several administrative enquiries before walking back to his office deep in thought. He was convinced of Mitchell's guilt, and no way did he want him slipping the net through lack of evidence. He hoped this degree of urgency had been conveyed to the team. This wasn't the time for anyone to think of taking their foot off the gas.

He dumped his papers on the desk and took a seat. He was on the point of waking up his pc when Sean Houghton walked in.

'Angus, I got your message. Well done for arresting and charging Steve Mitchell.' He strode over, grabbed Henderson's hand and shook it. It was a firm grip, the strong wrist of a man who still played competitive rugby.

'Thank you, sir.'

'You've solved a non-domestic murder in less than two weeks. It has to be some sort of record.' Houghton turned and sat on a chair beside the meeting table. Henderson got up from his seat and perched on the other side of the desk facing his boss.

'It helped that Mitchell was known to most of Stuart Livermore's associates.'

'He's not someone they were likely to forget. He's a big bastard and with a nasty temper too. His criminal record is a long list of assaults and fights. Is this what happened, do you think? Mitchell lost his rag with Livermore and stabbed him?'

'It looks that way, but he's not saying, and forensics can't tell us one way or another. However, the stab wounds on Livermore's leg and slashes on his arms do suggest the attack was more premeditated than a simple explosion of anger.'

'It's an important point. A good defence brief could use it to blow holes in any violent temper scenario. That is, if the CPS decide to go with it.'

'This the reason why I've tasked the murder team with trying to find more against him. We also have a forensic crew taking his house in Sheffield apart, looking for the knife.'

'What about electronics? Has South Yorkshire offered to analyse them, or are they sending it all down here for our lads to do it?'

'Any laptops, iPads, or phones they come across, will be sent straight to us. It was hard enough getting them to allocate some of their forensic people to search the house, never mind trying to find space in their high-tech unit. In any case, they said if they were required carry out the analysis, they've got such a large backlog, they wouldn't get around to it for at least a couple of weeks.'

'You made a good call. We haven't got that sort of time to spare with Mitchell due to make an appearance in court on Monday.'

'It's a tight deadline.'

'It gives us less than a week to build a solid case against him. As soon as his laptop and everything else arrives, get them off to Haywards Heath.'

'Will do.'

'Who runs HTCU?'

'Inspector Dave Chivers.'

'What's he like?'

'Despite being in charge of a technology outfit, one capable of hacking into phones and password-protected laptops, he's no geek. You won't hear him talking acronyms and tossing jargon around in meetings.'

'Good, I hate talking to IT people,' Houghton said. He got up from his seat, walked to the door and paused. 'I'll call Chivers and persuade him to clear the decks.'

'Thank you, sir, it would be most helpful.'

'Goodnight, Angus.'

'Good night, Sean,' Henderson said to the vacant doorway.

Henderson turned and began tidying the papers lying on his desk in preparation for leaving. The adrenaline kick he received after arresting Stuart Livermore's murderer had dissipated, leaving him feeling lethargic and empty. Perhaps, a booze up with the team would change his mood. If not, he would stay a couple of hours, then go for a run along the seafront and take advantage of an early night.

Houghton would need more than a slice of luck getting any cooperation out of Inspector Chivers. Henderson would have told him as much if Houghton had decided to stick around a little longer. Chivers could be a spikey sod and didn't like being told what to do. Houghton would need to be at his diplomatic best to have Mitchell's gear analysed and the results available before Monday.

He picked up his jacket and headed into the Detectives' Room, looking for the revellers. It was Friday, but this coming weekend looked like another he would be spending in the office.

TWENTY-SIX

Henderson's culinary skills were limited to what most people would regard as staples: chilli, Bolognese, stews, plus dishes that could be heated in the oven. The previous Saturday, he had made a large pot of chilli. When it had cooled, he'd scooped four servings-for-one into resealable bags and stored them in the freezer.

This morning, he had taken one of the bags out of the freezer and allowed it to defrost. He was thankful for his foresight. The last thing he felt like doing this evening was cooking. He wasn't big on takeaways, but he felt so beat and, with a card containing a dozen or so takeaway restaurant numbers lying close by, he would have been sorely tempted.

He had learned to cook out of necessity, as apart from the period when he was living with Rachel, he had lived on his own since moving to Sussex from Glasgow. He couldn't rely on the staff restaurant at work to feed him. At the end of a tiring day, after conducting a tough operation or interviewing a cantankerous witness, it was too easy to reach for comfort food: pies, chips, and stodgy puddings. Before long and with much too much reliance on it, he wouldn't be able to get into many of his clothes.

Twenty minutes after popping the contents of the defrosted bag into a pan and doing the same to some rice, he carried a tray containing his own take on chilli con carne into the lounge. He also carried a large glass of water. He'd tasted the chilli and somehow, after a short stay in the freezer, it was much hotter than he remembered.

Henderson put the tray on the coffee table before switching on the television and the DVD player. After inserting a copy of the *Black Night* DVD which Carol Walters had managed to source, he returned to the settee. Picking up his tray, he lifted his fork and took a mouthful of chilli and at the same time picked up the television remote. He dropped the remote and immediately reached for the glass of water. The heat from the chilli seemed to multiply in his mouth. When it subsided, he stopped eating to fiddle with the remote and select the correct episode on the DVD.

Black Night was based on what became Stuart Livermore's most successful book. According to Hannah Robbins, when it was first published it had been a moderate success. Once the television programme had aired, the book shot into *The Sunday Times* top twenty. The programme also boosted sales of all his other books, and since then, every new release by Livermore could be found riding high in the book charts.

Henderson didn't have the time to view all eight forty-minute episodes tonight. It had been decided he would watch the odd-numbered ones while DS Walters would take on the even-numbered.

With Steve Mitchell in custody, he reckoned their viewing of *Black Night* would do little to strengthen the case against him. As far as Henderson knew, Mitchell had nothing to do with either the television programme or the book. However, it would be useful to try to understand more about Stuart Livermore and his world, with a view to considering just how he could have provoked Mitchell into killing him.

Ten minutes in and Henderson was starting to enjoy the programme. He had tried watching it when it first appeared on the BBC, but for some reason, it didn't grab him. Now he could see why. It focused on the disappearance of a brother and sister, ten-year-old twins, from a play park in Derby. He didn't like this part so much. No television programme could do justice to the real grief and anguish parents would feel when their children didn't come home.

Putting such reservations to one side, the banter between the two detectives - young, a good-looking woman, and an acne-scarred man, both with troubled pasts - was excellent and, despite the gravity of their task, at times funny. Their boss, by way of contrast, was unsmiling, uncompromising, and un-pc in the way he addressed everyone. He was particularly hard on the only female detective in the station, he bullied witnesses during interviews, and dished out more of the same as they were trying to make a statement.

The story was set thirty-five years back, so comparisons with modern policing methods weren't valid. However, it succeeded in shining a light on how things had changed in the way suspects were handled when arrested, questioned, and remanded in custody.

The hours flew by. A couple of times, he started watching the next episode, the one Walters had been allocated, so keen was he to resolve the cliff-hanger left by the previous one.

By skipping the opening and closing credits on each episode, along with recaps, he managed to complete his required viewing in a little over two hours. With his binge watching marathon now over, he took his tray through to the kitchen and loaded his plates and cutlery into the dishwasher. He poured a glass of whisky and returned to the lounge.

He switched the television and DVD player off, and took a seat on the settee. He picked up the Livermore murder file and flicked through it, trying to see if anything he'd seen on the screen resonated with something in the file.

Five minutes later, his phone rang.

'Have you finished watching?' Walters asked.

'Aye, I have, a few minutes ago.'

'What did you think?'

'To my surprise, as I didn't take to it the first time round, I enjoyed it. I thought the banter between the two detectives and the unconventional outbursts from their abrasive boss made it worth watching. Overall, the female detective was my favourite character.'

'You liked her, even though she was responsible for her brother's death?'

'C'mon, it was an accident.'

'Do you want me to tell you how it ends?'

'No thanks. If we get some slack after the Livermore case calms, I'll try to find some time and watch the rest.'

'I think I'll do the same. It's one of the better detective programmes I've come across.'

'What do you think it told us about Stuart Livermore?' Henderson asked. He took a sip of whisky, enjoying the familiar burning sensation. It was a warm, pleasant glow, and not the 'petrol explosion in the mouth' effect of a cheaper variety, or, for that matter, his home-made chilli.

'I'm not sure it told us much. Running down our list of things to look out for: no one was stabbed in the same manner as Livermore, no living person was insulted, no character gave us a lecture about politics, religion, or sport, and no one made fun of any minority group.'

'With the story being set in the early eighties, he did take some liberties with the misogynist superintendent, and the lack of women and ethnic minorities at the cop shop. I got irritated by the way he led and bullied some witnesses, but that's to be expected. They didn't have PACE or the army of litigious lawyers we have to deal with on a daily basis nowadays.'

'I would say in summary, it was an excellent night's viewing, but I don't think it moved the case along one iota.'

'I enjoyed it too, and I don't think it did either. Did it make you want to read some of Livermore's other stuff?'

'It did, but nowadays I find I've got less and less time for reading. Maybe I'll buy one of his books and leave it in the middle of the coffee table to remind me to read it.'

'A guilt trip? Never fails. See you in the morning, Carol.'

'See you.'

Henderson lobbed the phone on to the settee and cradled his whisky glass. It was rare in any murder investigation, with the exception of a straightforward domestic fracas, for the Senior Investigating Officer to feel confident the individual now in the cells was, without a shadow of a doubt, the culprit responsible.

At this juncture, there was always a nagging uncertainty: did they have the right man? Could they do more to prove his guilt? What if the judge decided to throw out all the evidence and set him free? Despite his confidence in Mitchell's central role in Livermore's murder, he couldn't help but allow doubts to creep in.

TWENTY-SEVEN

The police patrol car turned into the rear entrance of John Street, Brighton's main police station, and stopped close to the door. Good job, no way did he want to be walking far. The misting rain outside would turn his straight hair into a lank mess, meaning anyone looking at him would automatically assume he was guilty.

The big bastard in the passenger seat got out first and hauled open the rear door. He reached inside the car and grabbed a piece of the back seat passenger's combat jacket, an attempt to hurry him along.

'Hey, get your fucking mitts off the threads,' Danny Carlyle said, pushing his hand away. 'I'm here of my own free will to answer a couple of questions. I'm not a fucking serial killer.'

'Well, get a bloody move on, mate. We've got a lot more of you perverts to bring in today.'

Carlyle smiled to himself at this little jewel of information. It confirmed the 'can you come down to the station and answer a few questions' routine wasn't simply an excuse to get him into their clutches. This before they huckled him off to a cold cell without so much as a by your leave.

The two miserable uniforms left him in reception while they both behaved like perfect schoolboys in front of the desk sergeant, a fat bloater with a ruddy face and boozer's nose. Carlyle was a betting man and would have liked to open a book on the sergeant's early demise. He'd give 3-1 he wouldn't make the end of the year. Problem was, his fellow attendees didn't look like they'd be interested: a junkie bird with greasier hair than his, two aggressive scroats with tats on much of their visible skin, and a confused old bat who thought she was waiting to see her doctor.

The two young hoodlums didn't frighten him one bit. He'd seen their type come and go, more the latter, at the point of a rival's blade, or in the back of a prison van. Such obvious tats had no place on the body of a serious criminal. Chances were, a frightened witness or victim wouldn't have a clue if you were black or white, fat or thin, tall or short. They would, however, have no trouble remembering the England flags on their necks, or the 'Love n' Hate' inked across each knuckle.

A few minutes later the leery copper came over and this time, without touching, informed him it was time to go.

'Thank fuck for small mercies,' he said getting up from his seat. 'If you'd left me there a bit longer with this group of sparkling raconteurs, I might have been more reluctant to move.'

He was led through a set of secure double doors and down a corridor, all around, the grey of an institutional establishment. It didn't matter which one: Social Security, Probation Service, Prison, they all looked and smelled the same. It was surprising to some people that his loathing of such places had not turned him straight, but as they say, that was a story for another time.

He walked into an interview room and was instructed to sit. Yes, he wanted a cup of coffee, milk and two sugars, but no, his patience wasn't unlimited. If his questioners weren't here in five, he would be heading for the exit.

The coffee arrived, and he gave it the once-over before taking a drink. Spitting into the cup was common enough, but hard to spot. If they'd pissed in it, there would be no foam. If they'd added a dash of floor cleaning product or, if feeling really vindictive, bleach, there would be a whiff of ammonia or chlorine. It looked and tasted fine.

He was reaching for a second sip when two detectives entered the room. He did a quick assessment. The bloke had thinning hair, a paunch from eating too much junk food, and a face no more acquainted with daylight than a vampire. Carlyle dismissed him without further thought. His companion, on the other hand, was hot with a capital H. Aged around thirty, she had short dark hair, a pretty face, pointed nose, and a tight blouse and skirt, both straining hard with the underlying pressure. Delightful. He was going to enjoy this.

'Good morning, Mr Carlyle, I am Detective Inspector Jim Hegarty. This is Detective Sergeant Suzy King. Thank you for coming along this morning. I say Mr Carlyle, but I understand you now go by the name of Steve Sutton?'

'Aye, changed it after my last stretch, didn't I? Too much baggage wi' the old name.'

'Notoriety, I think you mean,' Hegarty hissed.

'Call it what you like.'

'As Danny Carlyle, you were known as the Napier Rapist. Responsible for five rapes and the murder of a young woman in the Edinburgh area between 2001 and 2004.'

His anger rose like a boiling kettle. 'Why do you fucking people need to keep reminding me?' he said through gritted teeth, and banging his fist on the table for emphasis.

'Calm down there, Mr Carlyle, I mean, Sutton. I'm only repeating the facts that are here in black and white inside this file.'

'Facts, aye, but it's a constant reminder to me, a person,' he said, jabbing a thumb into his chest, 'who is trying to leave his past behind him.'

'Your determination to go straight is laudable, don't you think DS King?'

'I do, sir. It is.'

Ah, you can't win them all. A good-looking lass, let down by a scruffy southern accent.

'I assure you, Mr Carlyle, it is not our intention for this meeting to get in the way of your rehabilitation.'

'Then why are you still calling me by my old bloody name?'

'Force of habit. Now, Mr Sutton, we're part of a team investigating a series of rapes that took place in the Brighton area over the last eighteen months. The perpetrator has been called by most newspapers, the South Coast Rapist. In an effort to find him, we are interviewing everyone in Sussex who appears on the Sex Offenders Register.'

'So, you thought you'd just look me up did ya?' His voice rising in volume and shrillness. 'Don't you bastards ever let go?'

'Now, now, Mr Sutton, there is no need to get angry. This investigation is not exclusively directed at you.'

'I've only got your word for that.'

'I'm afraid it's all you're going to get. Now, we'd like to know where were you on the night of Wednesday, 25th September, between the hours of 10pm and midnight?'

'Why do you want to know?'

'We are focussing our efforts on the attempted rape of a young woman in Hollingbury. It happened just under two weeks ago, on the twenty-fifth.'

'About two weeks ago, eh?' Carlyle said, sitting back in his chair and adopting a pose as if he was considering the question while sifting through large memory banks. This wasn't the time for any smart-arse comments like, let me first check my busy diary, or, can I make a call to my appointments secretary? No, this situation called for a calm performance otherwise, Hegarty and his flat-foots would be all over him like a bad smell.

'Lemme think. Aye right. A week last Wednesday, my team, the boys in red, Manchester United, were playing the auld enemy, Liverpool, at Old Trafford. I watched the game at The Royal Oak in Hollingbury, my local. Afterwards, I went back to my mate's house with a couple of other guys for some beers. We gave the manager's selection and tactics a good kicking until about two in the morning. They played shite in the first half, and were lucky to walk away with all the points.'

'I'm going to have to ask you for the names of those other men you were with. I'm sure you understand.'

'Aye, no problemo. Gimme a pen and paper and I'll write it down.'

Ten minutes later, Danny Carlyle walked back into the reception area of the cop shop, a complimentary travel voucher tucked inside his pocket. It was the best he could do in the circumstances. They had turned down his request for a cop car or taxi to take him back to his house. He wasn't a happy about it, wasting time on his day off, waiting for a bus. Maybe instead, he would go into town and down a few jars. Something to make his trip worthwhile.

The old dear and the druggie bird had gone, but the two tattooed scroats were still sitting there. Their spotty faces were etched in sneers, as if it would only take one crossed word and they would explode. It took a strong bout of willpower not to give them the finger and test their mettle. He hoped whatever charges they were there to address carried a hefty custodial.

He felt buoyed by his performance as he walked out of the front door of the cop shop and into John Street. Hegarty and King had hung on to his every word, lapping them up like a pair of thirsty cats at a bowl of fresh milk. Following the aborted attack in Hollingbury, when the bitch surprised him by squirting pepper spray in his face, he did go back to his mate's flat and drank until two. Difference was, he persuaded them to tell the cops a little white lie if asked. They would say he had been with them earlier in the night watching the match in the Royal Oak, not at a sports bar in town.

He walked down Edward Street in the direction of the Steine. His mind was so fixed on a performance that could have graced a stage at the Edinburgh Festival, he failed to notice the BMW coming up the road towards him, and that it was slowing down. Before he could react, it stopped beside him and a big bastard jumped out. He grabbed him by the jacket, and bundled him into the back seat. Seconds later, they were motoring past John Street police station. No one was any the wiser. Where was a cop when you needed one?

TWENTY-EIGHT

'Can I ask, Ryan, where do you get the ideas for your books?'

Ryan Allison leaned towards the microphone, despite the moderator of the four-author panel of which he was a member telling him not to. The microphone was super-sensitive, or something, but old habits were hard to change. He cleared his throat.

'Can I just say, before I answer the question, how pleased I am to be here in Cheltenham for this 'Does Politics Have a Place in the Modern Crime Novel?' panel. I'd also like to say what a beautiful room this event is being held in. It's the first time I've been inside a lady's college...' he paused for a moment, '...at least in daylight hours.'

This drew loud applause from the one hundred-plus attendees: a mixture of die-hard literary festival followers and a larger group of book-loving locals. Allison always liked to start any public appearance with a touch of humour. It was a good idea, he believed, to get the crowd on-side at an early stage.

'In answer to the question posed,' he said when the laughter had subsided, 'I get my ideas from newspapers, television, incidents I have witnessed, and ultimately, the thoughts swirling around in my head. I might merge something I've read with something I've watched, add in a couple of things from my own experience, then roll it around in this,' he said tapping the side of his head. 'Eventually, out pops a story.'

'Can I ask Trevor...' another questioner asked, leaving Allison to heave a contented sigh of relief. He had fielded his first audience question, and hadn't made a complete dick of himself. He sat back, but didn't tune out. It was tempting fate to do so. With a tricky or contentious question, moderators often tried to pep things up a bit by randomly picking another member of the panel and asking for their take on the question posed.

Without meaning to, his mind began to drift. Stuart Livermore's murder had shaken him, while the warning given to him by Hannah Robbins as he'd left for Gloucestershire, 'to be careful', did little to calm his demeanour. He missed his best friend and still hadn't come to terms with his death, or the ghastly way in which he had died.

This was the first literary event he had attended since Stuart's murder, and he felt a little anxious. Not because he believed some psycho was out there targeting authors or friends of Stuart Livermore, that would stretch the credibility of even the most imaginative crime novelist. No, but if the police didn't know the reason why Stuart was targeted, how could anyone reassure him? He didn't know if he'd made the same mistake as Stuart, upset the same person, or witnessed the same incident, thereby also making himself a target.

'Let me ask other members of the panel for their thoughts on this important point,' he heard the moderator say.

He and Stuart had been the best of friends, and in many respects, their careers had followed a similar trajectory. They had both appeared in *The Sunday Times* book chart at the same time –

'So, if I can start with you, Ryan.'

He turned to the moderator in panic, hoping his shocked facial expression reflected his panicked thoughts - *What the bloody hell was the question?*

Thankfully, the moderator wasn't some local academic who would do little but say a few words of introduction, sit for forty minutes looking intelligent, before pocketing a cheque for a hundred quid. Graham Townsend was a fellow author and Allison hoped, good at the role.

'This gentleman asked if it was becoming harder for new novelists to make a name for themselves with so much competition out there in the marketplace,' Townsend said, an expectant look on his face.

Allison took a moment to compose himself, thinking as well as trying to calm down. He then trotted out a short list of the changes taking place in the publishing industry: the growth of digital publishers, the expanding power of Amazon, and the explosion in the number of self-published authors. He then pulled it all together into what sounded, to him, like a cogent conclusion. The crowd approved and responded with enthusiastic applause.

He was repeating a trick he'd picked up from an author on another panel. At the time, he'd believed the guy was flannelling, attempting to buy time and space to allow his booze-addled brain to shift into gear. He then delivered a brilliant response that drew resounding applause. In speaking to him afterwards, Allison learned he didn't do it by accident. When faced with a subject he knew little about, he would summarise the good points made by everyone else on the panel, package them together with a neat conclusion and present it as all his own work.

Never again throughout the remaining thirty minutes did Allison lose concentration. At the end, members of the panel shook hands before going their separate ways. Some were heading to a nearby hostelry for a few pints before dinner, and others, like himself and the crime and fantasy author, Trevor Melrose, into the foyer to do a spot of book signing.

'I thought it went well this evening,' Melrose said as they walked. 'Some panel sessions can be as dull as dishwater. The audience tonight were up for it, and I believe we panellists responded. I remember once I was on a panel in Carlisle. After introductions, we asked the audience for questions. The room fell silent. I didn't know where to look.'

'Evening sessions always seem livelier than the afternoon ones.'

'It's maybe because people have spent a few hours in the pub first. By the time the evening session comes around, they're raring to go.'

'You're probably right. I thought you dealt well with the woman who asked if you knew the best way to kill a vampire. She sounded as though she believed in them. I'll be searching the local papers in

Gloucestershire for the next few weeks to see if any locals have been found with a stake through their hearts.'

Melrose laughed, revealing a gap in his front teeth which somehow suited his bespectacled face. 'I get that all the time. People write to me claiming they're witches, or they think there's a couple of them living next door. Others say they can conjure up ghosts from the fireplace, or they've talked to aliens. To the bloke who said fantasy didn't have a place in a crime novel, and couldn't stand my books as they weren't in touch with reality, I say he didn't have a clue what he was talking about.'

'I think the majority of people in the hall agreed with you.'

Allison had attended several Science Fiction/Fantasy gatherings with Stuart, and could vouch for the strange beliefs and behaviours of a number of their adherents. Many would turn up dressed as aliens, or in the uniform of the Starship Enterprise crew. After talking to a few, he realised it meant more to them than a hobby.

The foyer outside the hall now resembled a pop-up bookstore. Tables were dotted around the room, behind which authors would sit and sign their books. At the far end of the room, a larger table, manned by staff from the local bookshop. It was piled high with books for sale by all the authors appearing at the festival over its week-long duration.

Allison was pleased to see a sizeable queue had already formed in front of his table. Katy, a marketing bod from his publisher, was there too. She ushered him into his seat.

'You did well in the last panel session, Ryan,' Katy said. 'I think you received more applause than anyone else.'

'It's kind of you to say so, but I know you're on my side.'

'Only a little. Are you ready?'

'As I'll ever be.'

'Good. Now remember, Ryan, if anyone wants to buy one of your previous books, or indeed a copy of the new one, we have the lot over there at the big table.'

'I saw a big pile of *Don't Look Back* over there. We'll have a job selling them all during this festival.'

'Yes, but we'll make a damn good attempt at it, won't we?'

Looking at the pictures of himself on the back of his books, it was obvious he'd aged, but this didn't seem to apply to staff from his publisher. The marketing and publicity people who attended these events, invariably women - his publisher seemed to be staffed almost entirely by women - were still the twenty-two and twenty-three-year-olds he'd met when first embarking on his career, a decade before. In nine months or so, Katy would be replaced by some other fresh-faced employee, not long out of university, as Sophie before her had been.

It was disconcerting. He was beginning to doubt if someone so new to the book publishing business could tell him anything about writing and editing, or indeed the activity they were engaged in today: selling a book.

He scanned the queue before reaching for his pen and squaring the pad of paper in front of him. He noted, with some satisfaction, the absence of members of a Sri-Lankan literary society who had appeared at the last festival he attended. Members of this group were related, cousins, not siblings, and he was forced to wade through a variety of twenty-five and thirty-letter surnames, most of which he had no hope of pronouncing without the services of an interpreter.

'Good afternoon madam,' he said, smiling at the first person in the queue. He reached over and in one fluid movement, removed the book from her hand. 'Did you enjoy the talk?'

TWENTY-NINE

Dominic Green rubbed a hand over his bald head, something he often did when deep in thought. He was standing in the dim light of the warehouse at Rema Foods, a business he had set up on his release from prison. It had been financed not from one of the charities championed by the likes of the *Daily Mail* for rehabilitating old lags, but from money he'd squirreled away. It had been hidden in a bank account in the Caribbean, the place where he'd once owned a villa, out of reach from the rapacious talons of the Proceeds of Crime vultures.

The business was involved in the import of bulk foods from Asia: rice, flour, tea, sugar, and a whole host of other items, which were sold to small wholesalers and larger independent shops under the *White Knight* brand. Rema were middlemen, using contacts in India, Pakistan, and Thailand, the names of which Green had acquired in prison, and not available to other businesses in the same field. He also had the finances to buy in large volumes, the savings from which were passed on to his customers.

He never allowed any deliveries to arrive after five o' clock, and never in the dark. He was formerly one of the biggest drug dealers in Sussex, and the powers that be would never let him forget it. If he stepped out of line, and a delivery arriving after nine in the evening would fit the bill, they would come down on him like a ton of bricks.

They would raid his business premises here at Shoreham Harbour, stick knives into all the large sacks which were now filling the warehouse shelves, not caring about the mess they made. Soon, his long list of valued customers would no longer be answering their phones. No, this time around a high-profile, public persona was out. If he needed to kill a rival or a grass, he would leave the body where no one would find it.

John Lester and Spike had been his trusty lieutenants from that previous time. John had been shot dead by armed police, while Spike was still in jail following a fight he had on the inside, when he'd blinded his fellow combatant in one eye.

Their places had been taken by Stu Linton and Henry Ford. Stu was known as Jack, on account of his passing resemblance to the actor, Jack Black. Henry was called Morris, due to his connection with cars. However, Morris knew sod-all about cars and was a terrible driver. It was down to Jack to drive him around.

His two lads, and a group of half a dozen men he could call on at any time, were sitting at the back of the warehouse drinking tea. The latest delivery had been unloaded and packed away. Green walked to the other end of the warehouse and unlocked the office. The guy who was gagged and tied to the chair was now wide-eyed and looking more frightened than aggressive. Good. Green wanted a sensible conversation later, not to provide Morris with another human punchbag.

He picked up the pile of money which had been sorted earlier and walked out, locking the office door behind him. He headed over to the resting workers, weary after their solid work-out. If he could see heat rising in the air of this cool building, it would be coming off them like steam from the kettle in the office.

Green handed out the money to the men, way more than any of them earned in their day jobs. He was not only paying for their muscles, but also for their silence, and to stop them helping themselves. Silence was his new mantra. There was nothing illegal for them to see, and even if one of them was persuaded to get into a cop car, they would have nothing to tell them. The fewer cops or anyone else, who knew about his business, the better he liked it.

The men departed, leaving only Morris and Jack. Green closed and locked the door, pleased to see darkness outside descending. He picked up the schedule from his warehouse supervisor's desk, a man who had left for home a couple of hours previously, and instructed Jack and Morris about loading the small van at the back.

Sacks marked with a discreet blue star were removed from the warehouse shelves and stacked into a false compartment under the floor of the van. This happened before the goods, destined for a succession of warehouses in North London and the Midlands, were loaded. When complete, Jack would drive the van to a secret location where the star-marked sacks would be unloaded at a lab owned by Green. The van, now containing only legitimate goods, would then be driven to the house of their delivery driver and left in his driveway, ready for the morning.

In addition to their legitimate purpose, the star-marked sacks also contained packages of heroin and cocaine, the foundation of his restored drug-supply business. This delivery operation was repeated a couple of times a week, sometimes with a van containing star-marked sacks, other times not. When he was starting to feel antsy, they would make the journey with an empty van. Green wasn't taking any chances. At the first whiff of cop trouble, he would torch this place even if it contained drugs, and would do the same to the lab.

He wouldn't say he'd had a hard time in prison, he hadn't, but no way did he intend going back. At the time of his trial, he'd been rich with a manor house in rural Sussex, a villa in the Caribbean, and a wine store which made the guy from Berry Brothers who came to see it, drool. This was all before the forces of law and order filched, as they thought, all of it.

Before being sent down, when he still had access to his fortune, he engaged the best legal brains in the land; and even Green had trouble recognising the staunch pillar of the community his barrister presented to the jury. Far from being the head of a Sussex crime syndicate, his gowned friend portrayed him as a mere pawn in a larger game, controlled by an anonymous Mr Big.

He could have laughed, but kept the straight face his counsel advised throughout the trial and ended up with a four-year stretch instead of a potential twelve, for the most part spent in an open prison. While he was away, the boys on the outside tried to keep the business running, but without his strong controlling influence they lost ground and soon dealers from London and Albania began to muscle in. He would deal with them in the fullness of time.

With the van now stacked, Jack set off to complete the deliveries. Green and Morris walked towards the office.

'We put that delivery away in record time,' Morris said.

'What d'ya want,' Green growled, 'a fucking bonus?'

'That would be good, Mr Green, but no, I'm just saying. How's the new house?'

'Better than the place we were in, but not a patch on Langley Manor.'

'Nothing could be, but you'll soon get used to it.'

'You know me, Morris, I can get used to anything. It's the wife who needs convincing. She doesn't like this less than ostentatious lifestyle.'

'She'll need to get used to it, won't she? You said yourself, even if you had the money now, no way would you buy it back.'

'You're right there, mate. It's called keeping your head down. C'mon,' he said, unlocking the office door, 'let's deal with this greasy fucker. I wouldn't mind an early night.'

They walked in. Morris headed over to untie and remove the gag from the man in the chair. Green had no worries about their prisoner overpowering Morris and legging it. Morris was ex-army, mad-keen on physical fitness, and a former boxing champion. He could look after himself.

Green switched on the kettle and spooned coffee into two mugs. The jolt of caffeine might stop him sleeping tonight, but as he wasn't a good sleeper at the best of times, he probably wouldn't notice.

'Now listen up, perv features,' Morris said. 'You only talk when we want an answer, not before. Resist the urge to scream, as no one will hear you. If you do, I'll be forced to give you this,' he said holding up a fist. 'Understand?'

'Right, right, but don't hurt me, I've done nothing wrong.'

'Don't tempt me, know what I mean?'

A few minutes later, Green handed a mug to Morris and took a seat facing his prisoner.

'Now listen up, Danny Carlyle. A friend of my daughter was raped by the guy the papers are calling The South Coast Rapist. You with me so far?'

'Yeah.'

'I know her, she's a nice girl. My daughter is very upset. I don't like seeing her this way, so I've taken it upon myself to find this bastard and mete out my own brand of justice. Yeah?'

'I hear you.'

'Now you, mate, were known as the Napier Rapist. Raped five and killed one. Tell me Carlyle, are you the South Coast Rapist?'

'No fucking way. I've made mistakes in the past, for sure, but I paid for it. End of.'

'Mistakes? How is raping five women a mistake?'

'I was young. The lassies coming out of Rose Street pubs and the Students Union at the university had skirts right up to their arses. If that's not asking for it, I don't know what is.'

Green couldn't argue with him there. He was at an age when that sort of provocation no longer had any effect. With young guys, their veins swimming with alcohol, drugs and testosterone, it was a different ball game.

'I remember reading something about it at the time.'

'Then you'll know, if you can't tell from my accent, I don't come from around here. I don't know the area well enough to do what that guy in the paper does.'

'Why did you move to Brighton?'

'Why do you think? To get away from Edinburgh where people know me.'

'My daughter's friend was raped during Brighton Pride, Saturday, August 3rd. I know where I was that weekend, keeping as far away from all those fucking bum-bandits and narcissistic extroverts as possible. Where were you?'

'Day or night?'

'Night. Around 11:30pm.'

He paused for a few moments. 'Working. When I left prison and with help from a charity, I got me a job at Gatwick Airport, humping cases. I remember when Brighton Pride was on. I quite fancied going there, you know, just to see what it was like. It's sort of iconic.'

Green gave him a disapproving look, but Carlyle's curiosity seemed genuine.

'I couldn't go. I was working night-shift. Started at seven on Saturday night and didn't finish a twelve-hour stint until seven the following morning.'

THIRTY

'I loved your last book, Ryan. DI Broughton grows on me more every time I read another one of your novels. I trust the latest one will be just as good.'

'I hope you like it. To whom would you like it dedicated to?'

'Can I just say though, I wasn't sure about the ending of the last one.'

It was approaching the end of Ryan Allison's book signing at the Cheltenham Book Festival. The small lady with the white curly hair and intense expression was last in the queue. It had been an exhausting session. Not only was his hand sore from writing, unaccustomed as he was to wielding a pen since all his books were written on a laptop, his jaw ached from smiling so much.

He hoped his frustration at still sitting there when all the other authors had disappeared, and even the folks at the big table were packing up, didn't show. He valued all his readers, and back in the day when he didn't have a deal and couldn't give away his books free with a Mars bar, he vowed if ever he became successful, he would never treat his readers with disdain. However, this little lady was attacking the ramparts of that hallowed principle with a large siege engine.

'It should have been that slime ball Josh who caught the 7mm slug in his gut and not Gregor. I liked Gregor.'

'I'll take that point on board for the next one.'

'Oh, my goodness, is that the time? It looks like everyone has left. I don't want to keep you Ryan, but could you dedicate *Don't Look Back* to George, my beloved husband. He loves your books as much as I do.'

'I'm glad to hear it. Of course, I will.'

'He's in a care home now. Even though his mind is clear, his legs have gone. Thankfully, he can still read, and he's read all your books. I'm sure he'll love the new one.'

'I'm sorry to hear he's not well,' Allison said. He handed the book back to her.

She clasped it to her chest, and thanked him before walking away.

Allison waited for a moment or two, expecting her to return because she had forgotten to say something else. When she didn't, he sat back in his chair and blew out a long blast of air.

'I thought she would never leave,' Katy said.

'Me too, but looking on the bright side, we must have sold a shedload of books.'

'We have. Which means your decision to stay over this evening is more than justified.'

'Many times over, I should think.'

He considered his next question with care, not wanting to sound the least bit suggestive. He was a forty-six-year-old man and didn't want his twenty-two-year-old publicist thinking he was trying to come on to her.

'Are you driving back tonight?' he asked.

'Yes, I'm afraid so. Our budgets don't stretch to a hotel room. I have somewhere else to be in the morning.'

'Another day, another literary festival?'

'Something along those lines.'

He picked up his things and extended his hand. 'Goodbye Katy, many thanks for all your help and support.'

'Thank you, Ryan. Have a good night in rockin' and rollin' Cheltenham.'

'Katy, don't knock it until you've tried it, but I'll do my best.'

The hotel booked by his publisher was clean and comfortable, but the restaurant was brightly lit with strong smells emanating from the kitchen. The place exuded all the charm of a seaside fish and chip shop. He met Trevor Melrose and another crime author, Bob Mathieson, at the college entrance. They started walking, making their way to The Beaver Inn, a traditional pub serving good food, according to a web search.

'Did you see the scores?' Mathieson asked in his broad Yorkshire accent. In the dark, Allison would swear it was the sheep farmer from the hills above Ambridge in *The Archers*.

'Yeah,' Melrose said, 'there was a goal in extra time. Liverpool are back on top.'

'Get away with you. I'm talking rugby league, a man's game, not a namby-pamby run-around by a bunch of over-paid arse-wipes.'

'C'mon Bob, tell us what you really think,' Melrose said.

'Ah just did...hey.' He stopped walking and poked a finger into Melrose's chest. Like being jabbed with a tent pole, Allison imagined. 'Are you fucking with me, Melrose, trying to wind me up?'

At five-ten, Melrose had to look up to Mathieson. He was about six-two and broad as a road-working navvy. 'No way Bob, I wouldn't dare.'

'Had you there,' Mathieson said, laughing. 'It's *you* I wouldn't mess with, mate. I'd be frightened if I upset you, you'd let loose one of your vampires or nightwalkers on me.'

They resumed walking.

'You've read my books?'

'Every bloody one.'

'You do surprise me.'

The pub was warm and welcoming. In the space of five minutes, they all had beers in front of them and the kitchen was busy making up their food orders.

'Bob,' Allison said, 'I saw on Twitter you've signed a big new deal with your publisher.'

'Aye, I did,' he said, enveloping the glass in a big mitt before draining the remaining contents. Boy, this guy could drink. Allison and Melrose were about the half-way stage while Mathieson was calling a waitress over to order up another round.

'What can I get you?' she asked.

'Three more pints, love,' he said to the young woman. Out of anyone else's mouth, the word 'love' sounded sexist and coarse. In Mathieson's Yorkshire burr it sounded fluid and natural.

'Coming up,' she said and walked off.

Allison waited for the big man to elaborate. 'They want three more books out of me and for doing it, gave me a cheque for a hundred grand.'

'A hundred grand! Fucking hell.'

'Fucking hell just about sums it up.'

'The reason I ask, is I've got a renewal coming up soon and everybody I talk to are saying that advances are down.'

'Maybe for the crap you write, but for me, they can't get enough.'

Allison looked at Mathieson's inert granite face. If he wasn't such a big lump and Allison was feeling rash, he might be tempted to take a swing.

The stone-hewed features dissolved into a big grin. 'Got you there, Ryan,' Mathieson said, punching him playfully on the arm. 'Only jesting. I think your books are bloody good as well. Although I have to say, I prefer your spy series to the crime ones.'

Allison smiled in return, but his arm ached. The banter continued throughout the meal, Mathieson showing a funny side which Allison had never seen before. By the third pint he needed to pee. He was sure with the amount of beer in his system, his contribution would be capable of raising local river levels by at least a couple of inches.

He left the table and walked to the toilets at the back of the bar. His eyes were drawn to a group of four women seated around a table. They looked familiar, maybe they had attended the evening panel session. One of them looked over and smiled at him, more or less confirming his assertion. He returned the gesture and pushed open the door to the toilets.

Allison finished relieving himself. He was in the process of zipping up when he received a solid thump in the back, forcing his head to bang off the porcelain tiles. He turned, his anger rising, ready to remonstrate with the drunk who had careered into him. He recognised the sour-faced man facing him. He had approached Allison's table earlier during the book signing. At the time, the name of 'John Smith' had only rung a small alarm bell as it sounded fake.

'What the hell are you playing at?'

A fist was driven into his belly, making him double up and retch.

'That's for Steve Mitchell. If he gets sent down, you'll also get this,' he said. He pulled him up by the hair and stuck the point of a blade into his cheek. 'You and your mate Livermore are a couple of fucking rats.'

'What?' he coughed, trying hard not to throw-up his dinner.

'And this is to make sure you don't forget what I said.' The attacker drew his head back and butted Allison on the nose. The grip on his shirt lessened and for a few milliseconds he felt nothing. Then, the pain hit him with the force of a steam hammer. Blood cascaded from his nose onto the wet toilet tiles, and his knees buckled. He collapsed unconscious on the floor.

THIRTY-ONE

Hannah Robbins removed her earphones as the train pulled into Brighton station. She had always enjoyed the sight of a train easing towards the buffers. It wasn't because it signalled the end of the working day, the line between work and leisure for her was often blurred. Did listening to the audiobook of one of her authors constitute work, or pleasure? She didn't know, but as sure as hell, her boss wouldn't be willing to pay her overtime for doing it.

She loved coming into the station for the sheer majesty of the place. She admired the beautiful curved glass of the roof, and the cavernous, cathedral-type space above her head. She loved the contrast between the measured, slow movement of the steel beast and the disorderly hurrying of returning commuters, keen to get their hands on that first bottle of beer, or to dig a fork into a plate of food. In this, her love of trains and stations, she and Stuart were on the same page, or would the appropriate term be timetable, she wondered?

Outside, it was a mild evening. The walk home to her flat near the seafront in Hove would be a pleasure. Tonight though, she had other plans. She walked over to a bus stop and waited. Ten minutes later, she took a seat downstairs aboard the number seven. She, and many other people she knew in the Brighton and Hove area, didn't own a car. It wasn't such a big place and most of the time she could walk to where she wanted to go, If she didn't feel like walking, or the weather was inclement, buses and taxis were plentiful and frequent.

In addition, Brighton was a delightful place in which to walk with interesting sights all around: the seafront, Royal Pavilion and the Lanes. She also liked the architecture, which could change from Regency Terraces to Edwardian villas in the space of a few streets. When she needed to travel further afield and, providing her destination was near a station, she could take the train. If all else failed, she would hire a car.

She got off the bus in Eastern Road and walked towards Queens Park. Stuart's house was in darkness when she arrived, which didn't come as a surprise as she knew no one was living there now. It still made her heart sink. It wasn't because she was expecting Stuart to be there, standing in the kitchen wearing his Wines of France apron while he cooked his evening meal. For once, it would be nice to think his brother or a friend had decided to stay.

Hannah turned the key and opened the door, before closing it behind her. It was depressing to see a pile of mail on the floor. She gathered it up. Flicking through, she spotted a royalty statement from his publisher, others that looked like invitations to speak at literary events, and another from a local college. She shoved it all into her handbag to be dealt with later.

She wiped away an unexpected tear and started her customary tour of the house. This to ensure it wasn't occupied by a group of homeless people, a colony of mice, or birds had decided to nest in the eaves. The broken window in the back door had been replaced, and she had spent an afternoon hoovering, dusting, and scrubbing. This, to remove the blood from the lounge floor and the black powder resembling soot, which the fingerprint people had spread over nearly every surface.

She moved upstairs and checked each of the rooms in turn. On the advice of Rob in the office, a keen DIYer, she also looked up at the ceilings. This was to see if there was any damp, a sign that an outside gutter might be blocked, a tile had become loose in the roof, or a pipe in the loft was leaking. Seeing nothing to set off any alarm bells, aside from the grass in the back garden which now looked overgrown and untidy, she headed back downstairs.

If previous visits were anything to go by, she would now open the door and walk out, head back to Eastern Road and wait for a bus to take her home. This time, she felt less spooked and not as lonely as she had been before. She decided to linger a little longer to try to rekindle the lovely memories she had of staying here. She went into the kitchen, deposited her bag on the worktop, took off her jacket and filled the kettle.

A few minutes later, she carried a mug of steaming tea into the lounge and took a seat in the armchair. If she could ignore the fact that a murder had taken place there, the brutal slaying of the man she loved, it remained a lovely house. It was bright and airy, warm and comforting in the wilds of winter, cool and lively in summer, especially with all the windows open and the sounds of the park streaming in.

She liked living in an upper-floor apartment. It was a place where she could close the door and know that nothing would have changed by the time she returned, either at the end of the working day, or after a few days away on business. However, the feeling of space and freedom which came from being in a larger property and having a garden, could not be replaced.

Stuart had asked her to move in with him several times, but she had refused. She would only do so when he felt the same way about their relationship as she did. To sweeten the deal, he had said if she finally decided to sell her apartment, he would sign-over a half-share in the house to her, whether she wanted to pay him for it or not.

Thinking about Stuart and his generous spirit was beginning to make her feel tearful, but the thought also triggered something else. Who would inherit the house now he was gone? She knew it was worth anywhere between eight hundred and nine hundred thousand pounds, maybe more, and with no mortgage to repay. Following the success of *Black Night*, he had paid it off.

From reading newspapers and crime novels she was aware that people had been killed for less. Only the previous week, a boy in London had been stabbed to death for thirty pounds and the old iPhone he carried in his pocket. Of course, murdering Stuart in order to inherit the house would only benefit those close to him, like his resentful children and his jealous ex-wife.

Jodie was sixteen, and she hated Stuart. This, he'd put down to his actions in breaking up the family unit, and more important, the drip-drip effect of the bile that Ellen had been poisoning her head with all those years. Her youthful appearance belied the fire of animosity that burned inside, reminding Hannah of cons she used to come across in prison where she had once taught English. They held on to their hate with the same intensity as old ladies gripping their mug of Ovaltine at night, and their handbags in crowds, often for the one who they believed had betrayed them.

Ellen Jacobs was a piece of work. Right from the off, she had tried to drive a wedge between Stuart and Hannah. It started with late-night phone calls, abusive texts and emails, before anonymous letters began to be posted through the door. They accused her of abusing children, buying and consuming drugs, and being drunk and incapable at work.

In essence, she wasn't only jealous of Hannah's prominent place in Stuart's affections, she wanted him back. This wasn't, Hannah believed, because she still loved him, or wanted him to be a 'proper' father to their children. He still saw them whenever they deigned him worthy, but because Ellen had missed out on Stuart's success.

In a sense, Hannah could see Ellen's point of view. Her own brother, Ben, had been divorced from his second wife, Heather, for a year when her mega-rich father died and left her ten million pounds. Ben had been inconsolable for months. The old man had been ill for many years, and all the talk at family gatherings was about how much each of them would receive when he finally passed away. In time, her brother had come to terms with his disappointment, found a new wife, and carried on with his life. He put all thoughts of the money behind him in a way that Ellen never could.

Ellen resented the success Stuart enjoyed with *Dark Night* and advised anyone who knew her, in person and in numerous social media posts, to avoid watching the programme when it was broadcast. This wasn't the action of someone who loved Stuart and wanted him back, it was the twisted logic of a woman who would do anything to get her hands on his bank account. Mercifully, her campaign of vitriol had petered out after a few months, but who knew what effect Stuart's death would have on her now?

Hannah put down her half-empty tea mug and walked over to the bookcase. She had tidied it after the police had left the scene and now, in its restored shape, looked more or less as it had done when Stuart was alive. Unlike DI Henderson, she didn't think anything had been removed. She believed it had been messed up by the killer to somehow frustrate and mislead the police. In this, she believed, the culprit had succeeded.

She was the one who had put back all the folders, papers, books, CDs, and DVDs in the bookcase, and so she knew the precise location of the item she wanted. She found it quickly, pulled it out, and walked back to her seat. She sat still for a second or two trying to compose herself, before reaching for the tea mug and taking a drink. She put the mug down and opened the folder.

At the back of a sheaf of legal papers, was Stuart's will. Stuart was a relatively young man to be concerned about what happened to his assets after his death. He had come from a middle-class family, but his father's gambling habits ensured they were frequently broke. The success of *Dark Night* earned Stuart more money than his father had made in a lifetime as a sixth-form college lecturer, and it weighed heavily. It made him feel better to know that members of his immediate family and friends would benefit if he did make an untimely exit.

Hannah had never seen his will before now, but believed that Ellen Jacobs would be cited as the main beneficiary. If so, Hannah would take this information to DI Henderson in the morning, no, tonight, and hand him the motive for Stuart's murder that he was so desperately seeking.

She stopped and cancelled that line of thought. The papers she was holding had previously been in the hands of the police. They would be aware of the terms of the will. Nevertheless, if Ellen was, as she expected, the main beneficiary, and Henderson had decided to do nothing about it, she would badger him until he did.

She speed-read the legalese at the beginning, before moving on to the meat of the document. She was shocked to find Stuart's ex-wife had been left only a small sum of money, and his daughter and son a sufficient amount to fund their university education should they decide to go. There was no mention of

Ellen receiving the house, a share of his burgeoning bank account or his portfolio of investments. His family, by way of contrast, had been left generous amounts. She hoped his father, when he recovered from his long stay in hospital, wouldn't spend the lot at the first bookmaker he came across.

She paused, picked up her cup, and steeled herself for a left-field delivery from Stuart. He was passionate about a lot of things: climate change, homelessness, medical research, and the poverty of families in the UK, living in deprived council estates with a dearth of decent, well-paid jobs close by. It wouldn't surprise her to find he'd donated the rest of his money to a homeless charity, the Wellcome Trust, or to Greta Thunberg.

Tears trickled down Hannah's face as she read yet another example of Stuart's unbridled generosity. He had left the house and a large part of his remaining estate to her.

THIRTY-TWO

Henderson didn't need to look at the clock in the car to confirm it was late afternoon; his rumbling stomach did the job instead. He was heading to the area where he used to live, Seven Dials. In fact, the address he was driving towards, Montpelier Crescent, was across the road from Vernon Terrace, where his old apartment was located.

Steve Mitchell's bail hearing had taken place the day before. Henderson was pleased when the magistrate remanded him in custody, denying him bail. It gave them a bit more time to find additional evidence against him. However, with the forensic examination of all the items bagged at Stuart Livermore's house now complete, and nothing to show for it, things were not looking good. He was now depending on the team who had carried out the search of Mitchell's house in Sheffield coming up with something he could use.

When he arrived in Seven Dials, he was surprised to find a vacant parking space. He realised he'd arrived in that little window between picking the kids up from school, and workers coming home after a long day at their place of employment. He got out of the car and walked towards the address he had written down on the piece of paper he was holding.

Montpelier Crescent might have only been a stone's throw from Vernon Terrace, but they were worlds apart in property terms. The buildings in Vernon Terrace had all been converted into multi-occupancy, in the main, one- and two-bedroom apartments. Montpelier Crescent on the other hand, still retained many of the original town houses. This was also reflected in prices: apartments in Vernon Terrace averaging around the £300k to £400k mark, while houses in Montpelier Crescent were selling from £1.5m to over £2m.

He found the house without too much difficulty. He walked up the path and then up a short flight of steps. Ringing the doorbell, he realised he'd never been inside one of these town houses, despite the time he had lived in the area. His curiosity was piqued.

The door opened to reveal a well-dressed woman, aged around mid-forties and wearing a green blouse and long skirt. Her short blond hair was cut so finely in a bob, he doubted the mild breeze outside could ruffle it.

'Good evening. I'm Detective Inspector Henderson. I'm here to see Ryan Allison.'

'Hello, I'm Stacy, his wife.'

She stuck out her hand and Henderson shook it, but he could have been holding a dead fish for all the life it displayed.

'Come in. Ryan's in the lounge.'

She closed the door, but Henderson still stood in the hall. There were a number of rooms leading off the hallway making him hesitate. He didn't want to make the mistake of blundering into a teenager's bedroom or that of an au pair, although he didn't know if the Allison's had either.

'This way,' she said, her voice sounding a touch irritable, as if he should have known which way to go.

She opened the second door to his left. He followed and entered a spacious, brightly-lit room. There was a large bay window at one end overlooking Montpelier Crescent, his old apartment in the distance. The coving was decorated with fancy cornices, while chintz and gold was much in evidence, an attempt, he suspected, to recreate the splendour of an Edwardian drawing room. It was perhaps an obvious thing to do in such a large and impressive house, but it felt much too cold and impersonal for his taste.

Stacy stood to one side while he walked over to see the patient. Ryan Allison was seated on a chair, his thin, narrow face and big glasses making him look like a middle-aged Harry Potter. The numerous bashes, cuts, and bruises on his face spoiled the illusion, although he would imagine Master Potter wouldn't look much different after a bruising encounter with his arch enemy, Voldemort.

'Hello Ryan, I'm Detective Inspector Henderson. We met briefly at Stuart's funeral but you might not remember. It was only an introduction, one of many on the day, I suspect. How are you?'

'Been better.' A hand crept out of the blanket that was covering him. Henderson shook it. It possessed a bit more life than Stacy's, but not much. More like a live fish than a dead one. It also wasn't bruised, suggesting he hadn't fought back, or he was left-handed. Henderson noticed a series of photographs on the mantlepiece behind the patient's head. This suggested Allison had two girls, aged about sixteen and twelve.

'Can I offer either of you tea or coffee?' Stacy asked.

'Coffee would be great,' Henderson said.

'Ryan?'

He shook his head.

'You have to eat and drink something, darling. You need to keep your strength up.'

'Don't fuss, woman,' he said in an irritable tone, and with a dismissive wave of his hand. 'I'll be fine.'

Stacy left the room in a huff at her husband's brusque manner. She then shut the door behind her with a force greater than was necessary. Henderson took a seat on the couch opposite Ryan. 'Can you tell me what happened?'

'I already told the Cheltenham police everything. Why do I have to repeat it?'

'They were dealing with an assault. I'm investigating a murder.'

'You think this is connected to Stuart's death?'

'You tell me.'

He sighed. 'I was sitting in a bar with a couple of authors after appearing at the book festival.'

'Which authors?'

'Bob Mathieson and Trevor Melrose.'

Henderson noted the names. 'They were also involved in the festival?'

'Yes. Trevor was on the same question and answer panel as me; Bob was on another.'

'Okay.'

'After the talk and a bout of book signing, we went to this pub, The Beaver Inn. Our intention was to have a few pints and an evening meal.'

'How much did you have to drink? Were you drunk?'

'No, I wasn't drunk,' he said, the annoyance at the suggestion, clear in his tone. 'Yes, I admit a lot of literary festivals can be boozy affairs. Sitting on an author panel or being interviewed by an academic or television personality can be stressful.'

'I'll have to take your word for it,' Henderson said.

'Suffice to say it's about as taxing as an author's life can be. So, in the evening, we often head down to a pub and have a few beers to unwind. I've been to enough festivals, and participated in a lot of heavy sessions, to believe I can hold my drink. The three pints I had on the night were only enough to get me tipsy.'

The door opened and the lady of the house entered carrying a tray. In common with the opulent surroundings, it was gold-embossed. Despite this, he was pleased to see his coffee was being served in a Costa-style mug and not in a small china cup with a handle too small to fit his finger through.

A fleeting thought went through his head: did Stacy hear his stomach rumbling when he first entered the house? It looked as though she had. There were sandwiches cut into triangles and a selection of small cakes on a plate. He decided, no matter what was inside the sandwiches, if it was something he didn't like, such as pork or prawns, he was hungry enough to eat it.

The conversation halted while Stacy was in the room. He suspected this wasn't because Stacy had heard all the details before, but because Ryan didn't want his wife hearing anything about his away-from-home drinking activities.

'As I was saying,' Ryan said when his wife had left the room. 'I think I can hold my drink. You can be assured I wasn't drunk.'

Henderson took a side plate and added a couple of sandwiches. He took a bite: egg mayonnaise. He'd have no problem eating this.

'Were you being, for example, loud and obnoxious? Could you have upset a few of the locals without meaning to?'

'No way. Bob Mathieson's a big man and talks in a loud voice, but he wouldn't offend anyone. To hear him speak, the locals would think he was one of them.'

'The next thing is you go to the toilet. Did you notice someone following you?'

'No, I didn't. I walked in, did my business, and on the point of zipping up my fly, I received a solid thump in the back. I thought at first a drunk had fallen into me, but when I turned to remonstrate, this guy punched me in the gut. He then pulled out a knife and stuck it into my face. He said I would get this if Steve Mitchell is convicted. He then did this,' he said pointing, 'to my nose.'

'Broken?'

'Yep, but I've got a good doctor. He says he can set it back the way it was.'

'That's good to hear. You're absolutely sure the attacker mentioned Steve Mitchell.'

'Without doubt. I didn't mishear or I'm mentioning it because I'm trying to frame Mitchell, or his name is at the top of my mind. The guy in the toilet definitely said the name of Steve Mitchell when he threatened me with the knife. He said, me and Stuart were rats.'

Henderson left the Allison household ten minutes later, feeling pleased with himself for not demolishing all the sandwiches and cakes. He didn't want to give Sussex Police a bad name.

The Cheltenham police report had mentioned the presence of the knife, but not the name of Steve Mitchell. This, he suspected, was Ryan Allison's attempt at keeping the assault report simple. The naming of Mitchell was a surprise to Henderson, making him wonder what the attacker's aim might be. Allison was not a key witness in Mitchell's prosecution, and threatening Allison, as far as he knew, would make no difference to the outcome.

This meant the attacker was either acting on false information, or he knew something Henderson didn't. For this reason, Henderson suspected the assault might be significant. He wasn't sure how.

THIRTY-THREE

Danny Carlyle was freezing his nuts off. He could understand it if he was back in Edinburgh. There, the wind would whip off the North Sea and rob you of your body heat in seconds. Sussex was supposed to be in the sunny south, for God's sake. It was the crappy car's doing. The heating was inadequate at the best of times, and now the fan sounded as though it was suffering from bronchitis.

It was his own fault. He had set out to do this job a few days back, a warm day for a change, but he'd got side-tracked. This time it wasn't the sight of a hot chick gasping for his attention, but a pub showing football. Not an ordinary match by any stretch: the boys from Tynecastle versus the other lot from the green part of Edinburgh. He didn't regret going in. It had been a pulsating game which in the end, Hearts won 2-0 to put them top of the league. He couldn't help it, but he'd got pissed that night.

He was sitting outside a building in his dilapidated Ford Focus, on the equally crappy Victoria Industrial Park in tedious Burgess Hill. The building he was watching was the home of Zama Video Productions. This was a company involved in making corporate videos, public service adverts, and programmes for television, according to their website. Most of it made jack-shit sense to him, but they had something which, by rights, belonged to him.

His plan was a good one. He would wait to see who locked up when they closed the premises for the night. He would then sneak up behind them before shoving his trusty blade in their face and forcing them back inside. Once there, he would recover his property. How this person behaved would determine if he used the knife only to threaten, or if he would give them something more. If instead, the person locking up was an attractive woman, he thought, a smile playing on his lips, a whole new set of scenarios would present themselves.

He fiddled with the radio, but most stations played crap after six-thirty on a Tuesday night: heavy metal, country, and wall-to-wall adverts. There was none of the good stuff he liked to listen to on a Friday evening, designed to get everybody up and ready before they went out on the town and hit the clubs. Multiple shots of Vladivar and some loud dance music; nothing could touch it.

He was so full of such good thoughts, he nearly didn't notice the door of Zama Productions opening. Shit. He scrambled around to find a safe place to put down his messy meat pie and can of Tango. No way did he want to have his trousers covered in greasy finger marks, or soaked in sugar-infused orange juice.

Two people emerged from the building, a man and a woman. This wasn't part of his well-thought-out plan, and for a moment, he felt flummoxed. The man produced a set of keys and, while talking to the woman, began to lock the door. Carlyle sighed and started the engine of the Focus, resigned to returning the following day, hoping for some better luck.

The woman turned. He clocked her to see if she was good-looking, a wee bonus on a wasted day. Instead, he recognised her from weeks spent casing the house in Queens Park. It was Stuart Livermore's girlfriend. Holy Shit! The bitch was on to him!

His first reaction was to flee. To turn the car around and head for the motorway. There, he would drive to London, Birmingham, or Glasgow. Get as far away from her as possible. He needed to do something, he couldn't just wait around for the cops to come and arrest him.

Calm yourself Danny, he heard a voice in his head say; you know how to do this. Inside the nick, he had been taught relaxation and yoga techniques by a prison visitor. He'd only gone along to the sessions to take a peek at a woman. Anything to make a change from the pasty-faced old lags who inhabited his wing, all fat guts and haggard expressions, most of whom would have done well to attract the attentions of a dog. Despite the woman's wholesome appearance, and having a body which she could twist in ways he wouldn't have believed possible, she didn't arouse as much as a hair on his arm. She did, however, get him hooked on yoga. Here was something useful he could do in the long periods spent alone in a cell.

He placed his hands over his stomach and started taking deep breaths, reaching down into the depths of his chest and expelling the air in a slow, controlled exhale through his nose. He repeated this several times until the anxiety vanished and his normal disposition returned. No, he wouldn't flee. He would follow this woman, search her bag and, if that didn't reveal anything, force her to tell him what she had been discussing with the people at Zama.

She got into the man's car. He was an employee of Zama, Carlyle reckoned, and more than likely the big boss. His car was a flashy BMW 5-Series and, providing he didn't decide to show off the Beemer's big engine to the lady, the bright red colour would make it an easy car for him to follow.

He hoped the driver was simply dropping the woman off somewhere, and they weren't heading out to a pub or restaurant. He had no intention of spending any more time in Burgess Hill than he needed; the place depressed him.

At the end of Victoria Way, the BMW turned right. Carlyle settled down for the long haul, picked up the remains of the pie, and started munching. When they took a left, and he realised they were on Station Road, the pie was soon forgotten. He didn't know Burgess Hill well, but Station Road in any town meant there had to be a railway station nearby. Why would the BMW driver take Livermore's girlfriend all the way to Brighton, where Carlyle knew she lived, when he could stop at the railway station and let the train do the work for him?

A few minutes later, his assumption proved accurate. They drove up a hill, and at the top he could see Burgess Hill railway station. Carlyle drove past what looked like a car park off to the right, but he didn't dare turn off until he could be sure what the folks in the BMW were intending to do.

The indicator on the BMW flashed right, before the car swung across the road and came to a halt in the small lay-by outside the station entrance. Carlyle brought the Focus to a halt and bumped up on the pavement opposite, allowing the car behind to drive past. He watched as the woman got out of the BMW. She gave the driver what he regarded as a business-style wave, with no hint of affection, and headed into the station. The BMW sped off.

When the road looked clear, Carlyle put the car into reverse. If this wasn't an attempt to draw attention to himself, he didn't know what was. Just as well none of the people he was following were in sight. He braked, veered the car across the carriageway and roared into the car park he'd noticed earlier.

He got out of the car, ran to the ticket machine and fed it five, one-pound coins. It seemed to cover the charge because the machine started to spit out a ticket. He ran back to the car, threw the ticket where an inspector would see it, and then belted towards the station.

Puffing like a twenty-a-day man, which he was, he bought a single ticket to Brighton. He knew he needed to come back for the car, but that was a problem for another day.

'When's the next train to Brighton?' he asked the ticket clerk.

The guy turned and looked at the wall clock. 'Ten minutes.'

Panic over, he let his heavy breathing subside before walking over to a newsagent. He bought a newspaper and something to eat. He wasn't a regular buyer of newspapers, but it would be useful for hiding his face. Who could recall the features of a guy on a train with his face buried in the sports pages?

From his seat on the train, he had a good view of the target, but in other respects, the journey was uneventful. He felt sorry for many of his fellow travellers. Some looked like young dads who would be arriving home after their small children had dropped off to sleep. Other older travellers looked weary and jaded, as if travelling on a later train was a deliberate act. This designed to spend less time arguing over the kitchen table, or looking blankly at the old boot who'd done nothing of note with her day.

He knew Livermore's girlfriend lived in the Brighton area, but he didn't know where. He also knew she didn't own a car. If she headed for a bus or taxi when they reached their journey's end, he would play it by ear. If she walked, it was game on.

His mind wandered with the repetitive clickety-clack noise of the train. A week back, he'd been picked up by a couple of goons working for a local hoodlum called Dominic Green. He was a crap interrogator, despite his beefy sidekick punching Carlyle several times for his impertinence, and no better than DI Hegarty, the copper he'd seen earlier the same day. It had to be down to Carlyle's great acting. Yet again, he walked out of there with barely a scratch, his reputation intact.

The train pulled into Brighton station. He took his time folding the newspaper, all the time keeping his eye on the target. When she rose from her seat and headed for the exit, he did the same, walking a few metres behind.

Hallelujah! His first big break. She ignored the buses parked in the road at the side of the station, and the taxi stand out front. Instead, she began walking down Queen's Road in the direction of Brighton town centre. Despite not having been born there, he tended to walk a lot, and knew most of the streets around the town off by heart.

She veered right and headed along Western Road. She continued walking straight for the next fifteen minutes or so, not turning into a side street and taking no interest in the numerous restaurants, shops and small supermarkets she passed. When they reached Palmeira Square, she turned left into St John's Road, heading down the slope towards the seafront.

Along Western Road, he'd been walking close, about two metres behind. There were so many shops and side streets in the area, he needed some notice if she suddenly changed direction. Now, he sought to increase the gap. They were away from the main drag, and many streets in this part of town could be quiet at this time of the evening.

St John's Road was replete with numerous car repair businesses, a hive of activity and vehicle movements during the day, but dead as an old car battery at night. The pavements on either side of the road were cobbled, not usually a problem, but there had been some rain the night before, and they could be slippery.

He closed the gap and sneaked up behind her. He wrapped an arm around her neck, and hauled her into the doorway of a closed garage. He turned her round to face him, pulled out his knife, and stuck it into her face.

'Gimme the fucking bag!' he snarled.

Her head bent back, leaning away from the knife.

'Here, take it,' she said. She lifted it towards him, before shoving it hard into his face. It was a big thing, full of heavy stuff, and the smack it gave him on the head forced him to lose his grip of the knife. She untangled herself from the bag's shoulder strap and sped off.

Dazed for a moment, he recovered quickly and set off after her. In a few seconds he was behind her, close enough for him to clip the back of her heels, the way he used to do to boys at school that he didn't like.

Perhaps due to her speed, or because they were heading down a slope, she did more than trip, she sailed through the air. There was a dull thump as her head made contact with the back edge of a parked car. He stood, stunned, as she slumped to the ground, a growing puddle of blood oozing around her head.

THIRTY-FOUR

Henderson's apartment in Burlington Street was close to the seafront. This meant whenever he went out for a run, he didn't have to go far before he was away from cars and heading east or west on a straight, level surface. He went running two or three times a week. It could be morning or evening depending on work commitments, and despite his preference for morning runs when he felt fresh and rested, evenings were a good chance to mull over the day's events.

The sun was dipping towards the horizon, leaving about a half an hour before it would be dark. A steady breeze blew off the sea as he headed west towards Shoreham. With the temperature hovering around ten degrees, it made good conditions for running, a bonus for early October. The breeze brought with it a chill, and so he was wearing several layers, any of which could be removed if the going proved too warm.

If not working on a big case, he would be wearing earphones and either listening to music or a podcast. He was a fan of rock music, had been ever since his teenage years, and he liked the various playlists in the rock genre which Spotify curated. He'd also been listening to several football-related podcasts for a number of years, almost to the point of regarding the Guardian's football correspondents as old friends. The explosion in the popularity of podcasts of late had also turned him on to others involving history, philosophy, and inevitably, running.

The fish and chip shops, burger bars, and trinket sellers lining the lower echelons of the esplanade were closed for the night. The only activity he could see when he glanced over the railing, was a couple of dog walkers, and a few patrons heading towards the clubs and bars that somehow survived on word-of-mouth recommendations. There was little passing pedestrian traffic after about six in the evening to even notice the businesses existed.

He passed a long row of brightly-coloured beach huts. Some were boarded up for the season, their interiors not seeing daylight until April or May the following year. Others, were used every weekend throughout the year. In the middle of winter, those hardy types could be seen sitting outside, wrapped in blankets, their hands gripping a hot brew, and their eyes fixed on the grey sea where only commercial ships dared to sail.

Tonight, out at sea, boats were still visible in the fading light. They looked from a distance to be dodging between the giant windmills of the Rampion Offshore Wind Farm. A flurry of sails as several yachts headed in the direction of Brighton Marina, and a grain ship looked as though it had just sailed out of Shoreham Harbour. Further out, a slow-moving oil tanker was bearing east, probably heading towards one of the big oil terminals on the European mainland, perhaps Antwerp or Rotterdam.

Henderson had been a detective long enough to know that in any murder investigation, a point would come when everyone involved would think that all their effort had been wasted. They seemed to be no closer to finding the culprit than when they started. With Mitchell in custody and no additional evidence having been uncovered, it felt as though they were in this position now. His job was to make sure no one in the team lost faith.

In fact, several of the sporting podcasts he listened to were helpful in this regard. Part way through a tough football, rugby, or hockey season, coaches were often faced with a similar situation. How to convince players who were tired and jaded, to get out on the pitch on another cold and windy morning to do the same thing over again.

Coaches had the added advantage of being able to take their squads to Spain, or Dubai, for some morale-boosting warm weather training, something Henderson couldn't do. However, this would only work if the coach had instilled into their players' heads, lessons which would serve them well until the end of the season. This was the bit where he needed to do better.

He was so wrapped up in his thoughts he didn't register he'd passed the King Alfred Sports Centre a few minutes before. He was now at Shoreham Harbour, the end of the first half of his run. He stopped for a breather, leaning against a wall while undertaking some stretching exercises. He heard movement behind him.

'Well, if it isn't Detective Inspector Henderson, or should I be calling you, Chief Constable Henderson now, after all the acclaim you received for putting me away?'

Henderson turned.

'Good grief, Dominic Green. I never thought I'd see your face around here again.'

'Why? Did you think I'd be lying dead in a toilet in pokey, with the end of some scroat's sharpened comb sticking out of my gut?'

Henderson smiled. 'No, nothing quite so dramatic. I thought you might have moved away from the area. Too many bad memories in Sussex.'

'I've lived here most of my life, I'm not sure I want to live anywhere else.'

Dominic Green was instantly recognisable, even in the dull light of a sodium lamp. He was a tall man with a bald head, intense hawk-like eyes, and a natty dress sense. In the past, he would also have added an all-year suntan from trips to his villa in Barbados, but this had disappeared under the auspices of the Proceeds of Crime Act. It was hard for ex-cons, even those who once had access to a Caribbean villa, to lose the grey pallor, a result of spending too much time indoors.

He looked thinner too, an improvement for a man of his age, when too much fine wine and good food had been edging him towards a brush with Type 2 diabetes. Henderson wouldn't go as far as to wish a criminal like Green better health. Green didn't give a damn about the misery and deprivation the consumption of the drugs he distributed had caused, often into the hands of the most vulnerable in society.

'Well, it was interesting seeing you again, but I must be heading back, my muscles are getting cold.' Henderson made to move, but knew Dominic Green wouldn't have bumped into him by accident. When a voice said, 'Hang on a tick there, Henderson,' he was expecting it.

The DI stopped and turned to face him, Green's sharp features looking menacing in the shadow of the artificial light.

'Know anything about the guy the papers are calling the South Coast Rapist?'

'Only what I see on our system and read in *The Argus*.'

'Not one of your cases?'

He shook his head. 'No, it's being investigated by a DI in John Street.'

'Jim Hegarty?'

'Despite a long spell out of circulation, your information sources seem to be in good working order.'

'Hegarty's a first-class prick. He couldn't solve the *Daily Mail* quick crossword any faster than my wife, and she takes most of the afternoon.'

'You know as well as I do, even if he isn't the sharpest knife in the box, there are good people around him.'

'There's been six fucking rapes, and what have they got? A big fat nothing. Are you telling me this bastard didn't leave them a single clue?'

'What's your interest? Not the welfare of the good women of Brighton, I imagine.'

'A friend of my daughter was his third victim. It's hit the kid hard, and it's upset my daughter.'

'I'm sorry to hear it, but in case you've forgotten, meddling in police affairs was the reason you got sent down in the first place.'

'Of course, I fucking remember,' he said, his voice rising in pitch and harshness. 'I don't want to be involved in this any longer than I need to. Can I ask you to tell Hegarty to get his finger out? Better still, why don't you take on the case? You're smarter than him by a long chalk.'

'It doesn't work like that, and you know it. He's got his job to do, I've got mine.'

'I'll make it worth your while, a donation to the police Orphans and Widows Fund perhaps?'

'This is where this conversation ends. I'll be seeing you.' Henderson turned and started running. He called over his shoulder, 'Have a good evening, what's left of it.'

THIRTY-FIVE

Henderson walked into the Royal Sussex County Hospital in Brighton. He hoped he didn't look as if he had dressed in the dark. It had been a bit of a rush to get there. He had just come out of the shower when he received the call from DS Walters about Hannah Robbins. He still had wet hair, and wouldn't be surprised to find his jumper had been put on back to front, or his shirt unevenly buttoned.

He found the Neurological Unit on the board near the door and headed that way. It was Wednesday evening, and not strictly a traditional celebration night. However, if universities and colleges were in-term, as they were now, it was their night for going out. In response, many hostelries in the town offered discounts on production of a Student Card. They did this in the main, to avoid any hostility between locals and students, the traditional clash between 'town and gown', and to stop their bars and clubs becoming overcrowded at weekends.

It was early evening but already, on just walking through reception, he could see several young people in need of attention. He spotted a couple of lads helping their semi-conscious friend, a few individuals with head gashes, and one poor bloke with multiple scratches and, what looked at first glance like a broken arm, as if he had fallen out of a tree or window.

By way of contrast, the Neurological Unit was serenely quiet. It resembled the atmosphere of a college library at exam time: not a sound while everyone beavered away in the background. Instead of rows and rows of inert books, in their place were lines of beds, filled with inactive bodies.

He approached DS Walters, sitting on a chair reading a novel. One of Stuart Livermore's, he was interested to note.

'Evening, Carol.'

'Evening, gov. Have you been to the pool for a dip?'

'You caught me just as I was coming out of a therapeutic shower.'

She closed the book with a snap, the loudest sound that could be heard in this place.

'I've heard of power showers, even thermostatic showers, but never a therapeutic one.'

'It just means after a run, I spend longer in there than usual trying to wash away the pain and massage my tired muscles.'

'I thought running was supposed to be good for you?'

'It is, but that's not often how it feels afterwards.'

'I'll remember that the next time someone invites me out for a run.'

'While I was out, I met someone we used to know.'

'Who?'

'Dominic Green.'

'My, my. I thought he would be long gone from Sussex.'

'Me too, but more about him later. Tell me about Hannah.'

'She was found unconscious beside a car in St John's Road at around eight-thirty yesterday evening, funnily enough by a runner.'

'Twenty-four hours ago?'

'Yep.'

'Why has it taken so long for us to find out?'

'I'm coming to that. She has a blunt trauma injury to the left side of her head consistent with being hit by something solid, like a bottle or baseball bat. However, the eagle-eyed copper who attended the scene suggested she may have collided with the side of a car.'

'She was knocked down by a car?'

'No, the officer thinks *she* collided with a parked car.'

'Collided with a car? How did she do that, did she slip? I didn't notice it was wet when I was out earlier. It certainly wasn't icy.'

'She might have simply missed her footing. The pavements around there in St John's Road–'

'That's the street with all the garages and lock-ups near Palmeira Square?'

'Right. The pavements around there are a bit uneven and covered in cobblestones.'

'With so many garages and lock-ups in the vicinity, is it possible there might have been a spillage of engine oil or hydraulic fluid?'

'It's possible, but something else makes me think she didn't slip.'

'What?'

'The officers at the scene haven't recovered her handbag. If she was on her way back from work in London, as we suspect, no way would she have gone there without a handbag. This is the reason why it took so long to identify her. The connection was made by one of her colleagues who called the hospital looking for her when she failed to turn up for work today.'

'Good job they did. Let me think about this for a moment.'

'You'll have to do it later, gov. Here comes a doctor.'

'Good evening to you both. My name is Graham Howlett. I'm the surgeon who operated on Ms Robbins last night.'

Henderson stood. 'Good evening, Mr Howlett. I'm Detective Inspector Angus Henderson and this is Detective Sergeant Carol Walters, Sussex Police.' Henderson shook his hand, and in his other, held out his warrant card. Henderson was always surprised to find a surgeon's hands, no matter if they were six-two and built like a boxer, to be as delicate as a woman, and a regular user of hand moisturiser.

Graham Howlett was in his fifties with a good head of hair, but a heavily lined face. He wore gold-rimmed spectacles which complimented the other gold items on his person: watch strap, pen in his top pocket, and the thick wedding band on his finger.

'You're both police officers?'

'Yes.'

'I take it you are not relatives of Ms Robbins?'

'No, we're not,' Henderson said.

'I wasn't aware her injuries were of interest to the police.'

'They may or may not be,' Henderson said. 'Hannah Robbins is the girlfriend of a murder victim, a case we are in the process of investigating. Her welfare is of some concern to us, and the reason for her being in here, may have some bearing on the case.'

'I'm not sure I should be talking to you prior to meeting her next of kin.'

'Let me make a suggestion,' Henderson said. 'If you can update me on Hannah's condition, I'll make contact with her relatives and inform them of her situation directly.'

Howlett paused for a moment. 'This sounds like a satisfactory compromise. It's not as if you're both journalists.' He pulled a seat away from the wall and sat facing them.

'The severe impact she suffered on her head caused hydrocephalus, a build-up of cerebrospinal fluid in the brain. We have stabilised the cerebrospinal fluid and replaced the blood loss, about two pints. In time, the swelling in the frontal lobe of her brain will reduce. I'm referring to this area here,' he said pointing to the left side of his head and wiggling his finger slightly. This reminded Henderson of a schoolboy gesture to indicate if someone was 'screwy', or a bit weird. 'In surgical terms, my work is done. That is, unless the patient subsequently suffers a relapse.'

'When can we talk to her?'

'There lies a question I cannot readily answer. She is, at the moment, on a ventilator in a drug-induced coma. Over the next forty-eight hours, we will gradually reduce the medication and remove the ventilator, allowing her to breath using her own lungs. In medical terms, this procedure may go without a hitch, but you have to be aware that, following such a severe trauma, there is a chance she will remain in a coma.'

'Oh, I didn't realise,' Henderson said, as the implications began to dawn. He knew of several people who had been in comas for years, two criminals and a former police officer. At least one was expected to continue this way for the rest of his life. If this was the case here, they might never find out what had happened to Hannah Robbins.

'What are the chances of her coming out of the coma when she recovers from the surgery and you withdraw the medication?' Walters asked.

'Reasonably high, I would say. I would, given the nature of her injuries and how well she responded to surgery, expect her to return to normal in time. I cannot, however say if this means in a day or two, or in a week, or a months' time. There is no way of knowing how long it takes for those deep comas to resolve themselves. I'm sorry to be the bearer of such uncertain news. Looking more short-term, the next two days will be crucial in terms of her overall recovery.'

The surgeon shook their hands once more and walked off, leaving the two detectives feeling stunned.

'We have no way of telling,' Henderson said at last, 'if Hannah's injuries are in any way connected to Stuart Livermore's murder, or it's a bag snatch gone wrong.'

'Nor indeed if it was simply a freak accident. Perhaps, a bit of both. Could be she was rushing home and slipped. Later, a scumbag comes along and makes off with her bag.'

'Let's see if we can narrow the odds a little in our favour. I'll send a forensics team down to St John's Road to search the scene. If her head did make contact with the car, and knowing how light car body panels are nowadays, such an impact is bound to have left a dent or a mark. If the paintwork was also damaged, we can check with the surgeon and see if he found the same particles in her injury.'

'Right.'

'See if you can pull whatever CCTV you can from the businesses around there. You would think with cars, spare parts, and expensive tools lying around, at least a few of them would have decent security. Between the two, forensics and CCTV, we should be able to confirm which theory is the one we need to be looking at.'

'Will do.'

'Now, in addition to the CCTV check, organise a team to conduct a bin and waste ground search around St John's Street and up towards Palmeira Square. If someone did snatch her bag, once they'd extracted what they wanted, they might have ditched it. Call her office and see if anyone can give us a description of the bag to help in the search.'

'No problem.'

'If this is connected to Stuart Livermore's death, does it also tie-up with the assault on Ryan Allison in Cheltenham? If so, this could be another attempt to intimidate witnesses in the future trial of Steve Mitchell.'

'It's tenuous at best, gov. The most we could hope from Ryan and Hannah, is for them to appear as character witnesses in support of Stuart Livermore. Nothing they've said so far would make a material difference to the case against Steve Mitchell.'

'I agree, and the reason why both of those incidents trouble me.'

THIRTY-SIX

His publishers were heartless bastards. Ryan Allison had written two series of books: one crime, and the other thriller. The crime series, featuring Detective Inspector Terrance Broughton was based in Eastbourne where Allison grew up. The eighth book in the series, *Don't Look Back*, was published three months ago, and the book Allison had been signing when he was in Cheltenham.

The other was a series of spy novels featuring rogue MI5 agent Brett Townes. Allison had sent the manuscript for the third novel in the series, *Dead Water*, to his publishers, over eight months ago. This wasn't unusual. Now and again, he would phone and they would tell him it was at the copy-editing stage, or out with advance readers. Sometimes they would say, while we've got you on the phone, would you like to come in and take a look at some covers? So far, so normal.

The publication date of any new novel would normally be agreed in consultation with him, but for months he'd heard nothing. He had assumed this was because they were waiting for the dust to settle on the latest Terrance Broughton publication. The logic being that when sales of *Don't Look Back* took their inevitable downward slump after the initial marketing and publicity buzz, along would come Brett Townes to pep up sales of all his books once again.

What the bastards had done was to pull out all the stops in order to release *Dead Water* only a few days ago. To anyone with a half a brain, even they could see this was a ploy to capitalise on the blaze of publicity surrounding Stuart Livermore's murder.

'Look on the bright side,' Stacy, ever the pragmatist, said. 'They did it for sound commercial reasons. If it's good for them, it's good for you.'

Yes, it was true, if they were talking about the death of a cabinet minister, a key element of the story in *Dead Water*, but not of his closest friend. Their actions were cold and heartless, more suited to the plot of a Halloween play than the actions of a supposedly reputable company.

He stared out of the car window as he trundled towards the centre of Brighton. Trundled being the operative word. It was six-thirty in the evening and no sooner had he left the house than he'd been caught in one traffic jam after another. No matter; he was a stickler for timekeeping and always made strenuous efforts to arrive early for any appointment. It just meant he would have to forego his planned calm-before-the-storm coffee in a quiet coffee shop of his choice. Instead, he would have to make do with a takeaway from the café in Waterstones, the place where he was scheduled to appear tonight.

At least he wouldn't be appearing alone. If so, some sections of the audience might be tempted to have a pop about the book's insensitive publication date. If he prevaricated and tried to blame his publisher, he would look like a frightened rabbit in the headlights, only encouraging them more. 'We're in this together,' Katy, his marketing associate never failed to remind him when his spirits started to flag. At least he wouldn't have to suffer her homilies gleaned from a marketing manual, as in this respect, tonight he was flying solo.

At last, he turned away from the seafront and onto West Street. Up ahead, he could see the welcome sight of the Churchill Square car park. This being Brighton, the vision of a dark, deserted car park where any number of abductions and murders took place, scenes so beloved of television thriller writers, didn't exist. This place was always busy no matter what time of day or night he entered.

Tonight, the place was packed, perhaps due to a concert taking place at the Brighton Centre. He drove around for a few minutes before finding one of the last spaces on the ground floor. This got his back up. For the prices they were charging, comparable to car parks in Central London, not only should he be allocated his own space, staff should be on duty to point out its location to save him driving around.

The distance from the car park entrance to his destination was no more than one hundred metres. This gave him no time to see something of interest in a shop, or to watch the activities of a street performer. Despite suffering a traffic-induced delay, he wanted something, anything to take his mind off his situation and blow away the black cloud hovering close to his head. He had to hope the reviving effects of a cup of coffee, or a bit of jovial banter with some of his fellow authors, would do the trick instead.

He walked through the door of Waterstones and was not as thrilled as he should have been to see a display of *Dead Water* in one of the bookshop's windows. It consisted of a large poster with prop knives, a piece of rope, and several copies of the book lying in front. He didn't stop to take a picture, as he would normally do before posting it on Twitter and Instagram. Instead, he walked straight up the stairs to the third floor. It would piss him off no end if the café was closed, but no, it was open. This forestalled the humiliating sight of a seemingly lauded author having a hissy fit in a public place.

He took the steaming cup and sat down on one of the seats. He would go downstairs to the place where the event was being held in a few minutes. For now, he needed a few moments by himself to compose himself, to calm ragged nerves and turn the control dial in his brain from thinking about his crappy publisher to start considering what he might say to his readers.

He was so deep in thought, he didn't notice someone approach, until he heard the scrape of a chair. He looked up to see David Cairns, an author and fellow member of tonight's panel, but someone he didn't know well. Cairns sat down at the opposite side of the table, positioning his latte in front of him.

Cairns too was a crime author, but while Allison's books were infused with humour and light moments, Cairn's plots were dark and menacing. Characters had no empathy with one another, and Allison often lost count of the number of mutilated bodies.

'Evening Ryan, looking forward to tonight?'

'I guess so.'

'I'm not sure I would, if I was in your shoes.'

'What makes you say that?'

'Haven't you seen the West Street window downstairs?'

'How could I miss it?'

'Bad taste, I call it.'

'Yes, but at least it's only here in Brighton. I can be thick-skinned for one night.'

'Uh-uh,' Cairns said, shaking his head. He reached into a jacket pocket and retrieved his phone. He tapped the screen a couple of times before turning it around for Allison to see.

He was horrified to see a list of Tweets condemning his callous action. Some were calling him a gold-digger, an insensitive bastard, a poor excuse for a friend. Others were demanding his books should be boycotted.

'Bloody hell!'

'That's only Twitter,' Cairns said, seemingly enjoying this a bit more than he should. 'It's the same on Facebook and Instagram.'

'This is crazy. It's only a book.'

'It might only be a book to you, Ryan, but it's my livelihood. I'd hate for some mindless action like this to jeopardise my ability to pay the mortgage. C'mon, we'd better go downstairs.'

At the start, many audience members stuck to the agenda, which was about the usual stuff: where do you find your ideas, is the plot more important than characters, and so on. Later, a few moved off-piste, and when one said, 'Call yourself a friend of Stuart Livermore? I hope none of my friends behave as badly as you do,' it was the green light for the rest of them to wade in.

He didn't believe there were so many ways to say it, or to criticise him, but questioner after questioner managed to make their attack sound fresh and barbed, sharp enough to stick another dart into his self-esteem. In some respects, using Stacy's logic, he could count the evening a success. He had commandeered the majority of the airtime, and this was with four other authors in attendance. In exasperation, at about the halfway stage, the moderator intervened and banned further questions about the publication of *Dead Water* unless they related directly to the plot of the book.

When the session finally drew to a close, he let out a long blast of air. He realised he had been holding his breath, like a football fan watching his team in the dying seconds of a tense match while defending a 1-0 lead. He was last to leave the table, positioned at the front of the room with a backdrop decorated with long posters highlighting each author's books. To skate out of the door without a word would only make him look guilty.

Waterstones had set out tables at the side of the room with small stacks of books of all the appearing authors. The panellists drifted towards their respective piles, and began shaking hands with smiling readers, posing for selfies, and signing their purchases. Ryan stood beside his life's work for several minutes, but he needn't have bothered. Not one reader approached.

'It was a tough gig for you tonight, Ryan.'

He turned to see Haden Couch, a successful author himself, and moderator of the five-person panel this evening.

'They say there's no such thing as bad publicity. We shall see.'

'I remember a similar thing happened about three years back to another author, Lee Mann. It didn't seem to do him any harm. Did you hear about it?'

'I don't think so.'

'Lee released a book based on a real criminal case. It concerned the disappearance and murder of a four-year-old. It hit the shelves the same week the police, after years of searching and several false starts, arrested the actual culprit. Lee was accused of cashing in, much as you are now. There was a furore for a bit, but a week or two later, it all blew over. Lee's doing fine, by all accounts.'

'Cheers, Haden. I'm glad somebody understands.'

'Yeah, but it's not me you need to convince, is it?' he said, clapping Allison on the shoulder. 'I'd better go, there's some people poking around my table, I smell a sale. Take care Ryan, and thanks for coming this evening. I know it couldn't have been easy.'

'Thanks, Haden.'

In common with similar literary events, the number of people milling around the book tables didn't take long to thin out. Unlike movie or pop stars, whose auras were based, to a large extent, on their personality, an author's was a feature of the words on a page. For some, meeting and talking to the author could often destroy the picture they had constructed in their mind. For this reason, despite enjoying the talk, many attendees didn't hang around at the end.

A few minutes later, Ryan decided he'd done enough; it was time to make his escape. There was an open invitation for the appearing authors to make their way to The Cricketers, a pub in the Lanes, for a few pints. Ryan was pleased to hear the offer had been extended to him. Feeling such a pariah, he imagined his fellow authors would also decide to shun him.

However, as much as he would have liked to join them, his black mood suggested otherwise. Instead, he headed back to the Churchill Square car park. He wasn't sure what booze they still had left in the house, but whatever he could find, he would drink most of it.

Ryan Allison was so mired in misery, so deep in self-loathing, he failed to notice the guy walking five metres behind him. The guy had attended the talk, but didn't ask a question.

When Allison left the car park, the man followed in his car. If Allison went straight home, he would call it a night; if not, it would be his turn to take centre stage.

THIRTY-SEVEN

'We need more on him, Angus. What we have at the moment isn't enough.'

'I know gov. I just need a bit more time.'

'You've had plenty of time. I'm under pressure from the press, the folks upstairs, and now the bloody Police and Crime Commissioner has stuck her oar in. They're all baying for a conviction. They keep telling me Livermore's a high-profile person, a credit to Brighton, so I should be pulling out all the stops. I appreciate what you and your team have done, Angus, but most of what they've come up with is so bloody circumstantial.'

'I know, but we've been working hard to put meat on the bones.'

Sean Houghton got up from behind his desk and started to pace up and down beside the window, the chief inspector's way of trying to calm down. He was a keen runner, way more dedicated than Henderson, taking part in half-marathons and 10k races every couple of weeks. Henderson supposed being on the move, albeit in the narrow confines of an office at Malling House, was his preferred state.

It was Lisa Edwards' old office, but gone were the pictures of family, and seascapes, and the occasional vase of fresh flowers. He couldn't put a finger on exactly how, but it looked more masculine; a no-nonsense room where fripperies and irrelevancies weren't tolerated.

'You've got him in Brighton, driving past Livermore's house–'

'Yes, and don't forget, Mitchell lives in Yorkshire.'

'I know, but he says he came down south every couple of months to see a mate.'

'A mate in Clapham and who's conveniently disappeared. He doesn't answer the door, or his phone. A neighbour the officer spoke to believes he has been backpacking in the US for the last five months. Putting this to one side, he can't give us a valid reason for driving around Queen's Park on the same day as Livermore's murder. The only logical conclusion is he was casing Livermore's house.'

'I see where you're coming from, but it's still circumstantial.'

'I don't like it any more than you do. I would love to have something else, a hair or a fingerprint, anything to put him inside Livermore's house. What other reason is there for him being there?'

'Forensics didn't come up with anything else?'

'Not a sausage, but when the high-tech unit analysed his laptop, they discovered a whole list of barbed phrases in a file which he was drip-feeding into social media. Many of them were derogatory towards Stuart Livermore.'

'Livermore had moved on, according to his editor, but Mitchell hadn't.'

'It seems that way.'

'You said before, the History file on Mitchell's laptop contained a lot of research about weapons and the effects of being shot and stabbed on the human body.'

'They found loads about guns, knives, and explosives. Plus, he'd downloaded a TOR browser for searching the dark web. I'm told some authors do a lot of background research. I imagine a good lawyer and with a lot of research, could probably connect his searches to specific passages in his books. However, I think a jury would find it hard to believe it was all innocent. People have been convicted for less.'

'Let me tell you something, Angus,' Houghton said, as he sat down behind his desk. Henderson wondered what was coming next.

'When I started out as a newly-minted DC, I was called to a house in Balham, the scene of a domestic murder. A husband and wife had been drinking and smoking weed, according to witnesses who'd overheard them. He was known by neighbours to go on about her flirting whenever they went out. She, in turn, told her friends about his poor performance in the sack and how he reacted badly when she goaded him about it. This was in the days before Viagra became freely available. It turned out, he suffered from erectile dysfunction.'

Henderson nodded.

'She was found battered to death with a poker. When we arrived, the husband was sitting in the lounge next to her dead body, the murder weapon on the floor. It was a slam-dunk conviction, another sorry tale to add to the ninety-odd percent of murders classified as domestic.'

'His prints were on the poker?'

'Yep, all over it, and her blood was on his shirt. My boss, DI Gary O'Donnell, now dead, was old school. Once he got a theory into his head, it was impossible to dislodge. Weeks later, when the husband finally came to terms with his violent actions, and the shock of his wife's death, he denied killing her, saying he wasn't in the flat at the time. He'd gone out with the dog for a walk, came back in and found her.'

'Was he convicted?'

'Yep. The judge handed out a meaty twenty-two years for what he called a brutal, cold, premeditated murder. You see, during the barney, according to the next-door neighbour who had turned off her telly to listen, his wife had gone to the toilet for about five minutes, presumably to wash her face and try to calm down. When she returned to the lounge, this is when the neighbour heard screams and blows being struck.'

'I can see where the judge gets the premeditated. What happened in the end? I feel this isn't the conclusion to the story?'

'If DI O'Donnell had been doing his job properly, he would have made a better fist of checking with neighbours to find out if they'd seen our suspect out walking his dog. A local man came forward about six months after the husband was sentenced. On the night of the murder, he had been walking in Balham, the place where he and his brother used to live, photographing landmarks. He flew out to Australia the next day to see his brother and start a new job. It was only when he returned to the UK for a visit that he realised the husband was in the background of one of his pictures, walking the dog.'

'Hence the long delay in him coming forward?'

'Correct.'

'So, who killed her?'

'The male voice the neighbours had heard shouting, wasn't her husband, but her lover, a highly-strung character who lived across the road. He nipped into the house whenever the husband was out walking the dog. He filled in all the gaps in the story when we finally arrested him, but the point I want to make is this. The case ruined the lives of three people, not counting the killer. The dead wife, obviously. Her husband, who'd spent time inside for a murder he didn't commit, and a few years later committed suicide. Finally, DI O'Donnell who was drummed out of the force in disgrace. He died eighteen months later of hypothermia in Colchester, a heroin addict, homeless and found sleeping in a cardboard box.'

'Christ, what a story, and what a case for you to cut your teeth on.'

'You're right, and you can imagine the atmosphere in the murder team office. Unbridled euphoria when the husband was arrested, as the story had been all over the papers, much like Livermore's. Later, when the guy came forward with his photograph, the recriminations started and everyone began watching their arses, trying to distance themselves from any involvement in the investigation.'

'I can imagine.'

'For a spell, O'Donnell saw me as the fall guy, after all, it's not much of a loss to the team if a new face gets the chop. In the end, the bloodhounds of the IOPC, then called the IPCC, saw through O'Donnell's shenanigans. There was a time when I could have walked away from the whole crappy mess, but I'm glad I didn't.'

'You made the right decision.'

'So, you see, there's no way I want to make the same mistake Gary O'Donnell did. My gut instinct tells me we're heading down the same path. I'm ordering you to let Steve Mitchell go.'

'But—'

'Let me finish, Angus. Today's Friday. I'll give you until the close of business on Tuesday. If you can't find any more evidence to hang round Mitchell's neck by then, Mitchell goes free.'

THIRTY-EIGHT

'I'm having a helluva time of it at the moment, Hannah, I can tell you. My stupid, asinine, fuck-dog publishers have gone and published my new book as soon as they could after Stuart's death. Social media is going bananas. They're saying I'm a cruel, heartless bastard, only in it for the money and trying to cash in on a tragedy. There's also a campaign to boycott my books. If Steve Mitchell wasn't still locked up in jail, I would suspect he was behind it. For the moment, it hasn't got off the ground, thank God. But I'm sure if lynching was still around, I wouldn't be talking to you today.'

'Talking' usually implied one person speaking and the other listening before replying. In this case, Ryan Allison was doing all the talking, whilst the comatose figure of Hannah Robbins didn't so much as flinch. Not so much as a little tremor in her face, a flicker of the eye, or the slightest movement of her finger. Nothing.

The doctors had warned him it would be difficult talking to a non-responsive figure. He'd joked he had plenty of experience of this with his father, an aloof, taciturn man who said little, and showed even less emotion. Joking aside, he reckoned it wouldn't be much different to standing in front of an audience at some book festivals. They weren't always the most enthusiastic of audiences, clapping from time to time when he'd made a good point, or downright frosty when he didn't. At the end, when he would invite questions or throw into the room what he regarded as a contentious issue, sometimes all he would receive in return were blank faces and stony silence.

This was way worse, like nothing he had ever experienced. It had been suggested to him by one of the nurses that it would be a good idea for him to read to Hannah. He had brought along a book with this in mind, another Bill Bryson which he had bought especially for her. However, he was still too wound up about his dramatic fall from grace to concentrate on the words.

'I called my agent. You remember Sean McTiernan, don't you? He's a big Irishman who drinks like a fish and makes as much sense as a goldfish when he's drunk. I told him about the rushed publication of *Dead Water*. He threatened to go over to my publisher's ivory tower with a baseball bat and smash in a few heads. I reckon he would after a few drinks, you know what the Irish are like. However, time keeping has never been his strongest suit. When he finally extricated himself from whatever pub he was ensconced in, the offices would be closed. Then, the only things he could find to damage would be the glass doors or the plant pots in the plaza.'

No response.

'Sean's all bang and bluster, fine for negotiating deals with commissioning editors, but he's a literary agent and not an SAS operative. I don't think when it comes down to it, he could hurt a fly. On the other hand, your friend Lucinda, a fellow member of the editors' union, makes people feel small for fun. As you know, she is my editor and works for the said, fuck-dog publisher. She gave me the 'there-there, Ryan, think of the money,' speech. 'Have a few whiskies and you'll soon feel better.' I've never met a woman who thinks the answer to everything is whisky. I know her father's Scottish, but if I said this to anyone, they'd accuse me of perpetuating a stereotype.'

No response.

'Stacy's fine, although quite upset in her own way about the *Dead Water* cock-up. She, of course, blames me. I've been so wrapped up in Stuart's death, she says, that I failed to anticipate their actions. This led to one mighty barney, I can tell you. I'm sure if you were in charge you wouldn't have shafted me, Hannah, like they've done.'

No response.

'Maddy and Holly are doing fine. Maddy's adjusting well to senior school. If you remember, and I expect you do, she moved up in the summer. Holly's started the GCSE syllabus and is finding it tough. She's always been a slow starter but I'm sure she'll get there in the end. Well, I've told you all my news. What's been happening with you? Been anywhere interesting? Talked to any nice people?'

No response.

He stood and looked closely at her features, but couldn't see a flicker of recognition. He decided to call it quits and come back the following day when, with luck, he would be feeling more positive. Knowing how she was, he would need to come better prepared, both with materials and in his head.

'Well, I'm going to go now, Hannah. I think I will take Lucinda's advice and go home and have those whiskies, although I'm sure Stacy will have something to say on the matter. She does on everything else.'

He leaned over and kissed her cheek before walking away, tears pricking his eyes. Hannah was one of the brightest and most optimistic women he knew, her bright spark dimmed only by Stuart's death. He'd felt confident it would have returned in time. Until this.

He headed out of the Royal Sussex County Hospital determined not only to have a few whiskies, but to finish the whole bottle. What he needed was to drink himself into a stupor and forget about his writing career and poor Hannah's coma for a few hours. If Stacy wanted him to sleep in the spare room, he couldn't care less. With luck, everything would look better in the morning.

He crossed Eastern Road and had to think for a minute where he had parked the car. There was so much movement in the area, the streets looked different to when he'd first arrived: the two large grey vans were gone, so was the lime-green Maserati sports car into which he had taken a good look, barely an hour before.

He carried on down Paston Place, the unbroken line of cars on either side of the road acting like a steel barrier to prevent residents crossing. Darkness had fallen in the time he had been in the hospital, lights twinkling in the apartment blocks he passed. Sensible people were at home watching television, or sinking a few in their local pub. In fact, with this being Friday, he imagined most of the pubs in Kemptown would be packed, some intent on drinking themselves senseless in the hour or so that remained.

He could see his car, ten metres or so further on. He liked cars, but Brighton and Hove City Council hated them. The Greens in charge had introduced twenty-mile-an-hour speed limits all around Brighton and Hove, and onerous parking restrictions. Boards nearby barked their instructions like cantankerous sergeant majors: 'Residents Only', 'Return Prohibited Within an Hour', 'Pay at Machine'. They had grown around the town like mushrooms and now were as common and as insidious as seagulls.

In response, he had sold his beloved Audi A5 and bought a small car, a Fiat Abarth. It was small in stature, but with a racy engine under the bonnet. This, could make it go like the wind whenever he managed to get away from the restrictions of the town.

Moving closer to the car, he reached into his pocket and pulled out the key fob. Around a car-length away, he pointed the fob at the Fiat and pressed the 'unlock' button. He was about to step into the gap between his car and the car behind, heading for the driver's side, when he heard a noise behind him.

'Hello Allison. Fancy seeing you here.'

He turned wearily. Not another disgruntled reader waiting in the shadows to berate him.

'Now, if all you're going to do is harangue me, I have to tell you –'

'Remember me?'

The speaker was a large man, about six-two and well-built. More like a docker than anyone who attended any of his literary events. Allison looked hard at his face and for a moment believed he recognised him. Surely not.

Before he could ask him what he wanted, something flashed in the light of the street lamp. The guy punched him in the chest. He felt the wind go out of his lungs, like being poleaxed by a front row forward in rugby. Strangely, for a simple punch, he felt as if all the energy in his body was leaking out. He dropped to his knees, the effort required to stand proving too much. The man loomed over him. He bent down and grabbed a handful of his hair. Allison saw him smile. He leaned closer, gripping a large knife in his hand.

THIRTY-NINE

This time, DI Henderson arrived at a murder scene before Walters. He had little excuse. He lived only a few streets away. A strange thought suddenly passed through his head. Livermore's murder scene was located close to Walters' apartment, and now this one, a few streets from where he lived. He dismissed the notion. It was too frivolous to give it serious consideration. Plus, it was too early in the course of a murder investigation to be jumping to conclusions.

He felt remarkably bright for having been woken from a deep sleep, but he reckoned he was only at the early stages. He presented his warrant card to the cop manning the barrier. The cop would need to be on his toes tonight, as many local residents had gathered, despite the late hour, to look and take pictures with their camera phones. Some looked as though they had just got out of bed, and others, as if they hadn't made it there in the first place.

To be fair to the partying fraternity, it was early, around 12:30am on a Saturday morning. He knew many young people didn't contemplate heading out to clubs until at least midnight, and a night out couldn't be considered a success unless they arrived home after 3am.

The pathologist was already at the scene, and Henderson was pleased to see it was his friend, Grafton Rawlings. The victim was lying in a gap between two parked cars, and if someone walked by and looked over, they probably wouldn't have noticed him. From a distance, it would resemble a bag of rubbish, a down and out, or a drunk sleeping off the effects of a night spent drinking. He bent down beside the pathologist.

'Morning Grafton, it's good to see you. Although, I would have preferred it to be under better circumstances.'

'Hello Angus. Are you well?'

'As well as to be expected when everyone wants a murder solved. I'm not convinced we're there yet.'

'I'm sure you wouldn't want it any other way. If there was a simple way to solve these,' he said, nodding at the blood-soaked corpse on the ground, 'you'd be out of a job.'

'I suppose you're right. What have we got here?'

'The victim received a four-centimetre wide stab wound to his chest which would have killed him in the end. I suspect, in a bid to hurry the process along, the killer also cut his throat.'

Henderson winced. It was a gruesome way to kill anyone. The carotid arteries were the main source of blood to the brain, neck, and face. Assuming the victim's heart was still pumping at the point when the neck was severed, blood would spurt out over the pavement, victim, and killer. He could see the mess on the pavement and the victim, what about the killer?

'I turned him on his front a few minutes before you arrived to see if he had any other injuries. He hasn't, so I'll turn him back. Are you ready for this? It's not a pleasant spectacle.'

'I suppose so. I doubt I'll be seeing my bed for at least another twenty hours. Do your worst.'

'Could give me a hand to move him?'

'Sure.'

'I'll deal with his head if you can take him by his shoulders. Take care you don't get your hand caught on the bumper of one of those cars, it's a tight space. Are you ready?'

Henderson nodded.

'Okay, 1-2-3.'

Grafton wasn't kidding about the spectacle now in front of him. Slasher horror flicks like *Nightmare on Elm Street* didn't do justice to the sheer awfulness of it. The head was lolling back as if only held on by the brain stem, the eyes were set in terror on a white face, and the inner contents of the throat were there for all to see. Pervading the air all around, the strong coppery smell of blood, most of which had now leaked out of the victim's pale body.

Moving his eyes away from the neck, he looked at the face. Even in the poor illumination provided by street lighting, he recognised him. It was Ryan Allison.

Henderson had seen enough. He wanted to move, but for the moment he felt queasy. He couldn't be sick or faint in front of all the onlookers. Many were armed with smart phones, ready to take a picture of anything unusual, something they could sell to *The Argus,* or have their three minutes of fame when it was shown on BBC South East. The sight of the lead detective throwing up his evening meal would only encourage the crowd of onlookers, and if such a photograph appeared in *The Argus*, it would be the excuse Houghton needed to shift him to Traffic.

He stood, but didn't move, waiting for the dizziness in his head and butterflies in his stomach to subside. One emotion surpassed all others, that of shock.

'Are you all right boss?'

He turned to see DS Walters approaching. 'Hi Carol. I think so. Take a look at the vic and see if you recognise him. On second thoughts, I wouldn't bother.'

'Why not?'

'It's Stuart Livermore's friend, Ryan Allison. He's had his throat cut. Take a look if you want, but I warn you now, it's not a pretty sight.'

'Ryan Allison?'

He nodded.

'My goodness, I didn't expect that, but I'll pass on the dubious pleasure of seeing him. I'll wait for Grafton's report, when I imagine the sight will be less gruesome.'

They moved away to the sanctuary of a set of steps leading up to an apartment building. This to allow the ambulance crew to move closer and make ready for the removal of the body. It also had the advantage of moving the two detectives out of earshot of any eavesdroppers.

'First Livermore is murdered,' Walters said, 'his girlfriend is attacked, now his best friend is killed, following an attack in Cheltenham. There has to be a connection.'

Henderson couldn't respond, he still felt queasy.

'You all right gov?'

'Let's take a walk towards the seafront, the breeze might get rid of the vile metallic taste in my mouth.'

They walked down Paston Place. The sea was a slow-moving grey mass which he could see in the moonlight and with the aid of streetlights still lit on the promenade.

'You realise the implications of your last comment?' he said a minute or so later. The fresh breeze was doing a good job of clearing the fog in his head.

'What do you mean?'

'It's hard to see how the murders of Livermore and Allison aren't connected. They're crime writers, the best of friends, and they both lived in the Brighton area.'

'Detective Inspector Henderson, I thought I spotted you and Detective Sergeant Walters walking down here. Good morning to you both.'

Henderson turned to see Rob Tremain heading towards them. He was *The Argus's* Chief Crime Reporter, and probably the last person he wanted to see at this moment. His head was so full of the implications of now having two dead authors, he would find it hard to play it down for Tremain's readers. They didn't need to know there was a connection between them, not yet.

'Morning Rob. You made it down here pretty sharpish.'

'I must admit I was in the land of nod when the call came through. Some bod in the office heard it on the scanner. Can you give me a usable comment about the corpse up there, one to justify the loss of so much of my beauty sleep? I'm told there's a sizeable quantity of blood on the pavement.'

Henderson was about to admonish the reporter, when he stopped. Such prior knowledge didn't indicate Tremain had taken a peek underneath the crime tape, or gained access to an apartment overlooking the crime scene. The person who had found the body, a man returning from a night out with his girlfriend, had been in the process of bringing up his earlier meal of chicken curry when Henderson arrived. An officer had taken his statement, but Tremain may have spoken to the man after the cop had walked off.

'There's not much to tell at this stage. Suffice to say the victim is a white male, aged around forty, and he died of stab wounds. At the moment, we don't know if it was a random stabbing or an altercation which has turned violent. The next step is to try to identify the victim and locate any witnesses. How does that sound?'

'I suppose, it's the best I can hope for at this early stage. Now, if I can ask a favour, when you do finally manage to identify him...'

'You'll be the first to know.'

'Many thanks. It's time to return to the crime scene and see if there is anything else I can include in my exclusive report. No one from any of the other locals or even from the nationals has shown up yet. Got to go. See you around.'

'We might need him,' Henderson told Walters when they were alone. 'If he manages to track down any witness before we do, it could provide us with a description of the attacker.'

'It would be good to have one, but it was dark, and the killer picked a good spot between street lights. You were saying before Tremain arrived, about the implications of a connection between the victims.'

'Was I? Oh, yes. If the murders of Livermore and Allison are connected, and the early indications are it looks to be the case, where does that leave Steve Mitchell? He didn't murder Ryan Allison, because he was safely locked up in Lewes nick at the time.'

FORTY

Henderson finished the morning team briefing. The main item on the agenda was adding the investigation into the murder of Ryan Allison to that of Stuart Livermore. He walked back to his office, grabbed his jacket and, with DS Walters beside him, they headed out of the building and over to his car.

'Gov, I know we need to give Ryan Allison's life the once-over,' Walters said. 'We need to talk to all his close friends, his literary agent, editor, and all the rest, but everyone knows his murder must be connected to Livermore's.'

'In which case, are you suggesting we should stop what we're doing and look for the similarities between the two men. Find out where their lives intersect?'

'Yes.'

'We can only do it once we've found out everything we can about Ryan Allison.'

'Why not right away?'

'A couple of reasons. I accept we can forget coincidence. I think the odds of two authors being murdered in the same town, within a few weeks and miles of one other, must be astronomical.'

'Agreed.'

They approached the car and climbed in. It was early October, but the weather hadn't reached the stage of being so cold that leaving the car in the car park for a few hours would require the windscreen to be cleared of frost. There had been a build-up of condensation, however, and they sat for several seconds while the high-speed fan did its work.

'Putting coincidence to one side,' Henderson said, 'I still think it's too early to suggest both men were murdered by the same killer.'

He negotiated the car out of the gates of Malling House and drove towards the A27.

'What makes you say that?'

'We need to approach every case with the same degree of professionalism and an open mind.'

Walters sighed. 'As you never stop reminding me.'

'I shouldn't have to. We don't know if Allison was killed by someone else for a different reason entirely, but we need to consider it. His murder could have been a copycat, a random act, an enemy of his and his only, mistaken identity, or something else entirely.'

'I'm not convinced.'

'Think of the place where Allison was killed, then compare it to Livermore.'

'The street versus inside his house?'

'Right. Now do the same with the knife wound.'

Walters thought for a moment. 'Livermore was killed with a narrow blade, about one centimetre across, a stiletto perhaps. Allison had his throat slit and a four-centimetre wound in his chest.'

'It's clearly two different knives.'

'Don't forget, Allison was also stabbed in the chest like Livermore, but I think I see where you're heading.'

'Despite the two murders looking, on the face of it, as if done by the same killer,' Henderson said, 'when we look at the detail, it's easy to argue it could be the work of two different killers. On the one hand, Livermore's was neat and sneaky. The killer broke into his house and confronted the victim in his lounge. On the other, Allison's killer appears to be bolder and stronger. It takes a different sort of confidence to confront someone in the street and slash their throat with a knife.'

'I agree.'

'In addition, with a bigger knife, it's easier to conceal and be handled by a larger person. Now do you see where I'm going with this?'

'Yep, I do. The motivation for both killings looks the same, but the dispatch of the victims suggests two different killers. If true, and thinking about the connections between the authors, it suggests the killers are on the same page.'

'Which is the reason why we must trawl through Ryan Allison's life. It also means Steve Mitchell should stay where he is. If he murdered Livermore, and I think he did, someone else must have killed Allison.'

'I have a problem with the killers being connected. It only works if they both have the same motivation, determination, and skills. We know the odds of finding such a pair are off the page.'

'It's a valid point,' he said, 'and a path we should be wary of heading down. C'mon, we're here, let's go and do what we came here to do.'

He couldn't find a parking space close to where he wanted, so he left the car in a Residents Parking slot and left a 'Police Business' message on the windscreen. It didn't usually cut much ice with traffic wardens, but there was always a first time They walked, neither officer saying much, the task ahead looming large.

Henderson rang the bell. He was confident the householder would be at home. With her husband not returning home last night, she would be loath to be away from the house or the home phone. What he wasn't so assured about was the whereabouts of their two children.

The door was flung open and Stacy Allison stood there, her well-coiffured hair of his previous visit still neat, but not meeting the high standard set before. Nor had her magazine-perfect makeup been applied this morning.

'Great. The police. So, you did get my message? I've been phoning the station non-stop all morning and only a few minutes ago got through. Have you found him? Is he all right?'

'Stacy, can we come in?'

'Why? Have you come to give me bad news? Is he injured?'

'Can we come in? This isn't the sort of conversation we should be conducting on the doorstep.'

'Sorry, you're right. I'm forgetting my manners. Come on in.'

They walked inside and Stacy closed the door. 'Go into the lounge, you know where it is. I'll make some tea.'

'No,' Henderson said. 'Come in with me. Sergeant Walters will look after the tea.' He looked at Walters, who nodded.

They headed into the lounge. It looked less tidy than it had been the other day. On the settee, he could see the home telephone, mobile, laptop, and an address book; key elements of a missing person search.

'Oh, sorry, let me move those things. I've been phoning everyone I know to try and find out where Ryan might be. You know how it is with some friends, you see them at school, you go to their house for coffee and sometimes out to dinner. Then, when something like this happens, you realise you don't have their phone number.'

'Stacy, please sit down.'

'I will in a second, just let me put some of those things away.'

She sat down on the chair opposite Henderson, who had taken a seat on the newly created space on the settee.

'We found Ryan, Stacy.'

'Oh, fantastic news! Where is he? Can I see him?'

'I'm sorry to tell you, Stacy, but Ryan is dead.'

An animal-like wail escaped from her mouth, before a scream, before she burst into tears. He looked around the room and spotted a box of tissues. He picked them up and positioned them on a table within easy reach.

Walters came into the lounge bearing a tray, put it down, and walked over to comfort her. This was one of the reasons, when delivering bad news, he liked to be accompanied by a female officer, especially someone as competent as DS Walters. In this age of the #MeToo movement, a male detective putting his arm around the partner of a murder victim could be interpreted as taking advantage of a vulnerable individual. It would further compound the problem if the woman, in her grief, turned and wrapped her arms around the detective.

'How did he die?' she sobbed.

'He was stabbed. We found him in a street in Brighton–'

'Near the hospital?'

'Yes.'

'He told me he was going to visit poor Hannah Robbins.'

For the next few minutes, Henderson sipped his tea while Stacy sobbed. When it seemed the tears were subsiding and her former composure was returning, he said: 'Can I ask Stacy, other than the incident in Cheltenham, has anyone ever threatened Ryan? For example, has he received any strange phone calls, texts or emails lately?'

'No. I don't think so. You mentioned the incident in Cheltenham. Could Ryan's stabbing have something to do with that? Ryan said the guy in the toilet pulled a knife on him.'

'The day before yesterday, a man was arrested by Cheltenham Police and charged with possession of a knife, assault and threatening behaviour. The person in question believed he was helping a man we currently have in custody, nothing more. I'm quite sure it's not connected to what happened to Ryan.'

'Oh, what am I going to do? What will I tell the girls?' She started crying again. Walters encouraged her to drink sweetened tea, the best medicine for shock available in any kitchen cupboard.

'Where are the children?' Walters asked.

'They both went for sleepovers last night. I'm picking them up later.'

The doorbell rang. Before Stacy could react, Henderson rose from his seat and said, 'I'll get it.'

He walked down the hall and opened the door. The serious but not unpleasant face of Family Liaison Officer, Jenni Black, greeted him.

'Morning, sir.'

'Morning Jenni. Come on in.'

'How is Mrs Allison?' Black asked him, as he shut the door.

'Not good. Two issues you should know about,' he said in hushed tones. 'There are two children in the family, and they don't know what's happened. She's due to pick them up later today after sleepovers. Also, you need to be aware, her husband was not only stabbed, he also had his throat cut.'

'Oh, gruesome.'

'If Stacy demands to see him, put her off until the formal identification. By then, the pathologist will have made the sight a lot more presentable.'

'Thanks for the warning, sir. Telling families they can't see the body of a loved one until the SIO says so, sounds so lame. They understandably become agitated and anxious. It's better if I can cut off any discussion before it escalates. Shall we go in?'

FORTY-ONE

Few detectives were left in the office following the early morning briefing. Most were out interviewing the friends, relatives, and associates of Ryan Allison. Like Stuart Livermore, Ryan Allison worked from home, while his publisher, editor, and literary agent were all based in London.

Similar to the questions Walters had posed, it was hard convincing the team about his chosen way forward. Henderson had explained the differences between the killings, and some were beginning to come around to his way of thinking. To the doubters, he posed another question: if seeking the similarities between Livermore and Allison was a shortcut to finding their killer, as most of them believed, how would they go about it?

It was like watching the lights switching on at dusk down the hill in Lewes. Answer? In the same way they were doing. Once they had found out everything they could about Ryan Allison's life, having already done the same for Stuart Livermore, only then could they see where the lives of the two men dovetailed. Once they had established those cross-over points, out would fall, he believed, a motive for their murders.

He picked up his car keys and phone and put on his jacket. He walked out of his office and headed out to the car park. Lunch was skipped today on purpose. Post-mortems were procedures that were grisly at the best of times, never mind a corpse that almost had its head chopped off.

The car park at the Brighton and Hove City Mortuary was a haven of calm. No more than ten metres away from where he was parked, Lewes Road was a metallic snake of cars, buses and lorries making their way into Brighton. Today, there was no time to enjoy the peace, or even to gather his courage. He got out of the car and walked inside.

In the quiet of the changing room, he donned a pair of paper coveralls and bootees and headed into the pathologist's domain. It was often thought by members of the public that such places had no need for the same strict anti-bacterial and anti-viral procedures governing hospitals; surely the dead didn't need protection from anything.

This was certainly true for corpses, but many living people worked there too. On a day-to-day basis this included pathologists and their assistants, cleaners and delivery drivers. On a day like today, it also attracted a police photographer, an observer from the Home Office, the Crime Scene Manager, and the Senior Investigating Officer, DI Henderson.

He was pleased to see there was no sign of Mrs Allison. Victim's families had no legal right to attend a post-mortem, but it didn't stop many from demanding it. The Family Liaison Officer at the Allison house had told him that Mrs Allison had wanted to be present, and, as she had been a former litigation lawyer, had made her demands with some vigour. The FLO was likewise firm in her refusal. Yes, she could see her husband, but only once the post-mortem procedures had been concluded.

Henderson watched as Grafton made a Y-incision in the chest of the body lying in front of him. This was one of only a few things Henderson wanted to see. The removal and weighing of organs would be more relevant if the cause of death was unknown. He would skip away to make some phone calls when that stage was reached, and come back later to listen to Grafton's conclusions. What Henderson needed to understand was how deep the knife wound penetrated, and anything he could learn about the weapon itself.

Grafton peeled back the chest skin and laid open the cadaver's chest before examining inside with his surgical probe. 'The knife penetrated the chest all the way through to his ribcage,' he said into the head microphone, 'breaking two ribs before entering the heart. This indicates to me,' Grafton continued, 'and I imagine is of interest to you, Detective Inspector Henderson, that the attacker used considerable force.'

In his head, Henderson ticked a box. Despite the murders of the two authors being inextricably linked, it was looking more and more likely they were carried out by two different people. If Steve Mitchell was responsible for the first, as Henderson believed, he couldn't have done the second. If they'd arrested the wrong man, as Sean Houghton was steadily coming around to thinking, they were still looking for two killers.

'The wound also indicates the knife was around four centimetres wide, extremely sharp with small serrations along one edge.'

This ticked another box. Unlike Livermore, stabbed with something long and narrow like a stiletto, this had all the hallmarks of something bigger and heavier, like a hunting knife. Henderson stayed for another twenty minutes before stepping out. He removed his overclothes before walking into the cemetery and taking a seat on a bench.

He pulled out his phone and switched off airplane mode. Whilst incommunicado, he'd missed a call from Steve Houghton, which he thought odd. His boss knew Henderson's movements today. He ignored it, and instead called Vicky Neal. She had been in London interviewing Sean McTiernan, Allison's literary agent, and now would be on her way back to Lewes.

'Hello Vicky.'

'Hi boss. I hope you're having a better day than me and Sally.'

'I doubt it, I'm at Ryan Allison's P-M.'

'Oh, yeah, so you are, rather you than me. I take it you've slipped out at the skull sawing stage. I can't stand the noise.'

'Can't you hear the buzz in the background?' he said holding the phone in the air for a moment. 'Only kidding, it's the roar of traffic on Lewes Road. How did you get on with McTiernan?'

'He's a big man, an Irishman with a strong Dublin accent, but quite unexpectedly softly spoken. However, whenever he starts to discuss a topic that gets on his goat, the volume goes up another ten notches.'

'How did he get on with our victim?'

'He said they were like a couple of brothers. They both liked a drink, and they both enjoyed going to rock concerts. He was surprised to hear he'd been beaten up by a friend of Steve Mitchell, as he wasn't involved in the sockpuppeting issue.'

'So, it was only Livermore?'

'Seems so.'

'It makes the attack on Allison in Cheltenham all the more bizarre. It's like he's guilty by association. Anything else?'

'You should be aware, although I don't know how relevant it is, Allison was in dispute with his publisher. This was about the publication of his new novel, *Dead Water*. They released it last week, a coincidence they said, but people on social media have been blaming Allison for trying to cash in on his friend's death. As a result, he's been receiving a number of abusive messages.'

'This is news to me, and also to his wife I suspect. When I asked her, she didn't mention it.'

'Some people have been calling for a boycott of his books, but one or two were threatening harm. You know how some of those social media nerds behave when someone is on the ropes and getting a kicking. McTiernan said Allison had been livid with his publisher, and so was he.'

'It's worth following up. However, calling for a campaign to stop buying an author's books is one thing, killing him for what looks like an error of judgement is something else. I don't see it being a realistic motive myself.'

'Me neither.'

'Thanks for the update, Vicky. Anything else?'

'Nope.'

'Good. Talk to you later.'

He was about to ring Walters when his phone rang. Thinking it might be his boss again, he looked at the screen and was surprised to see it wasn't.

'Hi Carol.'

'Hi gov, how's the P-M going?'

'Our vic looks a lot cleaner now than he did before. It still looks gruesome, but much better than it looked at Paston Place.'

'I'll bet. The reason I called was to give you an update on the meeting I had with Allison's editor, and also to give you a piece of interesting news.'

'Let's start with your interview of his editor.'

'Lucinda Beaufort.'

'Is that her real name?'

'Seems to be. If the name suggests someone who's a stuck-up, officious prig, it more or less sums her up. She spent most of our meeting talking about all the clearing up she had to do with Allison's manuscripts, more than she did talking about the man himself.'

'We all grieve in different ways. Could she throw any light on why Allison was murdered, or indeed why the same thing happened to Livermore?'

'Nothing of consequence. I'll take a second look at my notes when I get back to make sure I haven't missed anything. Livermore and Allison were the best of friends, but in professional terms, Livermore was in the Premier League while Allison was in the division below.'

'The Championship.'

'Yeah, that one. In her terminology, Livermore was a bestseller and Allison, mid-list, but I'm sure you catch the drift.'

'Does this mean the two men didn't move in the same professional circles?'

'Yep. Livermore was invited to the top literary events; one of his books was serialised on the radio and another adapted for telly. Allison, on the other hand, hadn't achieved either of those things.'

'Nevertheless, he looked to be doing all right. He lived in a big house in Montpelier Terrace, while I could only afford the cheap seats across the road.'

'According to Ms Beaufort, most of it is his wife's money. She used to be a top litigation lawyer in her day. She'd intended going back to work, but after her children were born, one with a mild form of autism, she decided to stay home.'

'Interesting. However, we still can't seem to find the elusive crossover between the two men. If we don't find it fast, or the press beat us to it, we'll have nothing to fall back on.'

'Would you like to hear some good news for a change?'

'I need it, there's not much around.'

'An officer at St John's Road has found Hannah Robbins' handbag.'

FORTY-TWO

Henderson walked back to his office and took a seat behind his desk. He removed the lid of the coffee cup bought on the way to work and took a sip: lukewarm. When he'd arrived back in Lewes after attending the P-M of Ryan Allison, he was called into Sean Houghton's office to put the final touches to another press release about his murder.

The incident in Paston Place had generated all sorts of speculation in the press due to the amount of blood spilled at the scene. This encouraged journalists to indulge in the most lurid headlines they could dream up, incorporating words like: 'bloodbath', 'massacre', and 'slaughter'.

Beyond the sensationalist front pages, they talked of a serial killer stalking the streets of Brighton, with editorials issuing warnings of the potential danger to other workers in the book business: authors, librarians, and bookshop staff. Despite some of the knee-jerk advice sounding ridiculous, Henderson couldn't ridicule it. He had tried, but couldn't yet come up with a satisfactory reason why a second author had been murdered.

It might have been the work of one of Steve Mitchell's friends, assuming there was someone else like the guy who had pulled a knife on Ryan Allison in Cheltenham, or for some other motive as yet unknown. What he did know, and the main subject of discussion at the last team briefing, was that his officers needed to go through all the interviews and research they'd done again and again until something clicked.

He finished the coffee, left his office and walked into the Detectives' Room looking for DS Walters.

'Hi gov,' she said when she spotted his approach. 'Have you come to see Hannah Robbins' bag?'

He nodded.

She donned a pair of nitrile gloves and lifted the bag on to her desk. She dipped inside and, with care, removed all the items inside and placed them on her desk. This included a bottle of Bvlgari Jasmin Noir perfume, a small make-up bag, an address book, a diary, a pen, a notebook, and a novel. By the look of the spaceships on the cover, it had something to do with science fiction.

'It looks as though everything worth hawking has been taken,' Walters said.

'Yep, pretty much. The bag looks big enough to carry a laptop, and going by the scratches and stretch marks on the leather, I would say it used to. If so, it's missing, along with her phone and purse.'

'Like I say, anything of any value has been stolen, but it does offer up one clue: her assailant was in all likelihood a man.'

'What makes you say that? Although, research would back you up. About ninety-five percent of bag snatches are carried out by men. Before you accuse me of being a nerd, it was included in a report I was reading this morning.'

'I was referring to the perfume. It's an expensive brand; any lass grabbing the bag would have nabbed it straight away.'

'Good point.'

'Also, the thief wasn't after her personal stuff. He left her address book and diary.'

'Maybe,' he said sitting up in his seat, 'we can still salvage something of value from this.'

'How?'

'Open the diary and see where she was last Tuesday, the night she was attacked.'

'Bloody hell, I should have thought of that. I just assumed she was on her way back from work.'

Walters flicked through the pages. 'At least she uses it, and doesn't keep everything on her phone as everyone else seems to do. It's full of work appointments. Last Tuesday... Ah, here we are.'

'Is anything written?'

'Yep, lots.' She opened it out in front of him. '10am - meeting with new author, Ben Ainslie. 11am - meeting with Dave Walker, Accounts. 1:30 - Lunch with Karen. 3pm leaving work early. 6pm Roberto Sanchez, Zama Video Productions BH.'

'Bingo!' Henderson said pointing at the last entry. 'It looks like she didn't head straight home from work after all.'

'Yes, guilty as charged for making assumptions,' Walters said. She turned to her pc and keyed the words, 'Zama Video Productions' into Google.

'Hang on,' Henderson said, after seeing the loaded screen, 'before you jump over to their website...'

Too late, the Zama website started to load. It was a glitzy, colourful affair, making him think they were printers of glossy publications, or something in the fashion business, and not a video production outfit as the name implied.

'Go back, I think I saw something,' Henderson said.

'Where?'

'Go back to where you were.'

Walters hit the 'back' button and the Google search appeared again with all the websites related to Zama Video Productions listed.

'There,' he said, pointing, about three results down. 'What's all this about a fire?'

Walters clicked on an article from the *Mid Sussex Times*. Like many news sites, it took an age to load. This was due to a plethora of adverts and pop-ups, a common feature of newspaper sites, keen to supplement their declining income, a result of falling newspaper sales.

'A mysterious fire ripped through the offices and studios of Zama Video Productions on Sunday night,' Walters read. 'Located in the Victoria Industrial Estate in Burgess Hill, the fire destroyed most of the building, but firefighters at the scene prevented it spreading to nearby businesses. Roberto Sanchez, MD of Zama, a video production studio engaged in the production of training videos for businesses, and programmes for television, said, 'This fire has been devastating. Not only have we lost our state of the art photographic and recording equipment, but our storage area too. This includes the tapes of all our training videos and most of the original film of our television programmes. The archive took years to build and most of it is irreplaceable. I'm heartbroken.' The source of the fire, which appears to have started in the archive area, is unknown, but the Fire Service are not ruling out an electrical fault, or arson.'

'So,' Henderson said, 'Hannah Robbins attends a meeting at Zama Video Productions on Tuesday evening, and on the way home she is attacked. A few days later, Sunday, the building is burned to the ground. Is this a coincidence or what?'

'How many times in the case have we said that? If they are connected, how?'

'See what you can find out about Zama Productions, and try to track down the guy in the newspaper article, the MD, Roberto Sanchez. Find out what he and Hannah were discussing. It could be something, or nothing. Perhaps she was there for something banal, I don't know, like renting some training videos for her company, or to ask them about making a video for a new book they were publishing. The fire adds a new and, dare I say, ominous dimension to this enquiry.'

'It sure does. Leave it with me.'

Henderson walked back to his office, his mind on the foibles of luck. It was this that had placed Hannah Robbins in the same location as a thief, and the actions she'd taken, or didn't take, which had landed her comatose in a hospital bed. He sat behind the desk, picked up the phone and called the Neurological Unit at the Royal Sussex.

'There has been no change in Ms Robbins' condition, I'm afraid to say, Detective Inspector,' the duty nurse told him. 'The surgeon expects her to recover in time. The trauma she has suffered was less severe, in brain-damage terms, than several of our other patients, some of whom are expected never to improve. It's a question of time, but we can't yet put a number on it.'

'Thank you for the update,' Henderson said. 'Goodbye.'

Henderson sat for a moment, his thoughts on the inert frame of Hannah Robbins and her fellow patients, wondering if they could see, feel, and hear the activity taking place around them. If they could, but couldn't respond to it, he imagined it would drive some of them mad in the end.

His concentration was broken when Walters burst into his office.

'What's happening? Is this building on fire as well as Zama Productions?' he asked.

'What? No. When we were talking earlier, you asked me to take a look at the company.'

'How could I forget? We spoke about it barely ten minutes ago.'

'I think I've found something. Come and take a look.'

FORTY-THREE

Dominic Green drove into the car park at Rema Foods. His staff called it a car park, but it was nothing more than five marked spaces outside a non-descript warehouse at Shoreham Harbour. He would have preferred to have stayed indoors tonight. It was a filthy night with high winds and heavy rain, but he had work to do. Not only this, his wife's constant nagging about the behaviour of one of his neighbours was doing his head in. He was glad he had an excuse to come out, even if it was only to have his clothes soaked as he walked out to the car.

Before being incarcerated in one of Her Majesty's houses of correction, a place reeking of piss, sweat, and stale cabbage the minute you stepped within ten metres of it, he'd lived a high life. Back in the day, he'd owned Langley Manor with over twenty acres of woodland, parkland, and lakes. There, he could shoot with any gun he fancied, fish in the lake to while away a quiet Tuesday, or dig out the binoculars and do a spot of birdwatching.

They now lived in a house in Henfield, a sizeable place with six bedrooms, set in half an acre. It was owned by a legitimate property company, which in turn was owned by his wife, and at one time rented out to visiting business types. When he was arrested, its ownership had been kept well hidden. The house had been gutted and remodelled since the departure of the last tenants, but his wife still found something to moan about: she didn't like watching films on a normal television and not in a private cinema, the new kitchen had only two ovens; the fridge didn't dispense ice cubes, and she believed the neighbour over the road was spying on her through the curtains.

He sighed. He unlocked the door of the warehouse and walked inside. He headed over to the cheeping box to silence the alarm. It would take a bloody smart detective to spot the difference between the sophistication of the alarm and the goods stored inside the warehouse.

The alarm system was state of the art, with sensors all over the place, and cameras outside producing high-quality colour pictures and dumping them straight to a secure hard disk. If the alarm sounded for any reason, an alert would ping on Green's phone. No matter where he was, he could activate any one of the seven cameras to see what was going on.

The incongruity related to what was being protected: on the face it, large bags of rice, pasta, flour, and tea. Even without any heroin and cocaine in situ waiting to be trucked out, he knew from experience and the wisdom of several drug dealers he had come across in the slammer, everything left traces.

The alarm system was there to protect him on several fronts. It would prevent a rival nicking his stash, staff helping themselves to the merchandise, and stop an undercover cop sneaking inside to see what Green's developing food business was really importing.

He made his way past the packing area where twelve workers had earlier in the day decanted the goods from twenty-kilo sacks into kilo and half kilo bags. Somewhat ironically, for a legitimate business being used as cover for an illegitimate one, the *White Knight* brand was selling well.

Some of their products had been stocked at a farm shop near Horsham. A man who had been visiting his sister nearby, bought a packet of tea and loved the flavour so much, he wanted to stock it in the chain of supermarkets he owned in the Oxford area. The work Green's people had been doing during the day was to fulfil the first order for this new customer.

Green switched on the light in the office and began making a brew. Before the kettle boiled, Jack and Morris arrived. Between them they dragged yet another pervert inside. This ugly creature would be number four. He hoped the cops working on the case were being just as efficient as he was, but he doubted it.

'Evening boss, and a fine evening it is too,' Morris said, his hair sopping wet.

'Evening guys. If this perv doesn't tell us what we want to know, tie him up outside. Five minutes of all that crappy storm, and he'll be singing like my old granny's budgie. Tea?'

'Aye, tea for me,' Morris said. He began tying the guy to the chair.

'Coffee for you, Jack?' Green asked.

'Champion,' a muffled voice said.

'Don't tell me you're eating again?' Green said, as Jack steadily demolished a long sausage roll.

'It's only a small snack to keep me going. I've got a feeling this might be a long night.'

'What makes you think that? Is our man here not being cooperative?'

'Like a bloody monk, he was. Not a peep out of him on the way over.'

'Well, let's see if we can change his disposition.' Green handed out the mugs to both guys and took a seat on the edge of the desk facing the guy in the chair. He took a sip of his brew. Lovely. An excellent antidote to the inclement weather outside.

'Who do we have here? It's Raymond Lawson. This slime-ball, would you believe, guys, raped two girls at the school in Brighton where he worked as a lab assistant. God, just saying the words makes me want to gut this bastard. You guys don't have daughters at school, but if you did, you would know where I'm coming from.'

'Despicable,' Morris said.

'Does this sound like you, Raymond? Or can I call you Ray?'

'I've moved on. I've got rights. You've got no business dragging me here in the middle—'

He stopped when Morris leaned over and slapped him hard on the back of the head.

'Awwww. You bastards.'

'Listen up, sonny. You left your fucking rights out there in a puddle in the car park. This isn't the cop shop where you're playing for time, waiting for your brief to arrive. There's only us. If I ask Morris to smash your face, or stamp on your balls, he will do so. Now, listen up and listen good. I'm looking for The South Coast Rapist, the bastard who's been raping all those young women in town.'

'I'm listening.'

'Is it you?'

'What? Don't be daft. I'm fifty-five, I'm overweight, and I've got a dodgy knee.'

True enough, Lawson was a big lad, in girth not in height. He didn't look so mobile, and his shape and dickhead hair style would stand out, giving any witnesses an easy job in recalling his description.

'Nevertheless, Raymond. Where were you on the weekend of Brighton Pride? A lass was raped in Ditchling Common on Saturday, August 3rd.'

'Saturday? I would have been at home watching telly.'

'You need to do better than that, Raymond.'

'I can't. My wife left me and took the kids after I was sent to jail; couldn't face the neighbours, she said. I've been living on my own ever since.'

'If you're looking for sympathy, you won't find it here.'

'I'm not looking for sympathy. It's just how it is. I live alone. There's no one around who can vouch for me.'

'Tsk, tsk. Too bad, but I'm not an unreasonable man. I'll give you another shot, the last one, I'm afraid, before my patience runs out and I let Morris do what he does best. Let's go a bit further back. During the Brighton Festival in May, another girl was raped on the Saturday night in Patcham. Hang on, am I seeing some sort of pattern here?'

'What do you mean, boss?' Morris said.

'Brighton Pride, the Brighton Festival, busy times are ideal cover for someone like our perv here. He can check out the women, watch them from a distance, see what they're wearing, how much they're drinking, the whole works.'

'Yeah, but this fat fuck would be crap at looking anonymous in a crowd, wouldn't he?'

'I can't argue with you there, mate. What do you think Ray?'

'I don't like crowds, never have. I get anxious if there are too many people around. When it's busy in Brighton, like at the Festival and at Pride, I keep well away.'

'You know, Morris, I think chunky here is telling us porkies. It's like he's got an answer for everything. Go on mate, do your thing.'

Morris walked over and punched Lawson on the face, one with his right, another from his left. In the army, he'd been a keen boxer. Not good enough for the professional circuit, but he could hold his own against bigger men than himself.

He punched Lawson in the gut, but even one of his pile drivers didn't make much of an impression there. For good measure, he kicked him in the knee. Green wasn't sure if it was Lawson's dodgy one, but nevertheless, it made the perv howl like a banshee.

'Stop, stop it,' he screeched.

'Why should we, you perv?' Green spat. 'People like you deserve nothing better than to turn up dead in the gutter.'

'It wasn't me,' he cried through tears and a blood-dripping nose.

'Convince me.'

'How can I?'

'If you stop telling lies it would help. Morris, seconds out, break's over. It's time for round two.'

'Don't hit me again! Don't hit me! All right, all right, I'll tell you. I think I know the name of the man you're looking for.'

FORTY-FOUR

Henderson was back in Sean Houghton's office. His deadline for gathering more evidence against Steve Mitchell having expired the previous night. Houghton was standing outside the office talking to his administrative assistant in hushed tones. Perhaps they were discussing the paperwork needed to issue Henderson with his P45, or they were arranging his move to another unit, such as Road Safety or Schools Liaison.

It wasn't like Henderson to be so pessimistic, but he had been convinced all along about Steve Mitchell's guilt, he had pinned his colours to the mast. He was firm in his belief that it was only a matter of time before some better, compelling evidence against Mitchell presented itself.

The lack of forensic evidence had left the DI uneasy from the start. The photographs taken of the inside of his untidy house and car in Sheffield, didn't stack up with the meticulous individual who had broken into Stuart Livermore's house and left ziltch in the way of evidence. With hindsight, Henderson should have given this issue more credence, but it was one thing to ignore compelling evidence, another to draw conclusions from the lack of it.

The murder of Ryan Allison didn't help. With the death of two authors, the press, social media, and anyone who had ever read a crime novel, were screaming, 'serial killer'. Henderson's belief in the two murders being different and, in his view, most likely committed by two separate killers, carried about as much weight as a straw house in a hurricane.

Houghton breezed in, his assistant right behind him. The chief inspector sat down at his desk while his assistant approached Henderson, coffee in one hand, and papers in the other. To his surprise she didn't hand papers, most likely a Transfer Request Form, but the coffee.

'Thanks Janine,' Houghton said. 'Could you please close the door on your way out?'

'Okay, Angus,' Houghton said after the door was closed. 'I assume no new evidence has surfaced to prove Steve Mitchell's guilt, or I trust you would have been banging my door down to inform me. Am I right?'

'You are. Everything we have is circumstantial: the acrimony between him and Stuart Livermore, and Mitchell driving down to Brighton to see where he lived. He still hasn't given us a satisfactory explanation for his presence there. I believe, even if he didn't kill him on the night, because there's no forensics to put him inside Livermore's house, he was there to do him some harm.'

'I have to agree, he is an unpleasant character who settles disputes with his fists and not his head. All those minor cautions and convictions are testament to his anger issues. Those concerns aside, I believe in this instance, he is an innocent man. Let him go.'

'I'll sort it out,' Henderson said with a heavy heart. He wanted to leave Houghton's office right away to complete the necessary paperwork before the effect of his actions could sink in. He didn't move, he had a feeling his boss had something else to say.

'I have to tell you, Angus, this case has become something of an embarrassment to me.'

'Why? Arresting a suspect for a crime and then confirming their alibi, or with luck, finding the actual culprit responsible, is part and parcel of police work. We aren't always in possession of the full picture when we arrest someone, and so we keep them in custody to stop them harming others, or to prevent them fleeing. It's unfortunate for Steve Mitchell that he had to spend a couple of weeks on remand, but I fail to see any other problem.'

'The problem is, this is my first big case since moving to Sussex, and, not unreasonably, I think, I wanted an early conviction. The ACC expected the same. Call it the new manager effect. When a new manager is appointed at a rugby or football club, results are improved. He and I expected the same.'

Henderson liked sport, but Houghton's analogy didn't hold water. Players working with a demotivated football manager were lacking confidence, and the resultant tail-off in league results only compounded the issue. With the appointment of a new manager, optimism about the impending changes he intended to make added impetus for the first few months. If this resulted in improved league results, it would lift their confidence higher.

No murder team Henderson had been in charge of lacked enthusiasm or motivation to do the job in hand. If heads started to drop due to a lack of progress, it was his job to keep them motivated. A new 'coach' would have a pep-up effect here, but nowhere else. What stopped his team from closing a case was the lack of leads, suspects, and evidence. How could this area automatically benefit from the appointment of a new chief inspector?

'My team are working flat out,' Henderson said. 'This isn't a case where we've been short of leads. It takes time to sift through them all to try and find out if they're relevant or not. It's firm evidence we're short of.'

'The new lead you were telling me about earlier.'

'Zama Video?'

'Yeah. Tell me again.'

'The night Hannah Robbins ended up in hospital, she had earlier in the day been to a meeting with a company in Burgess Hill called, Zama Video Productions.'

'What for?'

'I'll come to that in a minute.'

'Okay.'

'A few days after Hannah's appointment, a fire burned Zama to the ground.'

'An electrical fault, you said.'

'The fire burned too fiercely to be sure, but this is what the Fire Investigation Officer is edging towards.'

'Okay.'

'When we looked at their website, we discovered they'd been commissioned by a digital television channel to make a series of programmes called *Blood Lines*. In each of eight episodes, a different author talks in general about their work, and more specifically about a real crime which had been the inspiration for one of their books.'

'Ah yes, now I remember. One of the programmes featured Livermore and another Allison. Right?'

'Right. On the website there's only a short clip, but enough to see an author talking about his or her life and writing technique. It then goes into a few details about the crime itself, talking to journalists and police officers who worked on the original case.'

'Okay, I understand, but you haven't been able to track a copy of the programme down?'

He shook his head. 'Neither the Zama website nor a search on Google allows us to buy or view the complete programme. From the information on the website, we know in episode three, Stuart Livermore appears, and in episode seven, Ryan Allison. It's the first time, beyond the obvious, we've found a connection between Livermore and Allison. It was Allison's appearance on the programme that prompted Hannah Robbins to go to Burgess Hill and talk to Zama. She wanted a copy of the episode featuring her boyfriend.'

'I see the connection between the two authors, but it doesn't sound much like hard evidence, does it? Two men are murdered because they appeared on a television programme? I don't buy it.'

'I can't judge how valuable it may or may not be, until I can track down the programme and watch it.'

'I think this sounds like another dead end,' Angus, 'and symptomatic of the problems which have dogged this investigation from the start,' Houghton said. 'I have to tell you, it's proving prohibitively expensive to run, what with overtime, drafting in uniformed officers from John Street, and the number of detectives you have working on the team.'

Henderson seethed, but said nothing. If he was being truthful to himself, this was the reason he didn't apply for Houghton's job. In his opinion, murder cases couldn't be reduced to pounds and pence; they involved real people experiencing serious grief, and criminals who realised how high the stakes were and used every trick in the book to avoid arrest.

On the other hand, perhaps the cost issue wasn't so much part of the job, but a feature of Houghton's management style. It was hard to progress up the police ladder, in fact, any public service ladder, without sound knowledge of where the cash came from and how it was spent. Henderson wasn't the world's best when it came to budgets, but he couldn't live with himself if he failed to catch a killer when, because of a budget overspend, he hadn't allocated enough detectives.

'The point is,' Houghton continued, 'I'm losing faith in your ability to deliver a result. I'm giving you a week, Angus. If you can't give me the name of this killer or killers, I'll replace you with someone who can.'

FORTY-FIVE

They met together outside the warehouse of Rema Foods at Shoreham Harbour. In the twenty-four hours since the pervert Raymond Lawson spat out the name of Danny Carlyle, they had been busy.

In addition to finding out where the man in question lived, they'd got themselves tooled up. Later, when they turned up at his house, Carlyle would know the reason why they were there. They'd spoken to him already, and he would do everything he could to try to escape.

Dominic Green kicked himself for not seeing through the pervert's well-rehearsed lies-act. He'd given them some cock-and-bull story about working at Gatwick on the night of Brighton Pride. Problem was, Carlyle didn't look like Green's idea of the South Coast Rapist. He looked too small and weedy, somehow.

If Green had to kill the scroat in his own house, he would do so. What he wanted to do was take him down to Shoreham for questioning. Armed with their new information, they would get a confession out of him. No way would Green then hand him over to the forces of law and order. Instead, they would beat him senseless, before putting him in a sack. They would then take him out to the harbour and load him on to the *Gypsy Queen*, a boat belonging to a friend. Somewhere out in the Channel, they would weigh him down with stones and chuck him over the side. He'd seen Morris truss up prisoners before and not even the great Houdini could escape from one of his sacks.

If somehow they'd made a mistake and the police then arrested someone else for the rapes, he wouldn't lose a wink of sleep over killing Carlyle, nor, he suspected, would anybody else. However, he would soon be joined in his watery grave, by the body of Raymond Lawson, the perv who'd given them Carlyle's name. Green couldn't abide anyone telling him porkies.

Green got out of the Range Rover and climbed into the car Jack was driving, an anonymous Nissan saloon.

'I've never seen this one before, Jack. When did you buy it?'

Jack snorted. 'No way. Nicked it from Brighton station car park. If we're going to smoke this bastard, Carlyle, no way are we leaving any evidence for the rozzers to find. After, I'll take it out to the woods at Poynings and torch it.'

'Good man.'

Christ, Green thought, was he losing his touch? First Carlyle gets away, and now the car. Back in the day, he would have instructed his lieutenants, John or Spike, to nick a car, not expecting them to think about doing it themselves. Morris, being the smart bastard he was, he'd been in Army intelligence, would have spotted his error and filed it away for future reference.

Green hadn't known these boys long. He'd hired them on the recommendation of a friend he'd met inside. He couldn't yet say their relationship was based on trust. With John and Spike, they had a bond and would look out for one another. With Jack and Morris, he hadn't reached that stage. Green still regarded them as mercenaries. They would do a job as long as they were being well paid, but he couldn't say with any level of confidence if they would take any risks on his behalf.

The car doors were closed and the guns and other equipment stored out of sight. They set off at a sedate pace, no sense in drawing attention to themselves. Three geezers in an old car in the early hours of the morning would be enough for some cops to pull them over and take a look.

'I can't believe we had the perv in the office,' Green said, 'tied to a chair, and we let the bastard walk off into the night.'

'Waddle off, more like,' Jack said. 'If I remember rightly, Mo booted him in the nuts.'

'That was just a taster. I would have cut them off if I thought he was the guy.'

'Thinking back,' Jack said, a first for him as he didn't often think about anything, 'he fooled me. He sounded well convincing when he talked about all that airport stuff.'

'Yeah,' Green said, 'even when you smacked him around a bit, Morris, he didn't change his story. He said he'd moved to Brighton to start a new life and was now working at Gatwick Airport as a baggage handler.'

'No matter,' Morris said, 'when we get him down to the warehouse tonight, he's gonna talk. I guarantee it, even if I have to pull out every nail in his hands and feet.'

'You have such a soft spot for torture.' Green laughed. 'I imagine you sit up at night thinking up new techniques and methods you can use to terrorise people.'

'When I was in Iraq,' Morris said, 'we, the smart British, were supposed to use psychological torture techniques. The Americans were the brash ones using the rough stuff, but like, when you're in a bit of a rush, it's about the only thing that works.'

'I see where you're coming from, mate. I've done the same myself. I usually don't have time for the psychological stuff. Jack, how are things going over at the lab?'

'The new batch we delivered last Friday has been cut and bagged. Kieran was out earlier tonight with his team selling.'

'Good to know. Tell him to come and see me when he's got a minute. I want to find out how the competition are reacting. Make sure you guys are there as well, so we can sketch out our response if Kieran's been getting some heat.'

All thoughts of losing his touch disappeared out of the window at hearing this piece of heartening news. He was back and doing what he was good at: building the infrastructure for a team of lads and lassies to make good money giving the public what they wanted. If this wasn't private enterprise in action, straight out of a Milton Friedman textbook, he didn't know what was.

They drove up Ditchling Road towards Hollingbury. It was half-past midnight, a time when most people would be in bed. Danny Carlyle needed to be up sharpish in the morning to start an early shift at the airport, clocking-on at six-thirty, and so this would include him.

The best time to nab a suspect, according to Morris, quoting from his army manual, was between the hours of three and four in the morning. By then, most people would have been in bed for four, maybe five hours, and most likely enjoying deep REM sleep. If this was interrupted, they would feel drowsy and disoriented for several minutes. Any earlier, and they wouldn't have yet made it into deep sleep, any later, and they would be closer to the waking-up point, both situations leaving them less dozy and potentially more troublesome.

In this part of Brighton, built on the slopes of the South Downs, everywhere was hilly. Using the incline, Morris turned the engine off and coasted the car into a space opposite and down the road a bit from Carlyle's house. It didn't do to alert any insomniacs as to the presence of a strange car in the neighbourhood after midnight.

Hollingdean Terrace appeared to be split into two parts. The lower section down the hill consisted of sizeable semi-detached houses, some with garages. The houses in the upper part, where they were, were in the main of white painted terraces, a style common in many parts of Brighton and Hove.

They sat without saying much, each man assessing and analysing the task ahead. Morris wound down the window to listen. The target house was unlit, the curtains upstairs drawn, suggesting the occupant had gone to bed. The neighbours weren't night owls either, with only a few lights illuminated, and some of those would be nightlights for kids, or security devices on a timer.

'Right, I've seen enough,' Green said. 'Let's get tooled up and grab the bastard.'

They had brought a mixture of guns and knives. The guns were to scare Carlyle, but if that didn't work, knives would be deployed. It wasn't clever to let off a firearm in the dead of night. For all they knew an off-duty copper could be living close by, and he or she would know in an instant what piece of kit had made that sound.

'Everybody clear on how we're gonna do this?'

'Yep,' Jack said. 'I'll head around the back and make sure he doesn't try to scarper. You guys go in the front.'

Green was about to grab the door handle when Morris said, 'Hold on a second there, boys. I think I hear a car coming this way.'

They watched as the lights of a car headed towards them. As it approached, Green could see it wasn't one, but two cars driving close together: a black Mondeo and a police patrol MPV.

'Fucking hell,' Green hissed, 'somebody's clocked us. All the weapons under the seat, now!'

'We're fucked in any case, boss,' Jack said. 'If they ANPR the reg, they'll see it's been nicked.'

'Guys, don't do anything rash. We'll sit tight and find out what they want. Although, now thinking about it, I don't see why they would send two cars to book us for a busted tail light.'

The two vehicles moved into spaces across the road and up the hill from where the Nissan was parked; a bad tactical error in Green's view. At the first sign of trouble, Jack would be out of the space and down at the bottom of the road before they got their big arses back into their cars. Jack was a former Formula Three driver and Green had every confidence in his ability to lose them, even in this crappy pile of cheap Japanese engineering.

'Hang about,' Green said, 'I don't think they're here for us.'

'They're making no attempt to cross the road,' Morris said, even though they were all watching. 'Fuck me, they're heading for Carlyle's house!'

They watched as one of the officers stepped forward with a door banger and started bashing Carlyle's door in.

'Bastards!' Green hissed. 'They've come to arrest the pervy fucker.'

'Result!' Jack said. 'It'll put the bastard out of circulation for years.'

'Will it hell, mate. If we'd got in first, I would have had the pleasure of planting my fist into that bastard's face. Later, and after a good kicking, we'd get him aboard the *Gypsy Queen* and roll the dirty pervert over the side, never to be seen again. This way, the cops will give him another ten years of bed and breakfast on the state. When he comes out, he won't be so old, he could start again.'

'You're right.'

'I've seen enough. Let's get the fuck out of here, Jack, before they clock us.'

FORTY-SIX

It had been a frustrating morning for Carol Walters. She had been left on-hold for ages by a company called Halo TV, the parent outfit of Real Crime TV. Nowhere on the web, or in any directories, could she find contact details for RCTV. She waited another twenty minutes while the not-very-bright-sounding Damien went off to check their archive. In part, it was her own fault, as she refused to leave her number. She wanted a response today, not by the end of next week.

In the end, it had all been for nought. Halo didn't have a copy of *Blood Lines* and referred her, as she expected, to Zama Video Productions. She felt as if she was going around in circles, another dead-end. She then went through the inventory of items taken from Stuart Livermore's house, but he didn't have a copy either.

In frustration, and to make her feel as though she was doing something useful, she grabbed her car keys and made her way out to the car park. The storm that had brought high winds and torrential rain to Sussex over the last few days had blown itself out, leaving the mid-morning weather cold, but calm. Ideal conditions for running, DI Henderson had told her, but this was another of a long list of New Year resolutions that hadn't made it past January.

She drove from Lewes to Brighton, the reverse of her morning commute. Unlike DI Henderson, who liked to listen to Radio 4, she found a pop station and turned the volume up high. When she arrived in Brighton, she headed towards her own neighbourhood, Queen's Park. She wasn't going home, and instead turned into East Drive.

The Livermore house was no longer a crime scene, but the police were still in possession of a key. By rights, it should have been returned to the owner, which they now knew to be Hannah Robbins. With her still lying in a coma in the Royal Sussex Hospital, this hadn't been possible.

Walters opened the door and walked inside. She picked up the mail and flicked through it. Some of it was the usual stuff she received herself, not surprising as she lived only a few streets away: Domino's vouchers, a circular from the council about refuse collections, a health screening offer from a private clinic. The rest of it was specific to Livermore: a letter from Harrogate International Festivals, and another which looked like a tax bill. It was often said, the only certainties in life were death and taxes. She could have added that the tax man still wanted his pound of flesh whether you were currently with us or now six feet under.

She placed the letters on the hall table and headed into the lounge. She walked towards the bookcase, the only area of the house known to have been of interest to the killer. If, and it was a big if, there was something incriminating in the *Blood Lines* programme, perhaps the killer had come here to steal

Livermore's copy. She shook her head at her stupid thinking. What was the point of taking Livermore's copy when the programme had been broadcast on television?

For sure, Real Crime TV was only a minor digital channel with probably no more than a few thousand viewers. Even still, there could be perhaps tens, or hundreds of copies out there, either copied to DVD, or sitting on viewers' Sky boxes. What would have been the point of the killer taking Livermore's copy? That said, the programme was aired so long ago, most people would probably have forgotten about it by now.

She skimmed her way through Livermore's large DVD collection. A few minutes later, she found a copy of *Dark Night,* the BBC and Netflix programme which she and Henderson had enjoyed, but she could find no trace of *Blood Lines.* She looked through other parts of the bookcase, the books, CDs, and papers, thinking one might have been secreted there, but without success.

Livermore owned a television and a DVD player, but there was no satellite box of any kind. She knew some parts of Brighton and Hove were conservation areas, and restricted the erection of exterior equipment such as satellite dishes, but she didn't know if this was the reason behind Livermore's decision not to have one.

Drawing a blank, her next stop would be Livermore's ex-wife, Ellen Jacobs. If she had a copy, it would be kept out of spite, to show her friends and have them agree what a bastard her ex-husband was.

If Ellen didn't have it, she would, with some reluctance, be forced to call on Stacy Allison.

According to the Family Liaison Officer who was working at the Allison residence, Stacy had gone to pieces since her husband's murder. For no obvious reason, she would start shaking and crying at various points in the day. If food was cooked and placed in front of her, only then would she bother to eat.

Walters admired the work of the FLOs. It was good training for any young constable. It taught them a lot about human behaviour, and stopped them becoming arrogant or acting blasé when faced with a serious crime, but she wouldn't want to do it.

Not finding what she wanted, she walked outside and closed the front door. She made a point of ensuring it was locked. If the house was subsequently targeted by burglars, she wouldn't want to be the one carrying the can for a moment of carelessness.

'Hello Detective Walters.'

She turned and saw Steph Wallace standing there, kit bag on her shoulder. Her youthful face looked flushed, as if she had run part of the way home.

'Hello Steph. You've got a good memory for names.' She walked down the path towards her.

'I have to in my business. I meet so many new people every day. I use little memory techniques based on facial features, but I won't tell you how I remembered you.'

'I'm not sure I want to know. Finished work for the day?'

'Yep. I often have three appointments in the afternoon between two and five, but the last two cancelled. There's some stomach bug going around Brighton.'

'Don't you work in the evenings as well? The gym I go to doesn't shut 'til ten.'

'Same for us, and some, would you believe, are open twenty-four hours?'

'Amazing, but you wouldn't catch me pumping weights at three in the morning, no matter how badly I'd slept. I suppose it's to catch shift workers at Gatwick, and people in places like ours who work shifts and odd hours.'

'I used to take clients nearly every evening, but Mark decided we should have at least one night in the week when I don't. Get a take-out and watch a movie, he said. He thinks we should be spending more time together.' She pulled a face to show her feelings about that idea. 'Me, I'd rather be working and earning money.'

In Stuart Livermore's will, the house had been left to Hannah Robbins, but he had also gifted a generous sum to Steph. Walters wondered if her easier working schedule had been influenced by her unexpected windfall. She doubted the news of their neighbour's generosity would have gone by without some serious questions being asked in the Wallace household. Nevertheless, no way would anyone in the murder team reveal to Steph's husband her true relationship with her neighbour.

'Well, it was good seeing you, Steph, but I must get back to work.'

'Can I ask, what were you doing at Stuart's place? I thought you guys had finished in there.'

'We are, but I was looking to see if he had a copy of *Blood Lines,* a programme Stuart made with Real Crime TV.'

'Is it important to the case?'

Walters shrugged. 'It could be, or it might be yet another false alarm. We've had so many in this case, but we have to chase down every lead we get.'

'I've got it.'

'Have you?'

'Yeah, I've got every programme Stuart ever made for television, his audiobooks and every one of his books.'

'Brilliant! Could I borrow a copy of *Blood Lines*?'

'I don't normally let anyone touch or borrow Stuart's stuff, but as you're trying to find out who killed him, I'd like to help where I can. C'mon inside. I'll make us a cup of coffee and dig it out.'

FORTY-SEVEN

Henderson drew the blinds and put his phone on silent. Tonight, there was something he needed to watch on television, and he didn't need any interruptions. However, the aroma emanating from his Dhansak curry was one distraction he would allow. This time it wasn't a dish he'd made from scratch or bought from his usual takeaway in St James's Street, but a Tesco meal for one with a side dish of chickpeas and a piece of naan bread.

In celebrity interviews they often asked the star, if they were on Death Row, what would be their last meal? If he was ever in this position, not likely as he wasn't a celebrity or a death-row prisoner, this would be his. It would also include a haggis and black pudding salad starter, and something stodgy, like a jam or syrup sponge with oodles of thick custard, for pudding,

Beer was the best drink he knew to accompany curry. Wine was overwhelmed by the spices, and whisky tasted too sharp. In any case, he wanted to keep a clear head while watching the programme. The whisky would come later when he wanted to mull over what he'd seen. Tonight's viewing wasn't going to be a relaxing or vegetative activity, but active. To assist, he had a pen and notebook by his side.

Blood Lines was the first time they had discovered a strong connection between Stuart Livermore and Ryan Allison, bar their literary work and friendship. Now, he felt in his bones, the clue to their murders lay buried somewhere in this programme.

He pressed 'play' and the DVD started. When the menu was displayed, he selected Episode Two, the one featuring Stuart Livermore. He tucked into his meal as the opening sequence rolled. If he was in any doubt about the format of the programme, the presenter, another author by the name of Derek Walsh, dispelled it. This was a series in which eight authors would talk about their work and discuss one of their books which had been inspired by a real crime.

No surprises there. Henderson had been wondering, from a programme maker's perspective, how they could make this format interesting to the general viewer. He could understand how book lovers would enjoy spending an hour watching their favourite authors talk about their work, and finding out how he or she concocted their stories. For the rest of the viewing public he wasn't so sure.

This thought disappeared when Stuart Livermore appeared on the screen. Henderson was momentarily taken aback. In his experience, he couldn't remember seeing a murder victim in any case he was involved in looking so alive and engaging, excluding those victims he had known prior to their murder, such as Ryan Allison. In fact, Livermore spoke so well, Henderson was beginning to change the view formed in his mind's eye of the man, collated from the descriptions supplied by his love-struck neighbour, jaundiced ex-wife and grief-stricken girlfriend.

Here was a well-dressed, eloquent, and fit looking man talking about the craft he loved, sitting in his study at the back of his house, tapping away on his laptop. The author profile covered less than half the programme and soon they got into the meat of the episode.

The plot of Livermore's third novel, *Black Rose,* was based on a series of rapes which took place in Edinburgh during the late nineteen nineties, culminating in the murder of one of the rapist's victims. She was found in Rose Street, a street parallel to the more famous Princes Street, the 'rose' in the book's title. Henderson's own recollection of the case, formed as a PC in neighbouring Glasgow, was coming back to him as the story unfolded. They called the perpetrator the Napier Rapist, because the majority of his victims were attacked in an area to the south west of the city, centred around Napier University.

Not only did the programme discuss the details of the investigation and how Livermore used some key elements of the case in his book, the author and presenter were seen walking the streets around Edinburgh. There, they identified important locations, focusing, in the main, on the Rose Street murder.

Using interviews with a journalist who covered the case at the time, a forensic scientist at the Scottish Police Authority, and a clinical psychologist at the University of Edinburgh, they pieced together the murder. Then, it focussed on how the Edinburgh Police tracked down the killer. Next, they presented a psychological profile of the perpetrator - a man called Danny Carlyle.

He typified the background of many serious criminals. His father was an alcoholic and his mother a drug addict. Shop lifting brought him into focus with the law and it was only a matter of time before he committed something more serious and became incarcerated in an approved school. Soon, he graduated from there to prison. During one of his periods of freedom, he embarked on the six-month rape and murder spree, as portrayed in *Blood Lines*.

Henderson paused the DVD when Carlyle's picture appeared on the screen, the police mugshot he reckoned. Carlyle had a narrow face with prominent cheekbones, piercing green eyes and lank, straight fair hair down to his shoulders. Not a handsome man by any standard, and it seemed to the DI he had adapted his modus operandi to take account of this. Not able to appeal to women in face-to-face encounters with his charming features or magnetic personality, he attacked all his victims from behind. He did this in badly-lit, quiet streets, of which Edinburgh had more than its fair share.

When the credits rolled, Henderson turned the DVD back to the main menu then cleared away the debris of his meal. Far from it being a boring look at Stuart Livermore's writing, it was an absorbing and fast-moving programme with enough content to satisfy book lovers and real crime fans alike.

He had written down two things in his notebook. One was the name, Danny Carlyle. If he was still languishing in Saughton prison, the place he had been sent after sentencing, the idea taking form in Henderson's head would fall flat on its face at the first hurdle. His second note concerned the knife used on his victims. The programme went into some detail about this, and when the murder weapon was shown, Henderson paused the DVD. It was black handled with a long, narrow, pointed blade, no more than about a centimetre wide. He could see it was similar to the knife used on Stuart Livermore. So far, so good.

The knife would have ended up in the hands of the Edinburgh Police, and most likely would have been destroyed after Carlyle was convicted. However, while many criminals didn't covet a particular weapon, and would use whatever came to hand at the time, many favoured a particular type.

Gunmen who liked using Glocks would stick to this type of firearm. They knew about its reliability in difficult situations, and how to clean and maintain it. A similar weapon was made by Sig Sauer, and if the Glock wasn't available, they would use the Sig. In most respects, it would behave like the Glock.

A knifeman like Carlyle would favour small, narrow blades. He wasn't a big man, and knives like this were easy for him to conceal. They could also be described as sneaky, a word he had previously used to describe Livermore's attacker. Often, the victim wouldn't realise they had been stabbed until they felt the blood.

Henderson poured himself a glass of whisky and returned to the lounge. He selected Episode Seven on the DVD, the one featuring Ryan Allison, and sat back, cradling his glass.

He didn't feel the same sensation when the author came on the screen, as he had talked to him prior to the murder. Nevertheless, it was still interesting to see him in his element, writing and researching.

The Allison book featured in the DVD, *Lost Girls*, was based on the crimes of a Birmingham man, Greg Lewis, known as the Edgbaston Slasher. Although not a soldier, he had been turned down by the army after OCD was diagnosed, he behaved like one. He was frequently seen dressed in military fatigues, he built camps in the woods where he cooked and laid animal traps, and embarked on long hikes carrying a heavy backpack. Of the two killers, it was difficult to say which, Carlyle or Lewis, was the more unhinged.

Lewis's early life ticked all the crime psychologist's boxes. He came from a broken home, his father disappeared when he was two and his mother was a regular drug user. He spent a large part of his formative years in foster care and approved school. He started his criminal life at the age of thirteen as a terrible burglar, embarking on a series of burglaries and being caught every time. At eighteen, he enrolled in the Crime University, otherwise known as HM Prison Service. There, he learned to correct the basic mistakes he'd been making.

For most of his twenties and early thirties, he fell off the police radar, but still householders in the Edgbaston area of Birmingham where he lived, experienced high burglary rates. One night in summer, the sight of a naked woman asleep in a house he had entered became too much of a temptation. He raped her. When he made to leave, she began to scream, and Lewis slit her throat with the big hunting knife he carried. Henderson noted this.

The big knife came out on one further occasion but this time the woman miraculously survived. The sickening sight of Ryan Allison lying lifeless in Paston Place came back into Henderson's head with HD clarity.

When the credits rolled, he felt exhausted. It had been a difficult and tiring day, and then he had concentrated hard on two one-hour programmes, not too different from a one-to-one meeting with the chief constable. He was elated though, because for once in this case, he could see a clear motive.

Carlyle and Lewis were perhaps out of jail, using new identities and trying to start life afresh. Whether this meant legitimate work, or something illegal, it didn't matter. Then, *Blood Lines* comes along, throwing a fresh spotlight on their crimes. A stark reminder to everyone about what they'd done, and the kind of people they were.

For them to kill Livermore and Allison would achieve what? To exact revenge for writing a book about them, or maybe they had demanded money, a payment for being exploited, and both authors refused? It perhaps sounded a weak excuse for them to commit murder to a normal person, but Danny Carlyle and Greg Lewis were not normal people. In jail, if they knew one another, this was the sort of discussion that would keep them going through many dark days.

He was tempted to head into work now, access the PNC - Police National Computer - and find out the whereabouts of Carlyle and Lewis. If only one of them was still in prison, his nascent theory would be blown out of the water. However, he would be no use to anyone either if he arrived at the office in the morning looking like a half-shut knife. Instead, he went to bed.

FORTY-EIGHT

Henderson strode over to the staff restaurant for breakfast. He had called Walters first thing. She'd been thinking the same as he had when watching *Blood Lines* the previous night. She was convinced the 'outing' of the two murderers was the link between Livermore and Allison they had been looking for.

He knew at this stage it was only a theory, so they needed to temper the enthusiasm, but they would give it a good shake and see what fell out. It could all come to a crashing halt if one of the showstoppers at this stage of the investigation made an appearance: either the deaths of Carlyle or Lewis, or one, or both of them, were still in prison.

Walters had raised an important point which he was thinking about as he drove to work. Were Livermore and Allison the only targets, or did it mean the other six authors who also appeared in the *Blood Lines* programme were now in the firing line? He could imagine two criminals cooking up such a plan, but for four, five, or six criminals to do the same, was stretching the bounds of probability. Nevertheless, it would be negligent not to investigate.

They would first establish the whereabouts of Carlyle and Lewis, then expand the PNC search to include all the criminals identified in *Blood Lines*. If any had been released from prison, they would warn the author of the perceived threat. With those criminals still in prison, they would counsel the author to take sensible precautions around the date of their impending release.

He picked up his tray of scrambled eggs and toast, with a cup of tea on the side, and searched the sea of faces in the staff restaurant for DI Hobbs. He found him sitting at the window tucking into a typical English cooked breakfast: sausage, bacon, tomato, baked beans, and fried bread.

'Morning Gerry. I see the health kick didn't last long.'

'Oh, hi Angus, good to see you. Grab a pew.'

Henderson took a seat and removed the items from his tray before moving it to one side.

'I stuck with it for about two months, but when someone in the team brought in bacon rolls, I realised what I was missing.'

'They say it's the one thing veggies miss.'

'There you go, first-hand proof.'

'I think I would miss sausage. Not the link variety, as everywhere you go it seems to come in different flavours, but a square sausage. The kind they serve in Glasgow instead of a bacon buttie.'

'I like them too. The next time you're up there in the snowy north, bring us some back.'

'No problem.'

'I mean, I haven't ditched the healthy eating thing for good. I'll try to maintain it when I've got control over what's on my plate. If I do fall off the wagon, which happens from time to time, I won't beat myself up about it.'

'It sounds a reasonable compromise. How are things in drug enforcement? Are you settling back into working life after your accident?'

'It's like I've never been away. After confirming to the boss that I was feeling fine with no serious after effects, it was, 'here, take this anti-stab vest, let's go kick a few doors in.''

'Normal service is resumed.'

'I would like to think so, but even in the time I've been away, things have changed out there. Some dealers low down in the chain have been beaten up, and others taken to hospital with stab wounds. As usual, no one's talking.'

'What's the rumours? A new player moving in? A turf war between rival gangs?'

'We're not sure. Think it could be a bit of both.'

Henderson had a thought. 'What if I told you Dominic Green might be back in the game? I'm sure he's a name you haven't forgotten from your time in Serious Crimes?'

'Christ no, how could I? He's out?'

'About six months back. He collared me when I was out running.'

'What did he want with you? To tell you to take it easy with him this time around?'

Henderson laughed. 'No, he said he was concerned about the South Coast Rapist and asking why we haven't caught him.'

'That's Jim Hegarty's case.'

'I know.'

'Hang on,' Hobbs said, and paused eating as if something was bothering him. 'Yeah, I remember now. They pulled someone in for it. Brought him into John Street, late on Wednesday night.'

'Thank goodness for that. It should get Green off my back. He was looking for this guy too.'

'What's his interest?'

'A friend of his daughter was raped by this guy, apparently, and his daughter is upset. You know how he operates, any excuse to flex his muscles.'

'Good job we grabbed him before Green did. Otherwise, the culprit would disappear, and later turn up inside a skip or as part of the foundations of a new office block.'

'When he stopped me, he didn't look his old self. He looked a bit older and more haggard, but the confidence was still there. I think it won't be long before he's trying to muscle his way back in. You should keep an eye on the situation.'

'I'll mention it to the lads, don't worry. Confidence and money are two things Green was never short of. Plus, it's the business he knows best, so it wouldn't surprise me to see him up to his old tricks again. Thanks for the heads-up, Angus. I've now got something to tell my boss about those mysterious hospital admissions.'

After breakfast, Henderson headed back to his building, and up the stairs into the Detectives' Room. He walked towards DS Walters.

'Any joy with the PNC searches?' he asked her.

'Joy is putting it a bit strong.'

'Okay. Let's hear it.'

'There are eight criminals mentioned in the programme. Three are still in prison and one is dead. Other than our two suspects, this leaves another two unaccounted for.'

'Okay. What the story on our two suspects?'

'The programme we were watching about Stuart Livermore, featured Danny Carlyle, otherwise known as the Napier Rapist. He also calls himself Steve Sutton. He now lives in a house in Hollingbury.'

'He lives here? In Brighton?'

She nodded. 'Yep, he does.'

'Good God. Such an evil man. Why the hell is he living around here?'

'Who knows? Starting a new life, or resuming an old one?'

Henderson stood, thinking. 'I'll put a team together and we can head over to Hollingbury tonight and pick him up.'

'Not so fast, gov. He was arrested by detectives from John Street the night before last. They think he's the South Coast Rapist.'

'What, Carlyle?'

'If you don't believe me, by lunchtime, you can read about it yourself in *The Argus*.'

Henderson slumped back into the seat, his previous enthusiasm deflated. 'This is too much to take in. For once in this case, we've got ourselves a decent suspect for the murder of Livermore, and in the next breath you tell me he's been arrested for something else. Who made the arrest? Don't tell me, as Gerry mentioned something about it at breakfast. Was it Mr Personality himself, Jim Hegarty?'

'Got it in one, and now everything seems to have gone to his head. He's swanning around John Street like a cat with two tails. He's insufferable, according to my source.'

'He was insufferable before, what's new?'

'I told you I'd got a partial result.'

'Okay.'

'Danny Carlyle was the good bit.'

'Don't tell me, Greg Lewis is dead or he's still in prison?'

'No, he's not dead and he's not in prison.'

Henderson punched his fist into his other palm. 'Excellent! So, where is he?'

'I can't find him.'

'What do you mean you can't find him?'

'He's dropped off the radar. There's no sign of him in any of our systems.'

'Anyone in receipt of a life sentence and released from prison early does so under license. They are required to report to a probation officer and inform them where they're living.'

'I know, I know, but don't say this too loud, but with all the cuts to council budgets and the privatisation of the Probation Service, they haven't got the manpower to keep tabs on all the lifers on their books. They lost track of him about three months back.'

'Three months? Jesus!' Henderson paused for a moment, thinking. 'Hang on, didn't they say in *Blood Lines* he was a wannabe soldier, a guy who likes to camp out in the woods?'

'Yep. He builds camps and traps animals, a criminal version of Bear Grylls.'

'Who?'

'The outdoor guy from television.'

'This could be why we're having difficulty finding him; maybe he's hiding out in the woods.'

'Makes sense.'

'Try to get hold of someone from Probation Services, they must know something about him that could help us. Find out his last known address, if he's changed his name, any living relatives. Also, see if he and Carlyle shared a prison cell, or if not, if they knew one another when they were inside. At the very least, it should add another piece to this puzzle.'

'Will do.'

'Even if he is out in the sticks camping, it's near impossible to slip off the grid entirely. He'll need cash now and again, so he'll be forced to use an ATM, he might pay for groceries in a shop with a credit card, or pick up his phone and call his dear old mum. If he does any of those things, we should be able to find him.'

'I agree. I'll get Phil working on the traces once I've established if he's still using his real name.'

'There's a chance he's maybe still around here. If our scenario is right, he must have spent a couple weeks in the Brighton area tracking Ryan Allison's movements, before moving in for the kill. It looks likes Carlyle did, if he lives in Hollingbury.'

'Allegedly killing him.'

'You're right, I mustn't get carried away, even though the first two roadblocks have been cleared.'

'Yeah, it's a good theory, but speculation nonetheless. As you said, we need to keep an open mind.'

'Well, we should know if the theory's good or not once we get Carlyle into one of our interview rooms.'

'How are you going to do that? I don't imagine Hegarty will give him up without a fight.'

'You know me, Carol. I can be very persuasive.'

FORTY-NINE

Brighton's main police station in John Street rocketed to fame in October 1984. This was when many of the victims of the Brighton Bomb, an attempt by the IRA to kill Prime Minister Margaret Thatcher and members of her Cabinet, were taken. Photographs of the injured, many draped in blankets as they made their way into the building, were shown all around the world. In contrast to the place where Henderson worked, Malling House, a Grade II 17th century manor house, John Street was a bland 1960s concrete and glass affair, and often mistaken for the magistrates' court next door.

Henderson pulled out his pass and walked through security. He suspected he would have experienced a tougher grilling if they'd realised his true purpose in being there. A big arrest like the South Coast Rapist would keep tongues wagging in the building for weeks to come. For anyone involved in the case, it would result in any number of back-slaps and free drinks in the pub afterwards.

He made his way upstairs to the Detectives' Room. There, he found DI Hegarty holding court, regaling junior officers with his tale of late-night heroism. In some cases, arresting a difficult suspect could be regarded as an act of heroism, in particular when the target was prepared, armed and willing to take on the police. This reaction often surprised inexperienced officers who went in there gung-ho, so keen were they to make an arrest, ignoring the warnings highlighted at the Risk Assessment stage. With others, the most aggro an officer would experience would be the gobby wife or furious mother, first hurling insults, then any unattached objects they could find, at the departing arrest party.

In DI Hegarty's case, they now knew Danny Carlyle was a man who worked shifts at Gatwick and needed all the beauty sleep he could get. When the door was crashed, Carlyle would have found it hard at first to try to understand why heavily-clad men were standing in his bedroom, perhaps believing it was part of a bad dream. In the end, he came without a whimper, a smart move given the odds against him.

Henderson caught Hegarty's eye and he looked over.

'Can I have a word with you, Jim?'

'Take a seat in my office, Angus, I'll be there in a minute or two.'

Henderson had no problem complying, he'd heard enough about Hegarty's courageous action under fire. Hegarty's office looked to be about the size of his own, but Henderson's had a window. He liked having a window. It wasn't to stare out and daydream, he could do as much as he wanted at home with a glass of the good stuff. He used it mainly to determine the state of the weather before venturing outside. Their work often involved dashing out at short notice. If a quick glance suggested he should bring a jacket, umbrella, or hat, it was better than spending several hours being soaked to the skin, or freezing to death.

The other thing he noted about Hegarty's office was how untidy it looked. This wasn't his inner Marie Kondo speaking, the place was a complete tip. He wondered how Hegarty ever found anything. This confirmed everything Henderson knew about the man: he flew by the seat of his pants and delegated wherever he could. In fact, he had no need to look for anything, his junior officers would find it for him.

A few minutes later Jim Hegarty breezed in, exuding with the air and confidence of a man floating on cloud nine. He had no inkling that his visitor was carrying a giant pin and soon he would burst his bubble.

'I heard about your capture of the South Coast Rapist, Jim, well done.'

'I appreciate it coming from you, Angus, but it wasn't only me. Everyone in the team contributed.'

'He came without a fight I hear?'

He hesitated, perhaps wondering whether he should try to embellish the story. 'He didn't have much choice once we were in his bedroom, but I put it down to good timing. When we first heard he lived in the Brighton area, some of my officers wanted to arrest him right away, but I said no. We should wait for nightfall. Take him when he would be in bed.'

'A good call.'

'Thank you.'

'What evidence do you have that makes you think Carlyle's the one?'

'We interviewed everyone on the Sex Offender's Register in the area, those matching the age and build of the suspect, at any rate. Even when we talked to Carlyle at first and let him go, he sort of stood out from the rest.'

'In what way?'

'He was one of a few who had convictions for multiple rapes, and murder, so we started to give his alibi a good shakedown. When we questioned him about an attempted rape, he told us he'd spent the evening watching a football match and drinking in a local bar with his mates. If you remember, Angus, about three weeks back there was an attempted rape, close to Hollingbury Bowling Club.'

'I do remember, the same case you collared me about.'

'C'mon Angus, I was only doing it as a joke. Now, as I was saying, we interviewed his mates, and tried to break their stories, but they didn't budge an inch. The victim of the attempted rape had taken a bus home, and she was sure her attacker had been on the same bus, and not standing at the bus-stop or walking along Ditchling Road. That bus came from the centre of town.'

'I think I can see where you're going with this.'

'We hawked Carlyle's picture around a number of bars in the centre of town. We got a match at a sports bar in the Lanes and, when we reviewed their CCTV for the night in question, bingo! There was Carlyle in the bar until about ten-fifteen, and later, on the same bus as our victim.'

'So, you've rubbished his alibi, what evidence do you have that he did the rapes?'

Hegarty squirmed in the chair, searching for comfort. It was obvious this part of the story didn't hang together as well as the piece before. 'We have a forensic team giving his house the full treatment as we speak. So far, they've discovered a knife, and clothes in a box matching the ones he was wearing on the night of two rapes, incidents where we managed to obtain a reasonable description of the attacker. They've been sent for testing.'

'Good. Anything else?'

'We managed to extract a sperm sample from an earlier victim which we expect will match with his DNA. They tell me with a fair wind it should be completed before the end of the weekend. So, don't worry, Angus,' he said clapping his hands together, a smug expression on his face, 'Carlyle's not going anywhere for a long time to come.'

'Congratulations, Jim, you've done a great job. The women of Brighton can feel a lot safer this evening thanks to you. I mean it, this guy was a real danger to women, not only for the rapes, but in Edinburgh he murdered one of his victims.'

'I know, and it's a point I need to make the next time I speak to the press,' he said noting it down. 'What's your interest in the case, Angus, or,' he said with a smirk on his face, 'are you pleased at last to be off the hook?'

'Don't start all that bloody nonsense again.'

'Sorry.'

'Next thing you'll be telling everyone he's one of my relatives.'

'No, no, rest assured that won't happen.'

'It better not. I'm here, Jim, because I want to take Danny Carlyle over to Lewes for questioning about a murder.'

'What! You can't do that. I haven't concluded my investigation yet.'

'You've had him since Wednesday night and all day yesterday. You said it yourself, you're still waiting for the results of DNA testing.'

'He's...he's not saying much. I need more time to break him down.'

'He hasn't played ball, laid out all his crimes on the table for you to see?'

'No, nothing of the sort. I remember him from before, he's a good actor, but I'm confident forensics will prove his guilt.'

'Which you haven't got yet. It means you won't mind losing him for a few hours.'

'A few hours? Don't make me laugh. If he gets into the claws of Serious Crimes, he'll never come out. I can't allow it.'

'Jim, it's not your prerogative to say if you'll allow it or not. This murder takes precedence. In any case, by the time we finish questioning him, you'll have your forensics back and you can throw the book at him.'

'Yes, but he'll be your prisoner. Everything will need to be done on your terms. I'm not happy, I'm going to escalate this.'

Hegarty was being obstreperous because he wouldn't be able to swan around John Street like a king surveying his latest conquests when he didn't have a prisoner languishing in his dungeons. It wasn't so bad, he still could make hay. It was his team that had captured the South Coast Rapist, and he was the person the press wanted to interview and photograph. However, it would perhaps feel like a hollow claim to fame. A king without a crown, or even a castle.

'I'm sorry I was a bit blunt the time I accosted you outside the staff restaurant. It didn't come out the way I intended.'

Henderson stood. 'You think I'm still sore about that?'

'Might be.'

'Don't be daft. I'm dealing with two murders and maybe another one or two to come. My personal feelings don't come into it.'

FIFTY

'Did Hegarty give Carlyle up without a fuss? I can't believe he would,' Walters asked as they made their way downstairs.

'To be fair to Hegarty, between Carlyle's arrest and us finding out about *Blood Lines*, he didn't have much time to question him, no more than a day. If Carlyle had been in custody for four or five days, we could have pulled him out of remand at Lewes nick and no one would bother. To do it within days of him arresting Carlyle, especially with a gaggle of journalists still hanging around the door at John Street, knocked a fair bit of wind out of his sails.'

'It couldn't happen to a nicer man. I bet you didn't lose any sleep over it.'

'Not for a minute. Any word on Lewis?'

'The Probation Service seems to have lost track of him, but the news isn't all bad.'

'How do you mean?'

'As far as they know, he still uses his real name.'

'Does he?'

They walked outside of the building and headed towards the Custody Suite.

'When his probation officer at the time suggested a change of name would be a good way for him to restart his life after prison and move on, he rejected the idea. He loved his mother, he said, and couldn't disrespect her memory by using a different name.'

'My my. Another evil villain who loves his mum. I should look up my old psychology books, the condition must have a name. Is Phil still on the case trying to trace a phone call or a credit card transaction?'

'Yeah, him and three others. We're pulling out all the stops.'

'Good.'

They passed through secure double doors and headed into Interview Room 1.

Danny Carlyle was seated beside his brief, a man Henderson had come across many times before, Jonathan Giles. Henderson didn't really like him, but respected his views. He was tipped for higher things in the legal profession. His commitment to ensuring justice was served and the law observed, knew few bounds.

They made their introductions and Walters fired up the recording equipment.

Carlyle didn't much resemble the emaciated figure in the mugshot the DI had seen while watching the *Blood Lines* DVD, and used by television and newspapers at the time. In fact, if his hair had been cleaner and cut in a more modern style, he might look, perhaps not handsome, but almost presentable.

'Danny, we're part of the team investigating the murders of two local authors, Stuart Livermore and Ryan Allison. Have you heard of them?'

'Tragic, it was. I read about it in *The Argus*. I could hardly miss it. The story was in every bloody paper, even the free ones at the airport.'

'I see from my notes you're from Edinburgh. To me, you sound more like a Glasgow man.'

'I spent my formative years in the company of many Glasgow boys in the approved school I was sent to. At such an early age, you pick up accents easy as pie.'

'You've got a couple of cuts and bruises on your face which look to me a few days old. I hope Mr Giles here isn't going to put in a claim for bad handling by Sussex Police. You haven't been in our custody that long.'

Carlyle's hand moved to his cheek where a large bruise had formed. 'Nah, that was a fight in a bar. Occupational hazard when you're an ardent Man U supporter in a town full of Seagulls fans.'

'I'm sure. I said before we're part of the team investigating the death of Stuart Livermore and Ryan Allison. Did you know Stuart?'

'Fucking hell! Do I look like the sort of guy who reads books, or moves in literary circles? Do I hell. I said before, I've never heard of him, not until the story appeared in *The Argus*.'

There it was, the first lie of the day. Carlyle was a good actor, but Henderson could see the deceit in his eyes.

'That isn't strictly true, is it, Danny?'

'What do you mean?'

'I think you had a beef with Stuart Livermore,' Henderson said, raising his voice. 'He made a television programme called *Blood Lines* highlighting your crimes and you hated him for it.' He leaned closer and pointed at Carlyle. 'Didn't you?'

'Detective Henderson,' Giles said, 'you're trying to intimidate my–'

'Course I fucking did!' Carlyle shouted 'How would you like all your dirty washing hung out in public for everyone to see?'

'And what dirty washing it is.'

'Go fuck yourself.'

'How did you hear about *Blood Lines*? It was first broadcast five years ago and repeated about three years later. You were inside all this time.'

'Another inmate told me.'

'And who might this person be?'

'Some guy. I don't remember.'

'Maybe I can refresh your memory. It was Greg Lewis, wasn't it?'

Carlyle looked at his brief for guidance.

'You are trying to put words in my client's mouth, Inspector. What evidence do you have?'

'Mr Giles, we know Mr Carlyle and Greg Lewis shared a cell together. C'mon Danny, everybody says you two were big pals in prison.' He almost said 'thick as thieves' but stopped himself.

He shrugged as if to say, what harm could it do? 'Yeah, okay, Greg told me. He found out about it from a visitor.'

'A relative?'

'No, a prison visitor. There are lonely, damaged women out there who write to dangerous criminals, if you can believe it. We've had a couple of weddings out of it.'

'So, Greg told you about the programme's content, but I don't suppose you could watch it. They don't show such things in prison, or do they now give you your own television and DVD player?'

Carlyle laughed, showing pointed, yellow teeth. 'Do they fuck. If they did, no way would they ever let us see a programme like that. No chance. It would have caused a riot.'

'Why, because they show people like you for what you are?'

'No,' he said, his face red and angry, 'because they drag up the dirt from the past and don't let us forget it. How can we move on with all this shit hanging over our heads?'

Henderson would feel a little sympathy if this was true. The UK had one of the highest rates of recidivism in Europe, and more was needed to be done to stop former prisoners re-offending. In Carlyle's case, though, it didn't look as though he was trying to go straight, if Hegarty could prove he was the South Coast Rapist.

'I take it you've watched the programme since you came out?'

'Yep.'

'What did you think?'

'I think I've been exploited. Livermore used my story to make shedloads of dosh. It's not right.'

Henderson smiled to himself; the right buttons were being pushed. Carlyle the actor could forget about trying to secure a part in a West End play. The moment he became riled, the façade fell away like a mask.

'I don't see how you can say you're being exploited,' Walters said. 'The things you did in Edinburgh are out there in the public domain. It's in newspaper archives, and on the web, if anyone can be bothered to look.'

'You don't get it, do you?' When we're inside the nick, we get forgotten about. When they finally let us out, there's no gang of journos and photographers hanging about outside, or any hoo-ha in the papers. They don't even tell the victims' families, if you can believe it. So, we can get on with our lives the way we want. See?'

'So, what happened?' Henderson asked. 'You came out of prison and people started to recognise you?'

'Course they did. Thanks to that fucking programme, I've had people pointing at me in the street and saying, to their kids, 'It's him. Keep away from him, he kills people."

'Did it make you angry?'

His face reddened. 'Of course it fucking did,' he hollered.

'Who did you blame for it?'

Carlyle banged the flat of his hands on the table. 'Stuart Livermore, that's who, for making that programme and putting my fizzer on everybody's television screen.'

'Did you and Greg, in all those boring nights with nothing to do, concoct a little plan to do something about it?'

'Nah, way too much hassle.'

Carlyle had gone from hurricane livid to becalmed in an empty sea in the space of a few seconds. If this was some kind of mental aberration, nothing about it appeared in his psychological assessment.

'You did, Danny. You and Greg hatched a plan for you to kill Livermore, and for Lewis to kill Allison. In time, providing the two of you got away with it, people would forget about the pair of you for good. Wasn't this your plan?'

'I object to this suggestive line of questioning, Detective Inspector,' Carlyle's brief said. 'Where is the evidence?'

Carlyle was shaking his head, but saying nothing.

'Yes, you did, Danny. You went into Stuart Livermore's house in Brighton and waited for him to come home. When he did, you stabbed him and rummaged through his bookcase until you found his copy of *Blood Lines*. Am I right?'

'You've got it all wrong, Henderson,' Carlyle spat, 'and so has that fucking idiot over at John Street. No way did I kill Livermore and no way am I the South Coast Rapist.' He leaned over table, a contemptuous look on his face. 'Let me go now, and I'll say nothing more about it.'

FIFTY-ONE

Henderson and Walters left the interview room and closed the door. They were met outside by Sean Houghton. He and several members of the murder team had been watching proceedings in the Viewing Gallery through the two-way mirror. Houghton took Henderson to one side and waited for the other officers to walk past.

'He's a tough nut to crack, that one,' Houghton said. 'He's a good actor, but a couple of times the mask fell and you had him on the ropes. What's the plan now?'

'Hegarty has had a forensics team over at Carlyle's house since early Thursday morning. If there was something worth finding, they would have spotted it by now. I'll give them a call and see if they've got anything I can use.'

'The problem for us is, even if the knife they found at his house is the murder weapon, it won't be back from DNA testing for a few more days. By then, we'll have John Street petitioning everybody they can to have Carlyle back in their custody.'

'I know, but we need to have something concrete to throw at Carlyle now. Otherwise, he'll just move back into acting mode and bat back any accusations I make until the cows come home.'

'Let's walk back to the office,' Houghton said.

They walked along the corridor, pushed through a succession of double doors and out of the building.

'You're convinced about their motive: the appearance of Carlyle and Lewis in this *Blood Lines* programme?'

'It's the only thing connecting Livermore and Allison. You heard the vehemence of Carlyle. He hated Livermore for effectively outing him.'

'I'm not so convinced. I'm keeping an open mind.'

Oh, don't you start, Henderson was tempted to say. Instead, he said, 'You saw the way he became angry and raised his voice whenever the subject was mentioned. It's definitely a sore point.'

'I can't argue with you there, he's an aggressive son of a bitch, but was it enough for him to kill Livermore?'

'This isn't the time for faint hearts, Sean. We've got Carlyle where we want him. All we need now is one thing to place him inside Livermore's house, then we'll have him.'

'I seem to remember having the same conversation about Steve Mitchell.'

They climbed the stairs in their building to the first floor; the turn-off to Henderson's office, Houghton's on the floor above.

'I hope you're right about this, Angus, for all our sakes. See you later.'

Henderson walked past his office and into the Detectives' Room. He ignored all the expectant faces, keen to know if their hard work had at last achieved a result, and whether they could now move from investigating a murder to preparing a court case. Instead, he went over to the little kitchen where the coffee machine was situated. Only when he had a decent cup of coffee in his hand, would he make the call to the forensics team.

As usual, the folks who didn't appreciate the appeal of a decent cup of coffee and preferred to spoon Nescafé out of a catering-sized tin, had left granules all over the worktop. He created a clean space with a cloth and removed his distinctive blue Brighton and Hove Albion mug from the cupboard. They had all been warned never to use it, but he checked, just in case.

He liked this time, standing in here making a mug of coffee, and hated being disturbed. With a problem to solve and a simple task to perform, it often engaged a part of his brain that seemed more creative than normal. He filled the holder in the coffee machine with a scoop from the pack of coffee beans and locked it into the machine. He put his mug underneath the spout, added some milk, and pressed the 'Start' button.

The grinding of the beans, the hiss of pressurised water being passed through them, and finally, the dribbling of golden liquid as it splashed into his cup, sent him to another place. On and on it poured, while Henderson turned over in his mind something that had been said, was it by him or Carlyle, he wasn't sure, in the interview. What was it? It was on the tip of his tongue, but could he grasp it? Suddenly, it came to him.

He scrambled out of the kitchen, leaving his mug under the spout of the machine, and raced back to his office. He picked up the phone and called the Forensic Team office. His enthusiasm was tempered somewhat when the person who answered left him on hold while waiting for the team leader of the Carlyle house investigation, Charlie Dean, to finish what he was doing.

Henderson tapped his pen on the desk, his irritation at being hindered getting the better of him. He stopped when he heard the sound of someone lifting the receiver.

'Detective Inspector Henderson, good day to you, sir. What can I do you for?'

'Charlie, I've been informed you're the man in charge of the search of Danny Carlyle's house in Hollingbury.'

'Your information is correct. We completed it about two hours ago, record time for us. It's a rental and Carlyle didn't seem to own much stuff to mess it up, although what he did have was a shambles.'

'Could you do me a very big favour?'

Despite sounding calm, he was a sea of emotions underneath. A refusal, or if things weren't as he suspected, would mean his plan to nail Carlyle would fail before it had left the starting blocks.

'Why are you interested in the South Coast Rapist? A stupid bloody moniker, if you ask me. The Brighton Bonker, or Shoreham Shagger would have gained more headlines, I'm sure. It isn't your case and, knowing DI Hegarty as I do, he doesn't like outsiders poking their noses in.'

Henderson could tell Dean was just trying to wind him up, add a little interest to a dull day. He explained to him the interview he was conducting with Danny Carlyle and his suspicions about him being the killer of Stuart Livermore. He then told Dean what he wanted.

'So, if it's there, you just want me to dust it for prints, nothing more?'

'Yes.'

'Seeing it's you, and my wife is a fan of Livermore's books, I'll call you back in ten minutes.'

**

Henderson and Walters were back in the interview room. Danny Carlyle and his brief facing them once again. In the break, Carlyle's cockiness had returned. If they allowed suspects to smoke and drink, Henderson was sure he would now be sitting back with a cigarette in one hand and a glass of brandy in the other.

'Back so soon, Inspector?' Carlyle said. 'If we go on meeting like this, people will talk.'

'Yes, we're back Mr Carlyle, but this time I don't think you're going to like what we've brought with us.'

'What's all this about, Detective Inspector?' his brief asked. 'You never said anything to me about new evidence.'

'I haven't mentioned it before, Mr Giles, as I've only just found out. So, if you don't mind, you'll need to bear with me.'

'I'll allow it for now, but if this is some trick to implicate my client, Detective Inspector, I warn you, I will stop this interview.'

'Point noted, Mr Giles. Now, if we can make a start. Danny, you told me when we spoke earlier, you'd never heard of Stuart Livermore until you'd read about his death in *The Argus*.'

'Aye, I did.'

'This isn't strictly true, is it?'

'How many times? I didn't know the man from Adam.'

'Later on, you said you'd heard about the *Blood Lines* programme while you were inside, and that you'd watched it when you came out of prison.'

'Aye, so what?'

'The episode on *Blood Lines* featuring your case, is number two. It starred Stuart Livermore. How could you miss him? I've watched it, and he appears in the first twenty, twenty-five minutes of the one-hour programme. He's there again at the end.'

'Oh, aye, you're right, so he is. It must have slipped my mind.'

'How convenient.'

'No need to be so flippant, Inspector.'

'Something else seems to have slipped your mind, Danny,' Henderson said, ploughing on. 'When I accused you of waiting in Stuart Livermore's house for him to come home, you denied it.'

'Too right I fucking denied it, I've never been in his fucking house,' he said, his face red and his voice shrill. 'I've told you people all this before.'

'You've never been in Stuart Livermore's house?'

'That's what I said, are you fucking deaf?'

'Has he ever been in yours?'

Carlyle threw his hands in the air in supplication. 'What the fuck? I admitted I'd heard of him. Is that not enough? Are you trying to say we were buddies or something? I don't believe this.'

'Calm down, Danny,' Henderson said, as Walters removed several papers from a file. She turned them round for Carlyle and Giles to see. 'I'd like you both to take a look at this.'

Giles and Carlyle leaned forward to look.

'I'm showing the suspect photocopies of a DVD cover and disk of *Blood Lines,* which was recovered from Danny Carlyle's house by the forensic search team,' Walters said. 'Both the cover of the DVD and the disk have been fingerprinted. The fingerprints of Stuart Livermore and Danny Carlyle are clearly marked to identify them.'

As Carlyle and his brief looked over the photographs, their expressions slowly changed. Giles was now displaying a face like thunder, that seemed to say, 'Why the hell didn't you tell me about this before?' Carlyle's, in contrast, was frozen in a state of disbelief.

Stuart Livermore and Danny Carlyle's fingerprints were there, clear as day. Carlyle's on the DVD cover, Livermore's on the surface of the disk. There was no doubt in Henderson's mind, it had been stolen from Livermore's house on the night of the murder.

The DVD was a special one-off version made by Zama, as the programme had not been commercially distributed. On the inside, a special message of thanks from Roberto Sanchez, MD of Zama Productions, to Stuart Livermore. This was the item Carlyle had been looking for when he ransacked the bookcase in Livermore's lounge. Its main value at this time, however, was in putting a cat among the pigeons.

'Fuck!' Carlyle said, his face red. 'It's a lie. You bastards must have fucking planted it!'

'Danny, shut up!' his brief said. 'You'll dig yourself into an even deeper hole. Inspector, I think it's time we had a break, don't you?'

FIFTY-TWO

Henderson and Walters left Danny Carlyle and his solicitor to stew for fifteen minutes. They walked out of the interview room and headed into the Viewing Gallery. Inside, they were met with smiling faces, slaps on the back, and expressions of congratulation.

'Well done, sir.'

'Brilliant move, boss.'

'Where did you get that one?' Houghton asked, shaking his hand, his face beaming. 'It was a master stroke.'

'It was a kind of reverse logic. Forensics couldn't prove that Carlyle had been in Livermore's house, but they might be able to prove Carlyle had taken something from it.'

'Locard's Exchange Principle.'

'Indeed, and it was about the only thing Charlie Dean in Forensics would do for us, since dusting the DVD would take him no more than a couple of minutes.'

'What now?'

'The ball's back in Carlyle's court. He could, of course, clam up and say nothing. Force us to wait for the knife and build our case against him. I believe he'll see there's no way out for him. The DVD proves he was in Livermore's house and the *Blood Lines* programme that he had motive. Once we have the DNA from the knife, we'll have enough for a conviction, but first, I want to hear him say he killed Livermore.'

'I couldn't agree more.'

'To sweeten the deal, I think I could offer him a trade.'

'Trade what?' Houghton asked.

'He's not only wanted for the murder of Stuart Livermore and for being the South Coast Rapist, but also the attack on Hannah Robbins and the fire at Zama Productions.'

'You think he was involved in both of those? I don't recall seeing any the evidence?'

'You mentioned Locard's Exchange Principle. I also abide by the coincidence principle, in that I don't believe in it. Zama were responsible for making *Blood Lines*. Hannah Robbins attended a meeting at Zama on the night she was attacked. She was the girlfriend of Stuart Livermore.'

'When you put it like that, it sounds like they're all connected.' Houghton looked at his watch. 'I think your fifteen minutes is about up. You better go back in there and hear what's he's got to say, but whatever it is, nail the evil bastard, Angus.'

It was a more subdued Danny Carlyle they met when they returned to the interview room. The cockiness was still there, but restrained, and a more tense expression on his face.

'My client didn't appreciate having the DVD and fingerprint evidence sprung on him at such short notice,' Giles said.

'Point noted. You may have spotted at the top of the page of the printouts, the document had only been sent to me five minutes before we were due to come back in here.'

'I'll accept your explanation, but I trust there won't be a repeat.'

'No, I don't expect there will be.'

'Good.'

'Danny,' Henderson said. 'What have you got to say for yourself?'

'Fuck all.'

'Come, come, is that your best shot?'

'Look, I'm out on licence. If I go down for Livermore's murder, I'll never see daylight again. I'm saying nothing.'

'Look at this way. You received a life sentence in Edinburgh for a murder and five rapes. Yet, here you are, and still in your early forties.'

Carlyle's face brightened. 'Aye, right enough, the criminal justice system moves in mysterious ways.'

'If you go into court with the least number of charges, you stand a better chance, if I can use your expression, of seeing daylight again.'

'I can't argue with you there. Yer talking about other charges. What other charges?'

'Tell me what happened to Stuart Livermore, and Greg Lewis. Then, I might be able to do something about the attack on Stuart Livermore's girlfriend and the fire at Zama Productions in Burgess Hill.'

'What attack? It was an accident.'

'You admit you were there?'

'I followed her from Burgess Hill–'

'Where she'd been meeting the MD of Zama Productions.'

'Yeah. I thought maybe he'd given her something. Maybe the master copy of *Blood Lines* or something. You know, as a keepsake.'

'Go on.'

'When she walked down a quiet road in Brighton, I tried to snatch her bag to see if she had it, but she whacked me with it and took off. She tripped and smacked headfirst into a car.'

'It wasn't wet or icy that night, Danny. How did she trip? Did you make her?'

'No, I bloody didn't. She fell all by herself. There's loads of cobblestones around there, it could happen to anyone.'

'We'll put that to one side for the moment. Tell me about the fire at Zama Productions.'

He shook his head. 'Nothing to do with me.'

'Danny, don't blank me. Zama are the makers of *Blood Lines*. When you realised Livermore's girlfriend didn't have the master copy, you knew they would have it. You set the place on fire to destroy it.'

'Bollocks.'

'Forensics have found petrol at your house, and I'm sure when the tests are completed, they'll find traces of the stuff on your clothes.'

Carlyle turned and said something to his brief, who nodded and replied. The suspect detached himself from the confab with Giles and sat there, a grumpy expression on his face. Clearly, he didn't like his brief's advice.

'Well?'

Carlyle shrugged as if telling himself it didn't matter. 'It was them who made that fucking programme, wasn't it? It's only right for someone to wipe them off the face of the earth.'

'Are you admitting you started the fire, Danny? I mean, petrol in the house, you waiting outside their premises in your car, all captured on CCTV.'

'I object Detective Inspector; show me your evidence.'

Henderson was bluffing. He didn't have any CCTV evidence, but Phil Bentley and his team were working on it.

'Your right, Mr Giles, I do apologise. However, your client has admitted following Stuart Livermore's girlfriend from her meeting with Zama in Burgess Hill. Chances are, he didn't just spot her by accident walking around Burgess Hill or Brighton. He must have seen her coming out of Zama's premises when he was casing the place. I'm merely filling in the gaps in his story.'

'Nevertheless, this is conjecture. Show me your evidence.'

Carlyle sighed. 'It was me.'

'Danny, I told you, admit nothing.'

'Forget it boss, I've got this.'

'You're admitting you set fire to Zama Productions in Burgess Hill?'

'Yeah, it was me, all me.'

'How about we do this? Let's say we drop the arson charge, and you tell me all you know about Stuart Livermore and Greg Lewis.'

'Hang on, what about the woman's accident?'

'Danny, you've admitted being there and your actions in trying to snatch her bag somehow caused her injuries. She's now in a coma, and doctors have no idea when she will wake up.'

Carlyle leaned over and whispered something to his brief. The lawyer responded and Carlyle nodded.

'Right,' Carlyle said, 'drop the assault thing and the fire and I'll tell you all I know.'

Henderson shook his head. 'No can do. We can do something about the fire, but not the assault. Before I make any decision, I first want to hear the victim's side of the story. If she agrees with you and says it was an accident, we won't pursue it.'

'She'll say it was my fault either way. Her word against that of an ex-con. It doesn't take a bloody Mastermind contestant to tell you which side you'll take.'

'Nevertheless, while I've got another witness, albeit one at present in a coma, it would be remiss of me not to use her.'

Carlyle sat there considering his options and perhaps coming to the conclusion he didn't have many.

'Right,' Carlyle said at last, 'to make sure we're on the same page, you won't be charging me with the Zama Productions fire, and with being the South Coast Rapist.'

'What?'

'Ha ha, just testing to see if you're awake. So, we can forget the arson charge?'

'Right. We're agreed, no arson charge in relation to the fire at Zama Productions. Tell me about Stuart Livermore and Greg Lewis.'

Henderson was offering only a small concession, although he would say nothing about it to Carlyle. The blaze had burned fiercely, on account of all the combustible video and film material in the building. DS Neal, in discussions with the Fire Investigation Officer, had been told their investigation was now complete. Barring the surfacing of any new information, a conclusion either way would never be reached.

'Greg's a big guy. I'm not so large myself, and he sort of took me under his wing in prison and looked after me. For a start, he kept me away from those bastards peddling spice. It didn't matter if you had no money, they'd give you a baggie for free. A couple of them and you're hooked. A month later, you're in debt. Then, they can do whatever they like with you. I've seen guys commit suicide over it.'

He spoke with some eloquence and from the heart, for perhaps the first time in the course of the interview.

'I told you how Greg found out about the *Blood Lines* programme from a visitor. Him and me hatched up a plan to shut their smarmy mouths. What the fuck did a couple of public schoolboys know about us? They're people who've never been in trouble in their lives. The only debt they cared about was a big fat mortgage on their big fucking houses. How could they write a book about us without talking to me or Greg first?'

'If Stuart Livermore had put in a request with the prison authorities, would you have spoken to him?'

He shook his head. 'If he could have helped me in some way to get out of stir, aye, I might have. Just to make him a bit more loot? Nah, no fucking way.'

'Did you kill Stuart Livermore and did Greg Lewis kill Ryan Allison?'

'That was the plan.'

Here at last, was the confirmation Henderson was looking for. Not so much two killers working in tandem, but two killers pursuing their own, but related, agendas.

'Danny, did you or did you not kill Stuart Livermore?'

He paused, perhaps not wanting his 'dirty washing' to be displayed in public once again, or feeling coy because he'd been cornered. 'Aye I did,' he said at last.

'What about Greg? Did he kill Ryan Allison?'

He nodded.

'For the tape, Danny.'

'Aye, he did.'

'How do you know? Did the two of you talk about it afterwards?'

'We went out for a drink after, to celebrate.'

'Where can we find him?'

'There lies the problem. He's a hard man for me to track down at the best of times. You see, he doesn't own a phone. When he wants to get away from it all for a spell, like after dealing with Allison, he just goes into the woods and sets up camp.'

FIFTY-THREE

They tracked Greg Lewis down to a place in the Ashdown Forest. The largest forest in Sussex, it was located close to East Grinstead, and part of the High Weald Area of Outstanding Natural Beauty. One part of the forest had a special place in the hearts of thousands of children, One Hundred Acre Wood, the setting for the Winnie the Pooh stories.

Due to this literary connection, the woods were always busy in summer. A police team wouldn't be able to move for groups of school children heading to Pooh Bridge to drop their sticks into the water. On this cold and blustery mid-October morning, Henderson expected it would be much quieter.

They had managed to locate Lewis because he hadn't changed his name, and he had used a debit card at a pub in the forest. Perhaps he believed only credit cards left a trace. His camp was located using an EDF Energy helicopter fitted with heat-seeking equipment.

This was a change from its day-job of detecting electricity thieves who were by-passing their electricity meter to light and heat illicit cannabis plants. The photographs taken by the helicopter's camera told them they were looking at a small camp, but without a positive ID of the man, it was impossible to determine if it belonged to Lewis, a boy scout, or another wannabe soldier.

Henderson had decided to approach the camp at first light. He would have preferred to do it in the middle of the night, which in summer wouldn't have been a problem. Then, there would have been sufficient illumination for members of the team not to walk into trees or fall into ponds.

The weather forecast for the next few nights left the sky full of thick rainclouds, which would have left the forest black as ebony, making any approach in the dark impossible. The use of torches was also out of the question, as it would be an obvious beacon to a man skilled at hiding from view.

Dawn hadn't yet broken when he and Walters had set off from Malling House in Henderson's car. A van was following behind containing six armed ART officers. They were all taking no chances. Henderson considered him armed and very dangerous. Both detectives were equipped with 17-round Glocks and, in the boot of the car, anti-stab vests.

When they arrived at the forest, they avoided parking in any of the designated car parks, not that there was one close by. With it being so early in the morning, Henderson's car and the ART van would most likely be the only vehicles in an otherwise empty car park. If Lewis was as devious as he sounded, chances were, he would be watching and checking. This was one of the negative views expressed at the Risk Assessment meeting. The optimistic viewpoint was he had just got out of his sleeping bag, and was busily scratching his balls while waiting for the kettle to boil.

They parked beside a farm gate. A note had been left in the window of the ART van with a number to ring if a farmer needed the vehicles moved. Henderson believed it wouldn't be needed. The entrance looked as though it hadn't seen vehicle traffic for several years.

They climbed the gate, not daring to open it for fear of the hinges being rusty and screeching if pushed. There was little noise at this time of the morning, save for the flapping of birds, the scrambling of small animals and the occasional plane heading for Gatwick Airport. To a man alert and hiding out in the woods, any unfamiliar sound would easily be picked up by his finely-tuned antenna.

A few steps into the forest, they found themselves threading their way through close-packed trees. Henderson and Walters were wearing stab-proof vests, but the ART had donned the whole works: helmets, thick clothing, and boots. They had a harder job making progress, at times they were forced to sidestep between neighbouring trunks.

Fifteen minutes of walking, and the DI was starting to sweat despite the cold chill of the morning. He looked down at the map in his hand for the umpteenth time. He then held up two fingers, a silent sign to the team that the camp was nearby.

A few minutes later, he held up five fingers. The camp was in sight. The officers began to fan out, and position themselves at various points around the camp. If Lewis was here and tried to make a run for it,

Henderson's plan was to ensure at least one member of the team would be close, and in a position to stop him.

Henderson waited a long ten minutes while the team moved to their stations. He then advanced on the camp at a slow pace. Through dappled light, filtered by branches, he could see it dead ahead. Moving a few paces forward, he could make out a small clearing. There was a makeshift hide, a tarpaulin suspended on several wooden poles, a small fire burning close by, and a couple of t-shirts hanging on a short washing line. It was a good place for a camp: level ground, surrounded by trees, well away and shielded from tourist paths and car parks.

Henderson's instructions to all members of the team were clear. No one was to advance on the camp unless they had their eyes fixed on Lewis. The logic being, if Lewis had nipped into the bushes for a pee, and returned to see strangers milling about his camp, he either would take fright, or invoke the Rambo scenario, and pick them off one by one.

This was a real fear in Henderson's mind, and something he had been impressed on everyone. Lewis had been released from prison on license for the murder of a woman. Police in Birmingham believed he had committed at least one other murder. If caught and sentenced for the murder of Ryan Allison, he would likely die in prison. Henderson was sure Lewis was aware of this. For him to kill another one, two, or three coppers today, would make no difference to the time he would spend inside.

The burning fire and the bubbling billycan suspended above was a positive sign of an occupied camp. However, despite focusing on the side of the tent for a full minute, Henderson could not see any movement inside. The ART officer who had moved to a position facing the camp would now have a better view of the tent entrance. The fact that the officer was not advancing into the clearing with his gun cocked, further confirmed the absence of their target.

This suggested Lewis was off doing his ablutions, checking his snares, or out searching for additional dry wood. In which case, the team would have to wait, and each needed to be sure Lewis didn't come up behind them.

He heard movement over to his left and eased on tiptoes to get a better view. It was just a rabbit, but there was nothing soft about the grip that wrapped around his throat or the knife sticking into his cheek.

'Drop the gun, copper and start walking,' a deep voice behind him said.

FIFTY-FOUR

'C'mon you lot hiding in the bushes!' Greg Lewis hollered. 'Show yourselves, or he gets it. I know you're cops, fucking hikers don't carry guns.'

'Don't listen to him! Everyone, stay where you are!' Walters shouted.

She stepped forward into the clearing and walked towards Greg Lewis. Lewis was standing in front of his makeshift tent, his left arm around the Henderson's neck, and in his right hand, a blade pointing into the side of Henderson's head. It was a hunting knife, large and with a serrated edge, she noted. Similar to the weapon used to kill Ryan Allison.

'You've come far enough copper, drop your weapon.'

Walters hesitated before placing the gun at her feet. She wasn't a big reader of crime books, but had read *The Onion Field* by Joseph Wambaugh, a book she believed should be required reading for any cop. It had been written by an ex-LA police officer, and concerned two cops who'd put their guns down at the perp's insistence and became his prisoners. One officer had paid for it with his life, while the other lived with the guilt of giving up his weapon and not saving his partner. As a result, he'd contemplated suicide. The situation today was slightly different. There were another six guns lurking somewhere in the trees, and she hoped all were trained on the figure of Greg Lewis.

'Greg, I'm Detective Sergeant Carol Walters of Sussex Police. You're surrounded by a team of highly trained armed police officers. I'm asking you to put the knife down. Let your hostage go.'

'You don't expect me to believe the word of a pig,' he sneered? 'You're like the rest of them, a fucking liar.'

Lewis was broad with the build of a middleweight boxer, his arms thick and muscled. He had sharp features, with high cheek bones and square jaw. His hair was cut to the bone, a crew cut in old money, and dressed in a t-shirt and camouflaged trousers. Lightweight attire for such a chilly morning.

'C'mon Greg, what you are doing is pointless. Do what I ask and you won't be harmed. Put the knife down,' she said slowly, 'and let your hostage go.'

'Go fuck yourself, copper.'

Walters decided to change tack. 'We've been having a chat with one of your mates, Greg.'

'Who?'

'Danny Carlyle.'

'Danny? Have you? How is he?'

'Oh, Danny's fine. We had a long chat. He told us all about the little agreement you and him cooked up in prison.'

'What agreement?'

'You've got a short memory, Greg. It was for Danny to kill Livermore, and you to kill Allison.'

'You're a fucking liar. Danny would never give me up. Not in a million years. He's my brother.'

'Brothers can be just as disappointing as friends. I know, I've got one of those.'

'Not Danny, he's special.'

'Maybe he is, but he told us about you and Ryan Allison. You didn't like him, did you?'

'Allison's scum. A fucking public schoolboy who lived a privileged life. How could he write a book about me? He knows nothing about being abused by your uncle, beaten up by gangs who'd steal your money and shoes, or being hungry every minute of every fucking day.'

This was more or less the same story Carlyle had told, not surprising since the two of them had concocted this plan together. It was becoming clear to her that Carlyle was the brains of the twosome, Lewis the brawn.

'Allison may have had his faults, but no way did he deserve to die.'

'Of course he fucking did, but don't you worry, he didn't feel a thing. Just like this one won't. This blade gets sharpened every day.' He looked at Henderson and a muscle in his forearm twitched, the one holding the knife.

'Shoot!' Walters shouted.

Before the echo of her voice had died out, a gun fired. The bullet entered the head of Greg Lewis from the left side and exited out of the right, blood and brain matter following its trajectory. Lewis dropped to the ground, seconds before Henderson did the same.

FIFTY-FIVE

It was Henderson's first day back at work since the shooting of Greg Lewis. He had been given a week off to recuperate. After three days of long sleeps, a few runs and walks along the seafront with his upstairs neighbour, Sharon Conner, he had returned to work. Sharon was an intelligent and entertaining woman; now that her recent divorce wasn't so fresh in her mind, and her ex-husband didn't feature so often in conversations. Who knows where they would take it in future?

Walters walked into his office before plonking herself down on the visitor's chair. 'Morning gov, glad to see you back. How are you feeling?'

'Right as rain.'

'I didn't expect to see you here so soon. If you've been given a week's holiday, it seems rude not to take it all.'

'If the boss had offered me time off a month or so back, I would have bitten his hand off.'

'How's your neck?'

He tilted his head back, and showed her the cuts and bruises. Lewis had held him in an iron-clad grip, and when he fell, the razor-sharp knife had cut into the side of Henderson's neck. A few centimetres further over and the consequences could have been so different, and not something he liked to think about.

The last few days had been beneficial. It had given him a chance to rest his voice. For a time after the incident, he sounded not unlike a Disney cartoon character.

'In any case,' Henderson said, 'just because Carlyle's in jail and Lewis is dead, it doesn't mean there isn't tons to do.'

'Don't remind me. I received a call from the CPS last night, they've given me a long list of questions. It'll take most of the day to sort them out. Then, there's Professional Standards, and the joy of the inquest to come.'

'I didn't get a chance to thank you for saving my life.'

'You already did, when I came to see you at The Royal Sussex.'

'Did I? I don't remember. It must have been after they stuck one of many needles into me.'

'So, your memory lapse sort of blows my promised pay rise out of the water.'

'Don't push it, I was never so zonked you could wheedle extra money out of me.'

'I could stand here and revel in all the praise, but it wasn't me who saved you. It was Bob Franks. He saw Lewis's arm move, and opened fire more or less at the same time as my shout.'

'I must thank him too, or have I already done so?'

'Who knows? It was a good job Franks fired. If it had been Dave Rendell, who was facing the back of Lewis's head, it's you who might not be standing here.'

'I know and I only realised the danger I was in when I got home from hospital. The whisky took a bit of a hammering these last few days, I can tell you.'

Walters departed a few minutes later and Henderson began sifting through the paperwork on his desk. Three days off and it had mushroomed. He'd left it tidy and now it didn't look much better than Jim Hegarty's. Thinking of Hegarty, there were a number of Post-It Notes sticking to his computer monitor and on the desk. Hegarty's name was prominent.

Henderson hadn't gone to see Hegarty with the aim of congratulating him on the arrest of Carlyle. In the same way, he suspected Hegarty's repeated calls weren't to heap praise on him for finding the murderers of Livermore and Allison.

Henderson picked up the phone, but instead of calling Jim Hegarty at John Street nick, he called the Royal Sussex Hospital.

'This is DI Henderson of Sussex Police. Can you tell me how Hannah Robbins is today?'

'I can. She opened her eyes this morning and started speaking. She asked for a glass of water, I'm told.'

'That's terrific news.'

'It's not often we have a successful recovery in this unit. It's so nice for friends and family when it does happen.'

'I'll come along later and see how she is.'

'I'm sure, Ms Robbins will be looking forward to seeing you then. Bye now.'

Henderson put the phone down. He'd last seen Hannah when he'd been kept overnight at the Royal

Sussex. She had looked as unresponsive as the day she had been brought in. For her to be awake and speaking was an unbelievable transformation. He hoped her memory and none of her bodily functions had been impaired. It was unfortunate that when all the gears finally engaged, it would bring back memories of her accident, or perhaps an attack, and the death of her boyfriend.

He wanted to hear her side of the story, how she sustained her injuries. Was it the accident Danny Carlyle claimed? If she believed her injuries were caused by the bag thief's actions, did she want to press charges against Carlyle? Some people wouldn't hesitate, not only to punish the criminal, but to attain some form of closure, an attempt to try and put the incident behind them.

Criminals like Danny Carlyle, who were in receipt of a life sentence and released early from prison for good behaviour, are released on license. If they break the terms of the licence by committing another serious offence, they are sent back to prison to serve the remainder of their original term.

In addition to this, Danny Carlyle would most likely receive another life sentence for the murder of Stuart Livermore. He would also be given many more years for conspiring with Lewis to murder Ryan Allison. The eighteen months or two years Carlyle might receive for the assault on Hannah would, in reality, make no difference to the amount of time he actually spent in prison. The judge would probably make the sentence for assault concurrent, meaning that by the time Carlyle had spent a couple of years in prison for murdering Livermore, he would have effectively served his time for the assault charge. No matter, he wouldn't be seeing daylight for a long time to come.

Henderson ignored the piles of paperwork and woke up his computer. As expected, dozens of emails were cluttering up his inbox. He spent the next half hour deleting, filing, and reading, before loading his web browser to check on a few things. At the point when the lure of the coffee machine was starting to beckon, Sean Houghton walked in.

'I heard you were back, Angus. I didn't expect to see you so soon.'

'In truth, I surprised myself. I thought I'd be happy with a week off, but after a couple of days I was itching to come back.'

'No after-effects from the incident?'

He shook his head. 'Just a sore neck. Lewis was behind me when the shot was fired. I heard it, but didn't see it. I only felt him falling to the ground.'

'You must have feared for your life, knowing the kind of man Lewis was?'

'It had crossed my mind once or twice I can tell you, but I had every confidence in Carol. She's a bloody good negotiator; friendly, but she takes no crap.'

'Her part in stopping Greg Lewis will be recognised.'

'I'm pleased to hear it. She deserves it.'

Houghton turned to leave.

'Sean, before you go. Did you hear the latest?' Henderson said, nodding at his pc. 'Steve Mitchell is suing Sussex Police for wrongful arrest.'

'What? The bastard.'

'It sort of puts a damper on things.'

'Not at all. It's nothing for us to worry about, Angus, let him do his worst. I think he played a bigger part in this crime than we know.'

'How do you mean?'

'I'm convinced once we've analysed all the effects taken from Danny Carlyle's house, and searched the Lewis encampment, or wherever he lives, we'll find a connection to Mitchell. Once we've gathered together some evidence, it won't be him suing us, it will be us going after him. Catch you later.'

Well, well, he had changed his tune, Henderson thought as he picked up his jacket. He made sure his car keys were inside and headed out to the car park, all thoughts of a decent cup of coffee now forgotten. He drove in the direction of Brighton, to the Royal Sussex Hospital. The actions of Steve Mitchell might not be a good news story, but the recovery of Hannah Robbins definitely was.

The End

About the Author

Iain Cameron was born in Glasgow and moved to Brighton in the early eighties. He has worked as a management accountant, business consultant and a nursery goods retailer. He is now a full-time writer and lives in a village outside Horsham in West Sussex with his wife, two daughters and a lively Collie dog.

Blood Marked Pages is the ninth book to feature DI Angus Henderson, the Scottish cop at Sussex Police.

For more information about books and the author:
Visit the website at: www.iain-cameron.com
Follow him on twitter: @iainsbooks
Follow him on facebook @iaincameronauthor

Books by Iain Cameron

DI Angus Henderson Crime Novels
One Last Lesson
Driving into Darkness
Fear the Silence
Hunting for Crows
Red Red Wine
Night of Fire
Girls on Film
Black Quarry Farm
Blood Marked Pages

Books 1-4 are also available as an ebook box set:
The Essential DI Henderson Box Set

Matt Flynn Thrillers
The Pulsar Files
Deadly Intent

All books are available from Amazon
In the UK: here
In the US: here
In Australia: here
In Canada: here

Printed in Great Britain
by Amazon